"I was wondering…"

"Yes?" Zeke said.

Those blue eyes were stormier now as she looked directly at him. "Are you doing anything?"

"Now?" he asked, and Jessica nodded. "No. Well, I need to see to the plane, and—" Her eyes changed as if she was closing the blinds, a flush crept up her cheeks, and he quickly altered his course. Clint could deal with his own plane tomorrow when he got back to town. "But that can wait. What did you have in mind?" Maybe they'd get a pizza at the Commodore. That would give them some time to get to know each other a little. Maybe see if they had something in common. Maybe it could even lead to someday seeing that pale skin below all those layers.

She stepped closer to him. "I wondered if you might want to follow me to my place. It's a little out of the way, in Eagle Harbor, but…" Her voice was low, as though she didn't want to be overheard even though they were the only two in the hangar.

Oh, she didn't want to drive home alone. Didn't want to enter her home in the dark. The sky was already turning dusky, the days so short in the winter.

But this was the Copper Country. People weren't careless, but neither were they afraid to go to their own home alone after dark. Still, an officer and a gentleman and all that.

"I'd be happy to see you to your home," he said. She squinted at him, her cinnamon-colored eyebrows coming together.

"No, not 'see me home,' but come *home* with me."

"Oh," he said, surprised, but trying not to show it. He'd certainly been propositioned before, had women make the first move plenty of times. Sometimes it was a turn-on, most times not. But at least in those experiences, he had seen it coming.

Trying to recover from his shock, he quickly nodded, getting some kind of movement out before his mouth finally caught up. "Yes. I'd like that."

OTHER TITLES BY
MARA JACOBS

The Worth Series
(Contemporary Romance)
Worth The Weight
Worth The Drive
Worth The Fall
Worth The Effort
Totally Worth Christmas
Worth The Price
Worth The Lies
Worth The Flight

Freshman Roommates Trilogy
(New Adult Romance)
In Too Deep
In Too Fast
In Too Hard

Anna Dawson's Vegas Series
(Romantic Mystery)
Against The Odds
Against The Spread
Against The Rules
Against The Wall

Romantic Suspense
Broken Wings

Countdown To A Kiss
(A New Year's Eve Anthology)

WORTH the FLIGHT

The Worth Series, Book Seven

MARA JACOBS

Published by Mara Jacobs
©Copyright 2017 Mara Jacobs

ISBN: 978-1-940993-03-4

For more information on the author and her works, please
see www.marajacobs.com

For Margo

Prologue

—✳—

Twenty years ago

"JESSICA, I HAVE A BOOK I THINK YOU MIGHT LIKE. IT was checked out, but just returned today, so I held it for you," Mrs. Stevenson said to Jess as she approached the library desk, her arms heavy with books.

"I think I have my limit today," Jess told the librarian, disappointed because Mrs. Stevenson usually had recommendations that pleased her. And she never even flinched when Jess routinely checked out books that no twelve-year-old should be reading.

The first time she'd done it, Mrs. Stevenson had asked Jess if her mother was aware of her reading selections. Jess had simply nodded, trying to look innocent.

The truth was Jessica's mother was just pleased that Jess spent so much time at the library and always came home on Friday afternoons with a backpack full of books. It meant that Jess's mother would have to spend less time with her daughter.

At least, that was how it felt to Jess.

"Maybe you'll want this one instead of one of these," Mrs. Stevenson said as Jess unloaded her selections onto the desk. She was nodding, but then stopped as she saw the choice that her favorite librarian had held out for her.

Julie of the Wolves.

It looked old. And for little kids. Jess was firmly in the young adult category of books now. Many times, she was beyond it if she could swipe one of her parents' paperbacks without them noticing.

"Um…thank you for thinking of me," she said. "But I really was hoping to read these this weekend." A little white lie. Jess had read nearly everything in the medium-sized neighborhood library in her affluent Chicago suburb of Winnetka. She was now down to checking out anything she hadn't yet read that was even remotely interesting to her. This was after she'd reread all the good stuff a few times.

But even books that were way, way down on her list (or not even on her list at all) would be better than the *baby* book that Mrs. Stevenson held out to her.

She made a show of flipping through it, but knew instinctively that she would not be trading in one of her heavier tomes on the desk for this book.

"Yeah, looks good. Maybe next week," she said, putting the book down and sliding it to the side. She pulled her library card out of the side pocket on her backpack.

Mrs. Stevenson didn't push her on the kids' book. She just nodded and proceeded to check out Jess's stack of books while Jess made room in her backpack for her new treasures.

On one hand, she could hardly wait to get home and start reading. On the other hand, she could wait for quite a while before walking into the house.

Into whatever mood her mother was in. Into whether her father would be home that evening for dinner. And when he did show up, would her mother give him the silent treatment or start a fight?

Jess took a few deep breaths, feeling a little stronger as she took the stack of books from Mrs. Stevenson and put it in her bag, then slung it over one shoulder.

"Have a good weekend, Jessica," Mrs. Stevenson said with a smile. Jess tried to return it, but she was sure her facial muscles weren't quite up to the task.

That was what thinking about going home did to her these days.

It wasn't that her house wasn't nice. It was completely awesome—her father's ego and her mother's impeccable taste saw to that. But it wasn't a *home* like the smaller house that they'd lived in until Jess had been ten.

Right when they moved into this beautiful home—two years ago, when the company her father had started had taken off—their little family had been fractured.

And Jess had found solace in books.

She'd made some new friends at school, but it was a fancy private school and some of the kids were just complete phonies, only being nice to Jess once someone told them that her dad was a new heavy player on the scene. But that fact wasn't enough for the old-money kids.

Like twelve-year-olds could even be *old money*.

When Jess got home, she called out a hello to her mother, got a Snapple, an apple, and a cookie, and headed to her room. No Oreos or Chips Ahoy for Jess's mother. Nor anything homemade—she had stopped spending any time in the kitchen with the arrival of all that New Money. But it had to be the best, so gourmet cookies were delivered twice a week from a Winnetka bakery for Jess's lunches and snacks. Her mom never touched them, but occasionally Jess saw her dad wrap one in a napkin and take it with him as he left for the office. He'd catch her eye and wink, as if it was their little secret that he was swiping a cookie. In those small moments, Jess could breathe, believing that there were still remnants of the parents that she'd known before.

Before they had everything they could possibly want.

There was no answer from her mom as Jess made her way to her room. She could be out, or she could be locked away in the huge suite her parents shared at the far end of the long hallway from Jess's room.

The suite her parents *had* shared when they'd first moved into the house. Jess was pretty sure her father slept most nights in one of the three guest rooms, but they were careful to not let Jess discover that fact.

They must've thought she was an idiot. The house was large and they shut the doors, but at times, she could still hear them arguing.

Still nothing from her mother as Jess entered her room and shut the door. Her bedroom was twice the size of the one she'd had before they'd moved. It was way more than one girl needed, but it was her own haven. At least half of the room was. The one side was your typical bedroom like she'd had before—bed, desk, closet, shelves. Jess had turned the other side of the room into a reading nook with a cool lava lamp, and other eclectic things she'd found at a secondhand store.

Junk, her mother had called it. But she'd let Jess keep it all, only sighing heavily whenever she'd glance at that side of the room.

Jess plopped down on the floor in front of the comfy chair that she would soon curl up on with one of her books. She looked through her backpack, taking the books out one by one, as if they were precious jewels being unwrapped from a black velvet pouch.

At the bottom, a thinner book slipped from her grasp, and Jess stared down at *Julie of the Wolves*.

She mentally retraced the steps of the exchange at the library desk and concluded that Mrs. Stevenson must have accidentally swept the book into her arms with the others that Jess had checked out.

She'd have to bring it back. She didn't want Mrs. Stevenson to get into trouble for giving Jess more books than she should have.

Tomorrow. She'd bring it back tomorrow.

She slid up the chair and tucked herself in. Might as well read it, then, as long as she had it for the night.

Three hours later, she still sat in her chair, tears streaming down her face. Not necessarily because of the book, but because Jess had finally seen in words the isolation she had been feeling the past two years.

And hoping, praying, that she could be as strong as Julie.

Because Jess now realized that her life would be one like Julie's—join the pack to survive, but never forget who she was.

The wolf pack was Julie's company, her family in some ways, but she was never completely one of them.

That was Jess, she saw now. Among her family and so-called friends at school, she could blend in, but she was never truly one of them.

Jess almost identified more with the wolves, secretly yearning for a pack of her own.

At the end of the book, it mentioned that there were two more in the same series. It was too late for Jess to go back to the library now, but she'd go first thing in the morning.

She looked down from her chair to the other library books spread out on the floor. They all seemed to dull at the thought of rereading *Julie*. But if she was going to take out the other two books in the series, she'd have to return two, so she might as well get them out of the way.

Then she could read *Julie* another time before the morning.

When she rode her bike to the library the next day, she was surprised to learn Mrs. Stevenson had put the other two books in the series at the hold desk for Jess.

So, it was probably not a mistake that *Julie of the Wolves* had somehow gotten in her stack of books.

Wishing Mrs. Stevenson was working so Jess could discuss the book with her, but knowing her favorite curator had the weekends off, she traded in three of her books for the next two in the series, hanging on to the first book in case she wanted to read it again.

Which she did, on Sunday. She read the entire series, only coming out of her room all weekend at her mother's insistence to eat her meals.

There were no sounds of fighting, but Jess might not have heard them anyway, as deeply engrossed in her reading as she was.

Tracing the title on the cover, if she squinted, she could pretend it read *Jessica of the Wolves* instead of *Julie*.

Yes, that would be her from now on. She would be a girl who lived amongst a pack, one of them, but on her own.

A lone wolf.

She made a mental note to look for books on wolves on her next trip to the library.

By late Sunday night, when she would typically be tied up with anxiety about a new week of wading through the minefield of an elite, private middle school, Jess was more and more convinced that it would now all be different.

She was a lone wolf. Julie. Someone who was a survivor. One who could adapt and move with the pack, even though she wasn't part of it.

On Monday, she moved through the hallways with a new, quiet confidence, no longer trying to meet the eyes of the popular girls, looking for breadcrumbs of recognition thrown to her. She wore her long hair down and loose instead of in her usual ponytail, liking the way it swayed against her back, as if it were fur. Her movements were more graceful, more aware, and yet she felt removed from the other kids, above it all.

That night, her parents had an argument that no amount of square footage or closed doors could muffle. Well after she should have been asleep, she clearly heard the door to the guest room slam shut, followed quickly by that of her parents' room.

Not all wolves mated for life, she'd learned. Some went from pack to pack, and some were destined to live alone.

That would be her. She'd never be in a position like her parents, where they couldn't even stand to be in the same room. Not even in the same enormous house.

Yes, she'd be a lone wolf in every sense of the word.

By Thursday, the people in her school had noticed the change in Jessica, though she was not aware of that fact. She was completely taken aback when, on Friday afternoon, Blake Michaels, a popular boy who resembled Leonardo DiCaprio, even down to the swagger and dimpled smile (though not in sinking to the bottom of the ocean, as Leo did in *Titanic*), asked if she wanted to go to McDonald's with him after school.

She'd planned to go to the library and get a backpack full of books for the weekend, but she only tucked a strand of hair behind her ear and nodded her agreement to Blake.

By the following Monday, she was Blake's girl, and those in his group quickly adopted her into their pack. Girls who hadn't looked at her a week ago—or had, but with disdain—were now treating her as the alpha.

She was a lone wolf no more.

One

ZEKE HAMPTON BROUGHT THE CESSNA AROUND THE edge of Isle Royale for the second time, getting as low as he felt comfortable, given the rocky hills that burst from the island in various areas.

"There!" the woman sitting next to him in the cockpit exclaimed. "There they are." She pointed west, and his gaze followed the direction her long, graceful finger indicated.

"I see them," he said, turning the small plane slightly so they could come up behind the wolves she'd spotted with her binoculars.

The two animals were heading out of an area populated with pines and through a patch of trees that were bare due to it being early March. They were easier to spot on the open snow than they would have been in the summer with the fully blossomed leaves covering the island with a leafy canopy.

"It appears to still be just the two of them," she said, taking the binoculars away from her face, but still looking out the front of the plane. "The female is seven, and the male is nine. They've already outlived the average life expectancy of previous Isle Royale wolves. Mainly because the moose—their main prey—are so plentiful right now, and it's just the two of them.

"He is both her father and half-sibling. It's not totally uncommon for inbred wolves to mate, but so far the female has seemed unwilling. At least, that's what the study has shown."

"Wow. That's some *Game of Thrones*-type shit right there," he said.

She laughed, and Zeke found he liked the sound reverberating in the small cockpit. "I know, right? But she's no Cersei. Due to her lack of interest, it's highly likely the wolf population will cease to exist on Isle Royale soon. There are proposals to introduce a new wolf population to the island, but they're under review."

He slowed down, coming up behind the two wolves as they trekked through the snow. The expanse they were covering was fairly open, with no large hills, so he was able to get low enough for his passenger to get a good look.

His passenger. Jessica Chapman. The woman who'd said barely three words to him since he'd met her at the airport in Hancock early that morning. Unless it was about wolves' mating habits.

He'd been expecting a man from Michigan Tech who was the premier wolf expert in the area. Ms. Chapman had shown up instead, telling him that since the plane was already chartered for the day, she'd be filling in for Ralph, who was out of town.

Zeke had gone about his business, readying the plane. He'd taken a few quick peeks at her, though, and even once caught her looking back. But she'd stayed mostly silent while he flew the hundred-plus miles over frozen Lake Superior and around Isle Royale so she could get a good look at the current wolf population on the island for an ongoing study.

As if two wolves counted as a population.

He was encouraged by her Cersei answer. The last bit about the wolves was the most she'd spoken all day. After about an hour, he'd assumed that the lady did not want to partake in small talk, and he'd just shut up and flown the plane.

The little Cessna was a far cry from the F/A-18 fighter jet that he'd spent the better part of the last twenty years flying, but nonetheless, it felt good being in the air. Even if his "copilot" was more interested in two slow-moving wolves below them than the man that was piloting her across Lake Superior.

After a minute of them following the animals, the wolves headed back into the pines, and Zeke lost sight of them.

Oh, how he wished he were strapped into a Hornet instead of this bug-smasher. The wolves' heat signature against the crusted snow would allow the F/A-18 to acquire and track them, providing a weapons solution to the heads-up display so precise that even Dumbo could deliver a laser-guided bomb with pinpoint accuracy. He subconsciously cringed at his own thought—state-of-the-art weapons employed on a species that humans had driven to the brink of extinction. Flying an F/A-18 for the U.S. Navy, with its array of sophisticated weaponry at his fingertips, could do that to a person—turn them into a weapon.

He'd seen it happen.

"Want me to circle back or head to the other side of these woods to see if we can get another look?" he asked.

Jessica was staring out the window down at where the wolves had entered the trees. Sitting back, she shook her head and dug into the backpack she'd brought with her. "No, that's okay. I can confirm both wolves are still alive, if not exactly thriving."

Zeke had thought they'd looked a little mangy, but not being an expert on wolves (those might have been the first two he'd ever actually seen in person) and being three hundred feet in the air, he hadn't been certain.

"If you could, though, would you take a couple-mile perimeter around the island? I'd like to see how far out the lake is frozen."

"Roger that," he said, peeling off from the middle of the island and heading north toward the side near Canada.

The island was a national park and was reached by boat from points in Canada, Minnesota, and Michigan. It was the Michigan side from which they'd started out. The Hancock airport was fifty miles from Copper Harbor, where many of the boats to the island docked.

Not this time of year, of course, with Lake Superior frozen over in many spots. Which was why if anybody needed to get to the island (which no one did), they'd have to fly and, Zeke supposed, parachute out. Nobody was fool enough to attempt that.

Jessica started writing something in a notebook she'd pulled from her backpack, looking up every couple of minutes as Zeke got further from the island on the north side.

"How far out are we?" she asked him.

"Two miles," he said.

She took note of that in her notebook and made a circular motion that Zeke took to mean this was the path she wanted to circle the island. Making a wide turn and heading clockwise, he took a look down at the lake. Ice had formed solidly until the point where he was now circling, the point Jessica had noted. From where they were, and for several miles beyond, there were patches of solid ice, but also a lot of blue where the lake was so deep it had not frozen over completely.

"Twenty years ago, this would have been solid ice, and wolves and other animals would have been able to cross it to get to Isle Royale," Jessica said. "Though wolves were introduced forty years ago." There was sadness in her voice, and she followed up her words with a soft sigh before closing her notebook and putting it away.

"Climate change?" he said. "That's what's messing with the wolf population?"

"Among other things," she said. "Moose and beaver population, vegetation. But yes, climate change has significantly hurt the island's wildlife population."

He guided the plane around the south side of the island, closer to where they'd first approached, and swept over to the west, seeing the same large areas of blue where the ice drifts didn't touch. Yeah, it'd take some moose and wolves with pretty damn wide leg spans to make it to the island from the mainland.

The circle of life had a major gap in its circumference.

They flew around the whole island, and Zeke looked over to his passenger for direction. She turned to him, looking him in the eye for the first time since she'd shaken his hand at the airport.

Blue. Her eyes were a dark and stormy blue, not unlike the dark and stormy waters below them. They seemed all the more prominent because her skin was so fair, almost translucent. Milky white. Pearly white. Which made sense, given the strands of red hair that escaped from the sides of the knit pom-pom hat she wore.

Red hair and blue eyes. A rare combination, if that was her natural color.

He would have liked to see more of that pale skin, and wondered if you could easily see the blue of her veins, but she was covered in a turtleneck and olive-green fisherman's sweater, both visible under the collar of her khaki parka. She wore jeans that looked large enough to be covering thermal underwear, and big, warm Sorel boots on her feet.

She wore rag-wool gloves with the fingers cut out—probably for note taking. Those fingers and her face were the only parts of her not sporting several layers.

And what a face it was. High cheekbones that showed a spot of red from the cold, as did the tip of her straight, pert nose. And her mouth. Well, hell, that was just a work of art—a plump pillow of pink flashing brightly against the white of her cheeks.

Shit, if he did this charter thing as a permanent gig, he wasn't going to be attracted to all his clients, was he? He certainly never had that problem with his Navy squadron.

Her eyes flashed from his to his mouth and back up, recognizing that he was doing the same to her.

Shit. She'd totally caught him checking her out. But…

She bit that plump lower lip then turned away from him, staring out her side of the cockpit. "That's probably all I need. We can head back," she said.

"You're the boss," he said. She wasn't interested. Which was fine with Zeke, if not a little disappointing. Typically, when he shared a look like that with a beautiful woman—one where eyes glanced at lips and beyond—it was a short step away from a night spent together.

Didn't seem like it was going to go that route with Jessica Chapman.

A surreptitious glance at her left hand showed no ring, or at least none that he could see with the fingerless gloves.

Maybe she just wasn't interested. He'd have to get used to that. His buddies had teased him that he was giving up tons of easy pussy by getting out of the Navy. That he'd have to hang up his call sign of Magnet. It was probably true. Though there were long stretches of dry spells when out on cruise, for the most part, just going into any bar near Oceana where pilots hung out was a quick, easy way to get laid. Being a chick magnet was not needed.

And when he came home to the Copper Country on leave, he was a returning war hero, which carried its own brand of groupie.

But now he was just Zeke Hampton, unemployed pilot. Taking a wolf expert to Isle Royale as a favor to a fellow pilot.

A wolf expert who might possibly have a small interest in him, but not enough to pursue it in any way.

He inwardly sighed. There was a lot to this civilian life that was new to him, having gone into the Navy right after graduating from Tech. His whole adult life had been spent as a fighter pilot. He supposed it would take more than a couple of months to come to terms with all the changes.

Like a Michigan winter, for one thing—it'd been a long time since he'd been in the Upper Peninsula this time of year.

And being around his family and friends for more than a week at a time. It had been hard for him to abandon the mentality where he tried to cram everything and everyone in. Permanence was what he'd wanted. What he'd desperately needed. He had time now. Time that spread before him like Lake Superior did below him.

They were silent for the flight back to Hancock, Zeke thinking about his new life mostly, with the occasional thought thrown to the woman beside him.

The woman who looked out her side of the plane the entire

time, her body turned away from him.

Hell, he wouldn't have been surprised if she asked if he had a parachute.

It was a smooth landing—he'd trained to land on decks of carriers in roiling seas, so a little airport with clear skies was a picnic.

He taxied to the hangar, where his friend Clint stored the plane Zeke was flying. After cutting the engine, he got out and waited to help Jessica. Clint's plane was different than the seaplane he was considering buying, with no floats, just a set of stairs that folded out when he dropped the door. He offered his hand to Jessica, but she ignored it and descended on her own.

"Thanks very much. I hope you got what you needed," he said. There was nothing else to say to her. The business end of the day was taken care of for Clint via the Tech wolf study offices. No need to say anything else.

He started to move to the front of the plane, but she cleared her throat as though to speak, and he stopped.

"I was wondering…"

"Yes?" he said.

Those blue eyes were stormier now as she looked directly at him. "Are you doing anything?"

"Now?" he asked, and she nodded. "No. Well, I need to see to the plane, and—" Her eyes changed as if she was closing the blinds, a flush crept up her cheeks, and he quickly altered his course. Clint could deal with his own plane tomorrow when he got back to town. "But that can wait. What did you have in mind?" Maybe they'd get a pizza at the Commodore. That would give them some time to get to know each other a little. Maybe see if they had something in common. Maybe it could even lead to someday seeing that pale skin below all those layers.

She stepped closer to him. "I wondered if you might want to follow me to my place. It's a little out of the way, in Eagle Harbor, but…" Her voice was low, as though she didn't want to be overheard even though they were the only two in the hangar.

Oh, she didn't want to drive home alone. Didn't want to enter her home in the dark. The sky was already turning dusky, the days so short in the winter.

But this was the Copper Country. People weren't careless, but neither were they afraid to go to their own home alone after dark. Still, an officer and a gentleman and all that.

"I'd be happy to see you to your home," he said. She squinted at him, her cinnamon-colored eyebrows coming together.

"No, not 'see me home,' but come *home* with me."

"Oh," he said, surprised, but trying not to show it. He'd certainly been propositioned before, had women make the first move plenty of times. Sometimes it was a turn-on, most times not. But at least in those experiences, he had seen it coming.

Trying to recover from his shock, he quickly nodded, getting some kind of movement out before his mouth finally caught up. "Yes. I'd like that."

She nodded once. "I'll wait for you in the parking lot. I'm in the Range Rover. You can follow me to my place." She walked out of the hangar at a steady pace, showing no sign of nervousness. Or excitement, for that matter.

Zeke didn't think about the latter too much. He just started closing up shop.

In record time.

Two

―⁓―

HER HOME WAS AMAZING. AN A-FRAME SITUATED DEEP in the woods, overlooking a jutting in Lake Superior. It was dark by the time Zeke followed her down her winding driveway and into the home, so he couldn't see the actual view. He guessed from the shapes of the ice and snowbanks below that she was raised maybe twenty feet over craggy rocks along the lake.

He couldn't wait to see it by the light of day.

Not that he wanted to rush this night.

It'd been a few months for him, not having made a connection since he'd been back home, with most of his circle married or in relationships.

There'd been a woman in Oceana the night of his farewell party, but that had been a blur.

This night with Jessica would not be that. In fact, he shook his head when she held up a bottle of wine. He wanted a clear mind tonight. Clear eyes to see all that alabaster skin.

She peeled off the layers of her parka and sweater, and, seeing her in her turtleneck, he regretted not taking her up on the wine, for his mouth was suddenly dry.

She looked at the empty fireplace, which took up nearly one whole wall, walked to it, and started to kneel as if to start to build a fire.

He walked over to help her, realized it was a gas one, and nearly collided with her when she stood up and turned to him.

"Guess I can't be all manly for you and show my fire-starting skills," he said.

She quirked a brow at him and then flipped a switch that set the flames rising. "Manly enough for you?" she said. He chuckled and nodded. "Don't need to be a Boy Scout for that," she added.

"No, but you'd sure look cute in the uniform. The little neckerchief and all."

"I actually—" She stopped, biting her lower lip like she had in the plane. He stared down at her, so close that he could hear the catch of her breath when he reached up and pulled a tendril of her hair that hung down. The flames of the fireplace couldn't compare to the vivid coloring of the soft, silky strands he let slide through his fingers.

"I'm glad you invited me here," he said softly, moving inches closer, watching her eyes grow wider as he did. She was looking at him like he was dessert and Christmas rolled into one, and the blood rushed to his dick fast enough to break the sound barrier.

"I…I'm glad too," she said. Her voice was tentative, almost questioning, as if she was trying to convince herself.

Hell, he'd just have to make sure she was convinced. Moving his hand to the back of her neck, he pulled her closer. But before he could close the distance between his lips and hers, she slid out of his grasp and took a step back.

Her chest was moving fast with her breath, and she still had that hungry look in her eyes, but she took another step away from him.

"Umm…maybe… Do you want to go upstairs?" she asked.

It seemed like a stall tactic to Zeke, but shit, that was where he wanted to end up anyway.

"You betcha," he said, pulling out his best Yooper accent, rusty as it was.

She smiled at him, and he started to reach for her again, not willing to wait until they climbed those stairs, but she sidestepped past him, switching off the fireplace as she did.

Pity. He would have loved to eventually peel off her jeans and that white turtleneck in the glow of firelight. Still, he didn't object when she motioned for him to follow. Which he did. Gladly.

JESSICA WATCHED AS ZEKE HAMPTON entered the loft of her beloved, newly completed home. He seemed to take up all the air in the opened-air loft.

She couldn't believe he was there, in her bedroom, about to take her to bed.

No, that wasn't what was so unbelievable. It was that she'd asked him—someone she'd met only hours earlier—to come home with her.

For sex.

For *only* sex.

Jess had never had a one-night stand in her life, and she couldn't believe she was about to have one now.

She stepped deeper into the room, wondering how she was going to go through with this. It had taken every bit of nerve she possessed (Jess, who used to put the fear of God into Wall Street with just a phone call!) to invite him to follow her—both to her home and up to the loft.

She wasn't sure she could continue taking the lead. Though she'd found Zeke to be laid-back—just a Yooper with a pilot's license—which deeply appealed to the whole "simplify" thing she'd been doing the past three years, she now desperately wished that he was an alpha male who would take the reins.

"This is great," he said, standing at the railed edge of the loft, looking down into the great room where they'd just been, and then beyond to the blackness past the windows.

He wouldn't see the view in daylight, but Jess knew it was spectacular. Stark and bold, Lake Superior crashing against a rocky shore, it both calmed and exhilarated her. As soon as she saw the lot, she knew it was where she would build. Her engineer and then her contractor had told her what a nightmare it would be, what heating costs would be in the wintertime. But she didn't care. The view would be her salvation. A balm to cure her of the past years' heartache.

But Zeke would not be seeing that view, though he was looking out at the lake now.

God, he wouldn't want to spend the night, would he? Surely not. She had no idea what kind of schedule he kept, but at the hangar it hadn't seemed like he was jumping to get ready for the next day's flight. If he didn't have to be back in Hancock in the morning, would he want to stay at her place instead of getting on the road so late?

Assuming it would be late. It was only seven now, and the situation they were in didn't seem to call for much conversation or foreplay.

Both of which Jess wanted to skip, and yet she felt uneasy about being with a partner she knew nothing about.

She'd bought a box of condoms when she'd moved in, more out of wishful thinking than anything. But those hours in the plane alone with him—the scent of pine and outdoors mingling with him—made her bold. That and his handsome, stoic profile and the dashing dimple in his chin.

Besides, she was just helping out with the wolf study. She'd most likely never have to see him again.

He turned from the railing and prowled along the room, his back to her. She thought about sitting on the bed, but that made her nervous, so she stood as he walked to her vanity table, a long finger trailing along the glass bottles and up the standing mirror.

It had been those hands, strong and firm on the yoke of the plane, that had done her in. And the dimple. And the scent. And the being so damn close to him for so long after not having been near a man in that way in months.

Years.

He picked up a bottle of her perfume and held the tip to his nose, breathing in. He set it back down, and his head dipped and then shook. Did he know that wasn't the scent she was wearing today? He repeated the routine with the other two bottles, each time waiting after the breath and then shaking his head. Looking around the table and not seeing any more bottles, he glanced over his shoulder at her with questioning eyes.

"Vanilla," she said. "I baked this morning before I met you. I dropped the cookies off at the Houghton office."

He smiled then, and she did everything she could not to gasp. She'd propositioned Zeke Hampton because he'd seemed simple and uncomplicated. And since she hadn't ever laid eyes on him in the nearly three years she'd been in the Copper Country, she felt it was safe to assume she'd never have to see him again after this night.

But that smile—no, more of a grin—and the intelligence behind those dark brown eyes, had her thinking that there was a lot more to Zeke Hampton than she'd first assumed.

Uncomplicated was looking a lot less likely.

He was still looking at her when he said, "I thought these were outlawed."

He lifted his hand, which was now holding her greenstone necklace that was hanging over the mirror. "You're not allowed to take greenstones from Isle Royale, that's true," she said. "You can buy the jewelry around here, and other places, though."

He turned fully toward her, but stayed at the table, leaning against it, crossing his long legs at the ankle.

His dark brown hair was short and looked like he was growing it out, with the top being a little longer than the sides. She hadn't really noticed that in the plane because he was wearing headphones at times, and a knit cap at others. She had a flash of running her hand through the thickness at the top, and wondered if the sides would bristle in their shortness.

Wait. What were they talking about?

His smile said he knew exactly where her thoughts had been, and she had to clear her throat before answering. "I've had that necklace for years. It was a gift." She didn't bother going into the complicated relationship she had with the man who gave it to her. No need for that kind of sharing with someone she'd never see again. This was not supposed to be personal. "But I don't wear it around the island much, just because I don't want people to think it's ill-gotten gains." And because it hurt to feel the weight of the stone on her neck, of all it symbolized.

He chuckled, the sound sending a spark through her. God, it had been so long since she'd been attracted to a man, wanted something more than just a business relationship from any man. And she wanted that with Zeke—wanted him all over her. And she wanted to be all over him.

"And her?" he asked, still looking at her. Jess froze, knowing without looking where Zeke's hand was now. On top of the frame of Cassie's school photo from three years ago. What would he see looking at a photo of Cassie? Just a twelve-year-old with braces and a cowlick she desperately tried to calm in a ponytail? "Yours?"

How to answer that? Feelings she tried to run from, tried to bury in the task of designing and building her own home, snuck up on her, clenching in her gut like she'd been punched.

The pain. It might have been the only emotion strong enough to replace the lust she felt for the man watching her. He must have read the emotional turmoil on her face, because he pushed himself away from the vanity and made his way across the large loft in four long-legged strides. "Hey, I—"

She shook her head, backing away from him. Hating that what had been lightness in his eyes now seemed to be turning to concern, even pity. "It's not that. She's not… She's… It's just complicated, is all."

He was in front of her now, and if she still had the smell of cookies on her, he had the outdoors clinging to him like a cloak of freshness.

"I'm sorry. I didn't mean to bring up anything painful," he said. She put her head down, but he ducked his lower so she would have to meet his eyes. "Or complicated."

He was not what she wanted, what she assumed him to be. No good ol' boy Yooper with not a care in the world, who was down for a night of healthy, hot-blooded fun. Oh, he may have been all that, but he wasn't *just* that. Seeing, knowing, feeling, understanding. Things she did not want in a bedmate.

Much as she wanted to wrap her arms around his neck and inhale that deep, piney smell, she just couldn't chance it. Not after she'd worked so hard to find her peace. Her solitude.

He placed a warm hand on her arm, and she jolted. She took a step back, her knees backing into the side of the bed.

"I think I made a mistake," she whispered. A little too softly, because he moved closer to her.

"What?" There was no censure in his voice, nothing accusatory, but he'd heard her. He wasn't asking her to repeat herself, but to explain herself.

The one thing she wasn't sure she could do. At least not without hours and hours of soul-searching. Not what he signed up for when he'd said yes to her invitation.

"I guess I thought I could do this," she said, motioning with her hands between the two of them, including the bed for good measure. "But I can't. I'm sorry that you drove all the way up here."

He made a hand wave of his own, but it was only to brush away her words. "Don't worry about the drive. Listen, why don't we start over. Go back downstairs. Sit. Have a drink or something. Turn that fireplace on after all. Let's just talk."

She would have preferred if he'd been pissed. Called her a tease or something and stormed out. The understanding in his voice, his wish to put her at ease? Little did he know that being a good guy was the final nail in his coffin.

"I really think you should just go," she said. "Again, I'm really sorry. This just isn't me."

He took another step back, raising his hands from his sides as if to show her he held no weapons. Oh, but she knew he had weapons—the kind that could seriously hurt her.

"It doesn't have to *be* anything. Really, Jessica."

The use of her full name, the reminder of her ex saying it with derision in his voice, pushed her over the edge. "Really, Zeke. It was a mistake. I'm sorry, but I want you to leave."

"Of course," he said, still with understanding in his voice. He walked to the edge of the loft and had one foot on the stairs when he looked back at her.

"I'm sorry too," he said very quietly. Then he was gone, his head disappearing as he walked down the stairs. She heard his steps across the hardwood floors below, his pausing at the mudroom for boots and jacket, and then the closing of the outside door. No slamming, just a quiet click.

She stood in the middle of the loft and heard his truck start up and drive off. Then she finally sat on the bed, stared at the photo of Cassie on her vanity, at the necklace hanging from the edge of her mirror, and rolled over.

She could almost still feel the tingle from when Zeke pulled her hair through his fingers, almost smell the earthy scent of him.

And she could almost imagine those beautiful brown eyes staring down at her as he drove into her.

Almost.

Three

HAD THEY EVEN KISSED? ZEKE COULDN'T REMEMBER. It'd only been twenty minutes since she'd all but thrown him out the front door. As he drove back to Hancock in his Dodge Ram truck, he tried to piece together what had happened with Jessica Chapman.

A mission. She'd been on a mission. She'd wanted a one-night stand, and then remembered she wasn't a one-night stand kind of girl. In a weird way, he respected that, though he wished she'd maybe figured that out about herself a little earlier.

No kissing, that was for sure. He would have remembered tasting those pink lips.

Zeke shook his head and turned up the heater on his truck. Oh, well. No harm, no foul, right? Just an hour or so out of his day.

So why did he feel so out of sorts as he drove the deserted stretch of highway away from Eagle Harbor?

If he were honest with himself, he'd been out of sorts since he got out of the Navy. No. Longer than that.

A year ago, he'd been home for a short leave. He'd been with his best friend Petey Ryan in the Cat's Meow, and it'd seemed like old times. Their friend from freshman year at Tech, Twain Beck, had been there too. Zeke had even gotten lucky that night.

All had been well then.

And then, just a month later, it wasn't.

Last summer, he'd been back and announced his intention to leave the Navy in six months. His parents, sister, and friends had been shocked, but ecstatic. He'd gone on one last six-month cruise, the carrier feeling both nostalgic and prison-like for the last time. He'd gotten out with no real plans, though most of the military pilots—Navy or otherwise—went on to become airline pilots. Zeke assumed that would be the route he'd take too, but something about hanging with all his friends last summer made him put that plan on hold for a while and head back to the Copper Country. Just for a few months or so to spend some time with everyone. Figure out which airlines would be the top targets, where he'd like to live. Basic life shit.

And then a weird thing happened.

He felt a keen sense of *rightness* back in Hancock. Hell, back in his childhood bedroom, though it did seem weird not to have his twin sister Lizzie hogging the bathroom.

And then another weird thing happened.

Fate, Lizzie called it. Dumb luck, Petey said.

Zeke, not entirely convinced that his sister and his friend didn't have something to do with it, reserved judgment on just how "lucky" it was that Bobby Richards, who owned one of the area's seaplane charter businesses, wanted to sell out and retire. He mostly flew out of Marquette, but had started developing a following in the Copper Country, which was where Zeke would concentrate the business. *If* he bought it.

Zeke wasn't entirely sure that Lizzie didn't plant the seed of retirement in Bobby's head herself, though she swore she'd only heard it through the Copper Country grapevine. A vine so strong it was really more like a steel cable.

So Zeke had sat down with Bobby and talked numbers. He'd

gotten his ATP—Airline Transport Pilot—rating, allowing him to fly planes other than Navy jets, and would get his seaplane quals in as soon as the lakes thawed.

And now Zeke was seriously considering becoming the owner (along with the local bank) of Richardson's Charters. First thing Lizzie's team was working on was a name change to Hampton Air Charters.

It was all happening fast, but it seemed like it could be a good fit for Zeke, who had always loved the area but never thought to do more than visit since moving away after college. Still, he wasn't quite ready to make Bobby an offer.

He was still at his parents' place, which was working well while he decided which path to take. If he did buy Bobby's business, he'd then have to figure out where to live.

He'd love something like Jessica's house, but the bulk of his savings would have to go into purchasing the business, so there'd be no way he'd find such a modern home with that tremendous view. Even if he had all his savings from the past fourteen years in the Navy for just a home—and he'd lived pretty sparingly, so he had socked a lot away—he wouldn't be able to afford something like Jessica lived in.

Did wolf researchers at Tech make a hell of a lot more than he thought they did?

Nah, probably not.

There was definitely more to her than met the eye.

He drove to the east end of Hancock and to the house where he'd grown up. He turned up the hill by Bob's Mobil, making note of the Bible verse that Bob had placed on the sign above the gas prices.

Conduct yourselves with wisdom toward outsiders, making the most of the opportunity.

After pulling into the plowed-out area by his father's car,

Zeke sat in his parked truck, thinking about Jessica Chapman and opportunity.

He'd like a do-over with her. Some time taken, some steps not skipped. And for damn sure some kissing. She obviously needed more time, and for now, he had that to give.

He had the number of the research department at Tech where she worked. He'd call first thing tomorrow. Or maybe wait a couple of days. No need to look desperate.

But he definitely wanted to see her again.

Four

—◊—

"YOU'RE DOING GREAT, ANNIE. LET THIS OLD MAN CATCH his breath, and I'll be right back out there with you," Petey Ryan said as he left the ice and joined Zeke on the bleachers just beyond the boards.

Petey was taking Zeke's niece, Annie Robbins, skating, as he did every Sunday night if he was in town and Annie was willing. Which she usually was, though now, at thirteen, there were times when Petey got bumped for some friend get-together or other. Though not related, Petey and Annie had grown close three summers ago when he championed the Annie Aide charity to help defray Annie's medical costs.

Zeke was letting his nephew, Sam, climb on the lowest bleacher, raising and lowering himself, looking up at his uncle intermittently for praise and encouragement. Deciding to crash the standing skating date, and give his sister and her husband a little date night (which probably entailed never even leaving the house and ending up with them making out on the couch), Zeke had picked up his niece and nephew.

Annie and her older brother Stevie were Zeke's niece and nephew by marriage, and he didn't know them very well, having only been home three times since Lizzie and Finn got married two years ago. He was hoping that being back in the area would allow him to have more of a relationship with them both. Though Stevie, being a senior at Houghton High, wasn't around much anyway, and next year would be living in the dorm at Tech.

At least Zeke would be able to see Annie more regularly during her high school years. She loved to skate and was in a club for that. She was also in the local swim club, planning on joining the high school team when the time came.

When Lizzie had first reconnected with her high school flame Finn, Annie had been in a wheelchair, waiting for a lumbar fusion surgery. Three years later, she was outskating retired NHL player Petey.

Eighteen-month-old Sam was a Hampton, with his sister's black hair and brown eyes that resembled Zeke's, though he might be a little biased. Just then, Sam climbed higher than he knew he should and looked to Petey and Zeke with a "Who's gonna stop me?" grin.

"He's got his uncle's blood," Petey said, voicing Zeke's thoughts. "God help him," they both said, then chuckled.

God, it felt good to just hang with his best bud, his niece, and his nephew on a Sunday night at the ice rink. He edged up one more seat in the bleachers, keeping his leg out so Sam could climb higher but still have Zeke to hold on to.

His tiny hands dug into Zeke's jeans and Sam leveraged himself, mostly on his belly, onto the next bleacher. Standing on the foot bench, he beamed at the two men. "Good job, little man," Zeke said, and Sam chortled at his uncle.

Uncle Zeke. It'd been an instant title the day Lizzie married Finn. Honestly, there were a lot of years where Zeke thought his parents were destined to never become grandparents. All through their twenties and early thirties, Lizzie was building up her business in Detroit and didn't seem all that interested in the idea of marriage and babies. Zeke was flying for the Navy and had no intention of being away from a wife and kids for the months at a time that cruises demanded. Lots of his fellow pilots in the squadron had a wife and kids (or a husband, in the case of some of the female pilots) and made it work. But Zeke didn't want that. If he'd met *the one*, it might have changed his mind, but he hadn't.

"So where do you stand with the mystery redhead?" Petey asked Zeke.

Zeke had told his friend about his night—hour?—with Jessica only because a preliminary check on intel about the woman ended with a big, fat goose egg. Zeke figured if anyone would know about a mysterious beauty in the area it would be his former-hound-dog best friend. But Petey hadn't heard of Jessica either.

"Nowhere. After nothing turned up on social media, I tried calling the wolf study offices at Tech. Turns out she doesn't even work there, but was just filling in for the head guy, who was out of town. She must be familiar with the island or something, but they wouldn't say. Wouldn't give me any information about her other than she didn't work there."

"Well, yeah, because, you know, you don't want to give out personal info to stalkers or anything."

Zeke gave his friend the universal jerk-off hand signal, then cringed when he saw Sam watching him and trying to emulate his uncle by waving his little wrist.

He'd have to watch himself now that Uncle Zeke was going to get some serious playing time. A little less sailor in this naval officer.

"I'm not stalking her. I just want to reach out and see if she wants to get together again. If not, no big deal."

"She flew with you, right?" Petey asked.

"Yeah."

The big man shifted on the uncomfortable wooden bleachers and waved to Annie on the ice as she whizzed by. "So she knows your name. And Clint's business is online, right?"

"Yep. Lizzie looked it up when Clint contacted me. He doesn't do seaplane stuff, but she wanted to get an idea in case I buy Bobby's business. She has her team working on the whole thing. Branding. I have a brand now."

"Of course she does," Petey said.

"Jesus, I might have a *brand* now. How fucked up is that?" At either the strangeness of the word or Zeke's emphasis, Sam's head whipped up to his uncle at the curse. With a puzzled look, his little mouth started moving as if to sound out his own F-bomb.

Yeah, Zeke would definitely need to tone it down.

"I mean, I told her not to do anything, that I wasn't even sure I was going to buy the business."

Petey shrugged. "You know your sister. She's going to be three steps ahead on the planning of this thing."

"Yeah, but still. It all feels a little too...real, you know?"

"Things change. We grow old. Grow up. The people we thought we were, we just...aren't anymore. You know?"

"Yeah," Zeke said. Petey knew what he was talking about. Although both of them logically knew they wouldn't be flying jets for the Navy or playing in the NHL their whole lives, it was an odd feeling to give up such a huge piece of your identity. It was like a retirement, but without the gold watch.

It had been a hell of a party, though.

"What I'm saying is, if she wants to see you, she knows how to find you, right?"

"I guess," Zeke said, admitting it to himself. It didn't feel great.

"Didn't you say she wasn't that into you in the end?"

Zeke shrugged, watching his nephew gnaw on one of the wooden planks, knowing he should probably stop him. But the kid really seemed to be enjoying eating the hell out of the wooden bleacher. "I'm not even sure it was about me. I think it just got real for her, and she freaked. Liked the idea of a casual hookup, but couldn't go through with it." He didn't mention that he'd triggered something by pointing out the picture of the little girl. And the necklace. Those pieces of information he kept to himself. It felt disloyal, in a way, to tell even his best friend about something that seemed very personal to Jessica.

Sex, yeah, he could talk about that—though not in the detail he and Petey used to share back in their college days.

"Besides, don't you know where she lives? Didn't you say you went to her place?"

"Yeah."

Petey snorted. "Of course you did. What else were you gonna do? Take her to your bedroom at your parents' place? 'Mom, Dad, this is some chick I just met. Not really sure about her name, but we're just gonna go upstairs and study in my room.'" He chortled at his own humor, and Sam looked up and smiled, wanting in on the joke.

"I knew her name," Zeke said. "It was dark when we went to her place and I was following her. There are a bunch of those little drives off M-26. I'm not sure I could find it again." Not exactly the truth. He had stopped at the road when leaving and pressed on his brakes so the red light would shine on the fire number sign. That was all that was there, no hand-painted sign with a name, like some of the other drives had. He was a Navy pilot, flying missions over places nobody had even heard of and finding needles in haystacks. He could find her place again. He just didn't tell that to Petey.

"Besides," he said, "that really would be stalker-ish, showing up at her house unannounced."

"Very true," Petey said. He took his eyes from the ice where he was keeping an eye on Annie and looked at Zeke. "But are you gonna do it anyway?"

Zeke took a deep breath and let it out. Sam was now attempting to straddle Zeke's thigh, so he picked up the little guy and tossed him, catching him easily and then settling him across his lap, causing Sam to giggle and clap his tiny hands together.

"I honestly don't know," Zeke finally said.

Petey studied him, then turned back to the ice. "Anything you want to talk about?" he said softly.

"About what?" Zeke asked.

"The last year? Something go down?"

Zeke shook his head. Sam grabbed onto his knit hat and Zeke took it off and gave it to his nephew, which immediately went into Sam's mouth. Zeke thought he remembered Lizzie saying something about teething. "No. Nothing went down." His best buddy since high school studied him, and Zeke ducked the look, not wanting to talk about anything deep. "Other than the regular fighter pilot saving the world, being a hero stuff."

Petey snorted, and Zeke smiled. It was a long-running game with them when they'd go out. Who could get more chicks—the war hero or the NHL player? They were shameless in the piling on of their exploits and dogging of each other.

But that was then. Now Petey was newly married to a woman they'd known forever. Alison Jukuri, who was one of Lizzie's best friends and had practically been a second sister to Zeke growing up. Katie, their third partner in crime, was also like a sister. She was now married to pro golfer Darío Luna, with a one-year-old daughter and another baby on the way.

What had Petey just said? *Times change. People grow.* That was for damn sure.

"When you were home a year ago, you never mentioned getting out. I thought you'd at least stay in to get your twenty. Then last summer, you say you've got one more cruise in you and that's it. Now you're acting like a chick moaning about wanting a one-night stand—and not even a successful one—to be something more."

"Just want to take the mission to completion. I was cleared hot then waved off at the last second. So maybe a two-night stand. That's it," Zeke said, but not with much conviction.

That was because he was starting to feel a change in what he wanted. What he *thought* he wanted. It had started, he supposed, when his twin got married and started a family. Katie became a mother, too. Then his best friend got married. It seemed like everyone he was close to, outside of his Navy buddies, were all settled or married, with or without children. Happy.

Zeke had never been one to feel restless. Though there were long stretches of sheer boredom in what he did, there were the times, in the air, in training, in operations, that were thrilling enough that he never felt restless.

And maybe that wasn't quite the feeling that he'd had ever since last summer, and even more so now that he'd been home a couple of months. But when he looked at Sam—and Peaches Luna, and Annie and Stevie—he felt a kind of emptiness that he'd never felt before.

As if knowing that Zeke was thinking of him, Sam wrapped his chubby hand around Zeke's thumb and burrowed his little back into Zeke's chest, making himself comfortable. His pale eyelids blinked several times, then he smiled drowsily at Zeke before his eyes softly shut.

Zeke loved being an uncle. But he was starting to think he wanted to be a father. And at thirty-eight, he better be on the lookout for that child's possible mother.

"A second night, that's all," he said softly, not wanting to wake Sam.

Petey chuckled beside him. "Yeah, right. Whatever you need to tell yourself, flyboy."

Zeke brought an arm up and around Sam's body, holding him close, liking the feeling of the boy's bulk easing into his.

He'd give it one more week to try to find a phone number or email or some kind of contact info. Then he was going to show up at Jessica Chapman's door.

Five

—⚭—

"YOUR ORDER'S NOT QUITE READY YET. WOULD YOU LIKE something to drink at the bar while you wait?" the bartender at the Commodore said to Jessica.

"Yes, I guess so," she said. She'd phoned in her order when she'd left the meeting at the park services office. But that was only a few blocks away, apparently not enough time to make one of their famed tostada pizzas to go.

"I'll have a glass of Merlot," she said.

"Which can be brought to our table," someone said from behind her. Before she even turned, she knew who it was. That deep, throaty, full-of-confidence voice was one of the reasons she'd invited Zeke Hampton home with her two weeks ago.

She turned around and tried very hard to keep her features from conveying just how happy she was to see him. Or how damn good he looked.

He was wearing a white turtleneck with a black three-quarter-zip fleece over it, blue jeans, and work boots. His dark brown, not-quite-black, hair was tousled in waves, like maybe he'd just taken off a knit cap. A chook, or toque, the natives called it. Jess had picked up a bit of the lingo in the time she'd been in the Copper Country.

The slight cleft in his chin seemed more prominent today, or perhaps it was because he was smiling at her and his dimples seemed to bracket the small dent in his strong chin.

Strong everything, she guessed, though she hadn't seen him naked the night they'd almost hooked up. Pity, because she could only imagine that sight.

"Join us, please? At least until your order's ready?"

Hmmm. Maybe she wouldn't have to leave seeing Zeke Hampton naked only to her imagination. Could she go through with it this time?

She did a mental flip through her personal grooming, and that of her house, as he motioned for her to follow him into the secondary dining room, the one that faced out onto the Portage Canal, which was still mostly ice.

Had she shaved her legs recently? It hadn't mattered to her last time, so really, what did it matter now?

Thoughts of when she last changed her sheets fell away the closer she got to the table to which Zeke was taking her.

He was on a date. Had to be. The table held another man—a huge man who even now was smiling an "Oh, oh, Zeke's about to get busted" grin as he rose and grabbed a chair from an empty table. There were two women. One who was clearly with the big man, seeing as once he placed the snagged chair down next to Zeke's empty one, he scooted his chair closer to the woman and draped his arm across the back of her chair. She was petite and had the mocha coloring of what Jess had heard referred to as a "dark Finn." Different from the Nordic-looking Finns that were prevalent in the area, but also plentiful. She gave Jess a smile, but cut a quick glance to the other woman, whose back was to Jess.

Zeke's date.

From the back, all Jess could see was that she had shoulder-length black hair and was taller—at least while sitting—than the other woman.

As they rounded the table, the woman looked over her shoulder first to Zeke. Love and warmth were all over the woman's face, and Jess felt her stomach heave.

God, she'd been so stupid. She'd propositioned, and almost slept with, a man in a relationship.

She'd looked for a wedding band while he'd flown, and his finger was bare. But she hadn't come out and asked if he was seeing anyone.

Why would she when she wasn't interested in anything beyond a night of mutual enjoyment with no strings attached?

Barely last names attached.

And why hadn't Zeke mentioned the fact that he was seeing someone? Why had he taken her up on her proposition?

Her stock in Zeke Hampton bottomed out. Definite sell mode.

Oh, well. She'd say hello, try not to look guilty when he introduced his girlfriend, get her pizza, and get the hell out of there.

And go another day (week?) without thinking about shaving her legs.

She really should have taken her coworker Reilly up on his offer to join him and his girlfriend for dinner after their meeting.

"Jessica Chapman, this is Petey Ryan and his wife Alison Jukuri." Zeke motioned to the couple, who nodded to Jess. "Sorry, Al, haven't quite gotten the hang of calling you Ryan yet," he said.

"No worries. I'm keeping Jukuri, anyway," the smaller woman said.

"It's still under discussion," the big man—Petey Ryan—said.

Alison gave her husband—her *new* husband, apparently—an eye roll and returned her attention to Jess. "Nice to meet you. Join us," she said, waving to the empty chair.

Zeke was still standing, his arm out to take Jess's coat, which she reluctantly took off and gave him. He set it on top of their pile of jackets just as the waitress delivered her glass of wine and put it down in front of her.

"And this is Lizzie Robbins," he said, nodding at the woman who was now on Jess's right.

"Hello," Jess said, picking up her glass of wine, hoping her hands weren't shaking. The woman was looking at her closely, as if sizing her up, and Jess knew that the redhead curse of highly visible blushing was once again betraying her.

"At least you got her last name right," Petey said.

"I've had longer to practice with her," Zeke said. He sat down and picked up his bottle of beer, took a long drink, then pointed the neck of the bottle toward Lizzie. "Isn't that right?"

Lizzie smiled at Zeke, and Jess almost gasped at the familiarity and emotion that passed between the two of them.

Oh, God, he'd been with someone for a long time. Did she owe it to this woman to tell her that Zeke was a no-good dog? Even though nothing had actually happened between Zeke and herself. What was the girl code on that?

Alison leaned forward, away from her husband, and caught Jess's eye. "Lizzie and Zeke are twins. Not identical, obviously, but they sometimes have that weird twin thing going on where they read each others' minds. Don't let it freak you out."

His sister.

Jess took a longer, deeper sip of her wine. Okay, a gulp. She took a deep gulp of her wine.

Not his date.

She looked at him, and he was watching her. When their eyes met, he smiled at her, softly, slowly, as if not wanting to scare her away with any sudden movements. She almost choked on her wine, but somehow got the glass from her mouth back to the table without doing a full-on spit take.

She looked over at Alison, who sat back in her chair, taking a drink from her bottle of beer, crossing her arms in a "my work here is done" posture, and giving a wink to Jess.

Lizzie was watching her brother, who, Jess could tell, was still staring at her. Alison and Lizzie looked at each other with knowing gazes, which Jess assumed were about her. And Petey laughed for no apparent reason that Jess could tell.

It was as if they'd never seen their friend/brother smile at a woman before.

"Jessica, I think you should change that to-go order. Stay and eat with us," Lizzie said. As Jess was about to demur with words about not wanting to interrupt, Lizzie told the waitress to change Jess's order then cleared some things on the table to make more room.

"Watch out for her," Zeke said to Jess, indicating Lizzie. "She's kind of bossy."

"I prefer decisive," Lizzie said, and both men snorted.

Jess's pizza was delivered at the same time as the others' food, and she was relieved to have something to do besides sucking down her wine. Maybe she could just quickly eat and get out of there.

She wasn't as riddled with guilt as when she thought Zeke was with another woman, but she still had no intention of hanging out with him and his family and friends. No need to form attachments of any kind.

"Take your time," Lizzie said to Jess as she put a piece of pizza onto her plate. "We've got all night, and I just love meeting new people."

Jess looked to Zeke for help, but he only shrugged, smiled, and leaned back, as if waiting for the show to begin.

Oh, God. Why couldn't she have just had dinner with Reilly?

ZEKE WASN'T SURE IF JESSICA was enjoying the company or was in pure hell. She was proving to be pretty tough to read. The last thing he would have thought that day on the plane was that she was attracted to him, not to mention would take him home with her. Only for her to suddenly change her mind.

And now, amongst his sister and best friends, he couldn't tell if she was enjoying herself or secretly wishing she'd chosen anything other than Commodore pizza for her dinner.

"So, you're not with the actual wolf study, then?" Lizzie asked her after Zeke had briefly explained how he and Jessica had met.

Wait, what? He guessed he'd better stop watching her and listen to what they were saying.

But it was an easy mission to stare at her all night. She was dressed similarly to how she'd been two weeks ago—turtleneck, earthy, heavy wool sweater, jeans, boots. Her hair was down and flowing in waves past her shoulders. It was the color of fire, with as many shades and shadows as flames.

"No, I'm with the National Park Service. I was only helping out with the wolf study program because they were all at a conference that week, and I happen to be interested in what they're doing."

Zeke leaned forward. "You're a park ranger? You don't work for Tech?"

"Right," she said, as if he should have known that.

Had she told him that when they'd introduced themselves? He didn't think so, but who knew? He'd been temporarily stunned by the paleness of her skin and blue of her eyes.

So much for spending the time trying to track her down through Tech offices.

"There much money in that?" Petey asked, which earned him groans from Lizzie and Alison, plus an elbow jab from Al worthy of any NHL defenseman.

"It's okay," Jess said to Alison and Lizzie. To Petey, she said, "Not really. We like to say we get paid in sunsets."

"That's so cool," Alison said. "Do you get to wear a uniform and everything?"

"And everything," Jessica said, smiling at Al. "A hat, too. It's very Yogi Bear."

A hat. She wore one of those big ranger hats. The image should have been a boner killer to Zeke, but it was anything but. Especially as his mind quickly went to thinking about her in the hat. Wearing *only* the hat.

He felt a swift kick on his ankle that came from Petey. A quick glance at his friend reminded him to get his head off images of Jessica in nothing but a hat, and to pay attention. Facts were starting to spill, and Zeke needed to soak up all the intel he could.

"What kind of education do you need for that?" Lizzie asked. "Were you a forestry major at Tech?"

Yeah, he definitely needed to pay attention. His wonderful

twin sister, through sheer nosiness of her own, or because she sensed Zeke was interested, was going to go all CIA interrogation on Jessica. And in true Lizzie style, Jess would not only never know what hit her, but she'd walk away thinking Lizzie was her new best friend.

And so would Lizzie.

A small chuckle came from Jessica, and Zeke felt it like a punch to the gut. No, lower.

"Business degree from University of Chicago. Didn't exactly prepare me for hiking on Isle Royale."

"Oh, Toto, you're not in Kansas anymore," Al said. This time Jessica outright laughed.

Yeah, definitely lower than the gut.

"You've got that right. I had come up here a few times with family when I was a child. But I was a city girl for sure." She took a sip of her wine, and Zeke watched the liquid make its way past her pink lips, the delicate movement of her neck as she swallowed. "And then I went through a pretty nasty divorce a few years ago and just needed to get away. I remembered this area from when I was a kid."

Okay, she definitely had his attention now. Well, she'd *always* had his attention, but now he was hanging on every word. Didn't mean he couldn't still stare at her mouth, though. That was where her words were coming from, after all.

"Oh, I'm sorry you had to go through that," Lizzie said, laying a hand on top of Jessica's on the table. Zeke watched to see if the contact would be too familiar to her, but she left her hand on the table until Lizzie removed hers.

"Thank you," Jessica said. "I guess I was just looking for a place to heal, think things through. I never expected to stay."

"Says pretty much everybody who lives here who isn't originally from the area," Petey said.

It was true, Zeke knew. And was part of the reason he was even considering Bobby's offer of buying out his business. Zeke loved this place, but part of what he loved about it was that it was where his family and friends were.

Jessica had no one up here, but had decided to stay.

"Any children?" Alison asked, something Zeke probably should have wondered about.

Jessica looked to be a few years younger than Zeke's thirty-eight. Shit, thirty-nine in a few months. When did he become almost forty fucking years old?

"No. No kids," she said. So, who was the little girl in the photo on her dresser? A niece, maybe? Zeke leaned forward, as if he could get a better read on the emotion in her voice. Lack of emotion, rather. "As it turned out, that was probably a blessing," she added, then picked up her glass of wine and took a small sip.

Nothing. No wistful sighs of regret. No tiny smile of pain.

Jessica Chapman was in total control of her emotions. And that was something Zeke could respect, even as he simultaneously wished he could break through said emotional wall.

"So, you stayed up here…" Alison said, nudging Jessica to pick up her story.

"I did. Two years now. At first, I just rented, but then I built a place on Lake Superior, between Eagle Harbor and Copper Harbor." She didn't once look at Zeke, not letting on that he'd been a guest in her home.

"I'll bet the view is spectacular," he said. She glanced at him, her straight nose angled as if she was not quite looking down at him. Truth was, it had been dark, and he hadn't seen the view from her windows.

Hadn't seen nearly enough that night.

"It is," she said, and returned her attention to Lizzie and Al. "And although it was in finance, my college degree was enough to become a ranger. I got on with the park service my second year here. I'm only seasonal, and part time even then, but it's been really enjoyable. I had no idea how much I'd come to love it."

"And you're mostly on Isle Royale?" Lizzie asked.

Jessica nodded. "Mostly. But I do some shifts here in town at the offices. Also on Mott Island."

"Where's that?" Petey asked.

"It's a support island for Isle Royale. It's where all the backup technology is. Power, phone, that kind of thing. They keep Isle Royale running. A small crew stays there during the season."

"Huh. Who knew," Petey said. He looked around the table. "We never did make it to Isle Royale, did we? Remember, we were going to go the summer after our junior year in college? Camp out for a week. What happened to that plan?"

Alison shrugged. "Life happened, as it does with many of our grand plans." She waved in Zeke's direction. "You were crazy busy training for OCS that summer, right? I never even saw you." He nodded and kept looking at Al, even though out of the corner of his eye he noticed Jessica's head swivel in his direction. "And you were on the U.S. national team that summer," Al said to Petey, who nodded and took a swig from his beer. Al then looked to Lizzie. "Katie stayed in East Lansing that summer to be near Ron, right?"

"That's right," Lizzie said. "I stayed there too, working at that PR firm in Lansing."

Alison looked at Petey. "So it was really just little old me, and there was no way I was going to camp on Isle Royale with the moose and wolves—and mainly mosquitoes—by myself."

"The mosquitoes are as likely to kill you as the moose and wolves are," Jessica said. "Maybe more so."

"Still, I can't believe I've never been out there," Lizzie said, then looked at Zeke. "All the more reason you need to stay and buy out Bobby—so I can get to Isle Royale."

Zeke rolled his eyes at his sister, then took another slice of pizza and slid it onto his plate. "Yeah, I'm going to base my entire future on the fact that you need a ride to Isle Royale. I'll get you a ticket on the Ranger, Lizard."

She sat back in her chair, a playful pout on her face. One she'd perfected at age five and Zeke had been ignoring—and instigating—for just as long.

"So, it's seasonal and part time," Petey said to Jessica. "Must mean you've got lots of spare time on your hands." He kicked Zeke under the table again, and Zeke shot him a "back off" look, which Jessica seemed to catch, but ignored.

Jessica wiped her hands off on her napkin and took a final drink of her wine, emptying the glass. "Until recently, I spent all my spare time on the building of the house, working with the designer, then the contractor, furnishing it. It's all set now, but I found while I was doing it how much I liked it. Loved it, actually. So, I'm entertaining the idea of doing some house flipping. Small-time stuff, nothing like what I built. A ranger friend of mine, Reilly—who helped me out with my house—and I are talking about doing it together."

Reilly? Who the hell was Reilly? Would she have invited Zeke back to her place if there were something going on with this Reilly? Or maybe that was why she'd called a halt to the evening?

"And once the season opens, I'll pick up as many shifts as I can."

To Zeke, it felt like she was shutting any kind of door as to a future get-together. And really, although she'd certainly been cordial throughout dinner and hadn't shied away from any questions Al, Lizzie, or Petey put to her, neither did she volunteer much else about herself or ask any questions of them.

Jessica Chapman was polite and conversational, but she did not want to hang with his group. She didn't want to hang out with him, either, if the way she'd all but shoved him out the door at her place was any indication.

Which stung a little.

But he was a goddamn naval aviator. Fighter jet pilot. Top fucking Gun. He wasn't going to get his panties in a wad because a one-night stand—that wasn't—wanted nothing more than that.

"Thank you for letting me join you," she said, gathering her purse and scarf from the back of her chair. She started to pull out her wallet, but both Zeke and Petey objected. She thanked them and then rose. Zeke rose with her and handed her her parka, trying to help her put it on. But she only took it from his hands and tucked it under her arm.

She couldn't get away from him fast enough.

"I'll walk you to your car," he said, but she was already moving away from him.

"Not necessary, thanks. I'm right out front. Nice to meet you all."

The other three at the table all said their goodbyes as Jessica left the main dining room and moved to the bar side of the Commodore.

Zeke stood for a second, watching her back until he heard Lizzie say, "Go after her, stupid."

Right. He strode across the restaurant, reaching Jessica just as she got to the outside door. He put his hand up on the door, staying her motion of escape.

"I tried to get in touch with you," he said softly. Low, so only she would hear. When it was obvious she wouldn't automatically bolt, he lowered his hand from the door and stepped to the side in case people came in.

She did too, facing him but saying nothing.

"You're a hard person to track down," he added. Again nothing from her. "But I guess that's because I was thinking you worked for Tech, not the park service."

"You knew where I lived," she said.

He nodded once. "True. But I got the impression you wouldn't have been happy to open the door to an unexpected visitor."

"Yeah, that wouldn't have been cool. So thank you for not taking that route."

He didn't mention that he had only been a few days away from taking that exact tactic. She looked at the door, then took a deep breath and looked up at him. She was a tall woman, but Zeke was a big man. Not Petey Ryan big, but big enough to be able to handle 7.5 G-forces without blacking out.

"Listen," she said, "I'm up for trying again if you are."

He knew his eyes were growing bigger, and he hoped he

didn't look shocked, but he was. And then he was tickled that he'd been shocked by this woman twice now.

It had been a long time since a woman had shocked Zeke.

At least in a good way.

"Definitely. Let me—"

She held up a hand. "Not tonight. Tonight's no good. But tomorrow? Or maybe—"

"Tomorrow," he said a little more quickly—and eagerly—than he liked. He cleared his throat. "Yeah, tomorrow works."

"Okay. Around nine? Do you remember…?"

"Why don't I bring up some dinner, make it earlier, and—"

Again with the hand up. "I don't want to date you, Zeke. No offense."

"None taken," he said. And really, it was true. She wouldn't be thinking about sleeping with him if she wasn't attracted to him. So what if she only wanted a fuck buddy?

Mission accepted.

"I mean it. You seem like a great guy, and your friends are really cool. But that's not where I'm at in my life. I don't want to hear the story of Zeke Hampton. I don't want to get to know your friends and family better. And I have no particular urge to tell you my story. But I would like…"

"Yes?" He leaned closer to her and down a little, watching as she ever so quickly pursed her lips in a moment that contradicted her assuredness.

"I would like to have you back to my home again. No food. No long evenings by the fire."

He moved closer still, brushing the top of her fiery head with his chin, moving to whisper in her ear. "Just some down and dirty fucking?"

She hid the little gasp, but Zeke felt it, being as close to her as he was. He had a momentary rush of regret, feeling like maybe he'd pushed her too far. Shit. He really wanted to see her again.

But then he felt her head move, her soft hair brush against his cheek. "Yes. Just that," she whispered.

"Aye, aye, skipper," he said. He stepped back and opened the door for her. "Twenty-one hundred tomorrow, then."

It took her a second to comprehend, but when she did, she gave a curt nod and walked out of the restaurant, sliding on her coat as she did. Her parka hit her mid-thigh, so he didn't have the view of her ass he wanted. Nor had he the night he'd gone to her place.

But tomorrow. Oh, tomorrow he'd take his time and bare every delectable inch of her.

Maverick might have felt the need for speed, but Zeke did not when it came to Jessica Chapman.

Six

—◊—

ZEKE WALKED BACK TO THE TABLE FEELING A LITTLE dazed. The feeling was not unlike what he'd felt driving home from Jessica's home two weeks ago.

That alone should make Zeke glad she was suggesting a hookup-only deal, but…it didn't.

"So that's her, eh?" Petey said the second Zeke was back in his seat. He only nodded and reached for his beer. "I filled the ladies in," Petey said, motioning to Al and Lizzie. Zeke nodded again. He knew that would have happened the second he'd followed Jessica out.

His sister leaned over the table and swatted his arm. "How could you not tell me you met someone?" Alison had the same accusing look on her face, though hers went back and forth from Zeke to Petey.

Obviously, Petey had kept quiet. Probably because he thought there was nothing more to it, and Al and Lizzie would get all caught up in the idea of finding someone for Zeke. A mission they'd had since they'd both found their happily-ever-afters.

"Throttle back, everyone. It's nothing more than two consenting adults getting together for a little playtime."

"'Getting' in the past tense or future?" Alison asked.

"Almost in the past and possibly in the near future," he said. When he saw the look that passed between his sister and Alison, he knew he had to put the hammer down. "But she just told me point blank she didn't want to date. Didn't want to get to know my family and friends. So please don't push this."

Lizzie seemed hurt, but Alison nodded and leaned back into Petey's broad chest, since he'd pretty much spread across both their chairs. "That makes sense," she said. "She had lots of opportunities to ask questions about Zeke, and all of us, but didn't seem interested."

"Maybe she's just shy," Lizzie said. Zeke could tell she was trying to find some reason why Jessica wouldn't automatically fall in love with them all. To Lizzie, the thought was inconceivable.

"It's probably more of what she's been through," Alison said, throwing Lizzie a bone.

Al was a psychologist, and beyond that, she was pretty damn astute about people. Except Petey. It'd taken her forever to realize Petey was in love with her.

But then, it'd taken Zeke just as long to realize it, and Petey was his best friend.

"Her divorce," Zeke said, and Alison nodded. "I mean, not putting my shrink hat on or anything, just going from what she said, it sounds like maybe it really did a number on her. So much so that she leaves everything—and everyone—she knows and comes to this remote area. And then doesn't take opportunities to get to know new people." She leaned forward, looking at Zeke. "The woman wants to be left alone."

"Oh, nobody really wants that," Lizzie said. But Zeke knew sometimes people needed exactly that. He had. Many times.

"Roger that," he said to Alison, ignoring his sister.

"Doesn't mean she's not still a woman with natural desires, but she's built herself a safe haven up here," Al said. "It doesn't sound like she wants to let anyone in for anything other than a night at a time."

Zeke nodded again. Lizzie humphed and sat back in her seat. Yeah, that was so not in Lizzie's world. She was a believer in the more the merrier and that problems could be solved with enough of her grandmother-in-law Clea's Bundt cake and some hugs.

Well, maybe she wasn't that naive, but she hadn't seen the shit that Zeke had. Thank God.

"You'd be wise to play by her rules, Zeke," Alison said to him. "Or, if you won't play by them, at least understand them and what breaking them might mean."

He sat back and took a long drag from his beer bottle, draining it. Shit. Al was right.

Petey burst out laughing. "Oh, man. This is gonna be good. Flyboy's about to be the one taking orders."

"I took orders all the time," Zeke said. Every naval officer did, all the way up. But not this kind.

"Not this kind," Petey said, laughing again as Zeke's expression gave away his thought. "Shit, son, I'm glad you're home," Petey said. He brought his beer bottle into the center of the table, and Al and Lizzie put theirs to his. Zeke tipped his empty bottle to the center, clinking and joining in with their toast.

He should be thinking about how good it was to be home— and he was. A little.

But mostly he was thinking about how soon he'd be taking off for Eagle Harbor. And Jessica Chapman.

JESS LET HERSELF INTO HER HOME and stood still at the doorway, as she did every time she entered. Waiting, listening, trying to feel if there was someone in her space.

If he'd followed her here.

She knew she should get a dog, that coming home to a big bundle of fur bustling over to her would be so much easier than opening the door to silence every time. Silence and her worst fears.

Fears that so far had not come true. And maybe never would. James, her ex-husband, had moved on, she was sure. But she hadn't been in touch with him in over a year, and the last time, he had made mention of paying her a visit sometime.

It had not been in the friendly tone of someone wanting to catch up.

Sensing nothing out of the ordinary, Jess moved into her

home, taking off her parka and boots in the mudroom, then making her way to the kitchen for a fresh bottle of wine. Having the drive ahead of her, she'd only had the one glass while she'd been at dinner with Zeke and the others. And because of said dinner, and the meeting before it, Jess was ready for another glass—or four—of Merlot.

After pouring herself a large glass, she made her way over to the spacious living room and turned on the gas fireplace. She then curled up on a loveseat right in front, pulling down a cashmere throw over her legs.

Yes, a big, floppy-eared dog would fit right into the picture she'd created.

James had forbidden the idea of any pets, wanting Jess to be able to accompany him on his many business trips all over the world whenever he beckoned.

At first, he'd beckoned all the time. Jess had loved the travel, even as it sidelined her own career at the firm.

The phone rang, chasing thoughts of the past away. But not for very long. When she looked at the caller ID on the handset, it showed "Unknown Caller," and a shiver ran down her spine. Still sitting in the loveseat, she picked up the phone as it rang a second time, holding it in her hand and away from her body as if she'd snatched a snake from the grass.

A third ring grated on her enough that she pressed the talk button and brought the phone to her ear.

"Hello?" she said, her body tensing, waiting for a reply.

Please let it be a wrong number. Or a telemarketer, even.

Nothing. No sound. Not even breathing. But also not the dead air you sometimes heard before a recorded voice came on.

"Hello?" she said again, willing her voice not to convey the dread that was slowly seeping through her body.

Nothing.

Hang up. Hang up. Hang. Up.

"Hello?" she said one more time. When there was still no sound, she finally pressed the button to end the call. She kept the phone next to her on the loveseat. She wasn't going to even have a landline put in when she built the house, but cell reception was so spotty this far north that she felt she had to have something in case of an emergency. The thing practically never rang.

Jess had lost touch with most of her friends long before she and James had split up. It had been the slow estrangement from all others that finally woke her up to her husband's controlling nature. By the time she'd left him, there weren't many friendships remaining to even try to salvage.

He'd isolated her, and she'd been too dazzled by him to notice.

She looked around her expansive A-frame. The loft where she slept and had her home office jutted out over the great room, all facing majestic Lake Superior. She was still isolated, but this was of her own doing, her own creation.

She didn't feel nearly as lonely here as she had in the penthouse of James's building on Lake Shore Drive. She'd been surrounded by people in Chicago. It was amazing how lonely she'd been the last few years of her marriage.

Here she could—and did—go days without seeing anyone. Yet she felt a peaceful calm that was new and soothing to her.

The phone rang again, bursting that soothing all to hell. She picked it up and pressed talk but didn't say anything. If that asshole wanted to hear her voice, see if she was scared or on edge, or one of the other horrible emotions he could so easily bring out in her, he'd wouldn't get the satisfaction.

She sat in silence, listening to nothing on the other end. She thought she might have detected breathing, but she wasn't sure. It certainly wasn't the proverbial *heavy breathing*.

After a minute, she hung up. She sank down deeper into her cushions, bringing the throw up around her shoulders, letting the phone fall from the balance of her knees as she curled up her legs. It bounced on the soft rug, only inches from the hardwood where it might have broken. Which might not have been a bad thing.

She stared at the fireplace, glad now that she'd let the

contractor talk her into a gas one instead of wood. He'd made the point that she'd have to deal with either chopping or buying wood each year and hauling it into the house on her own.

She wasn't afraid of that—neither the cost nor the hard work—and actually welcomed the idea of splitting logs in half. But then the contractor had mentioned the tracked-in debris from the wood, a fireplace, and getting up to feed a fire all evening, and she capitulated.

Now as she sat staring at the blaze and the phone on the floor, she was glad she did. She could lie here all evening and not have to get up to throw on another log, which was good, because it seemed as if those phone calls had robbed her of her ability to do anything but lie there and stare straight ahead.

She woke up in the morning stiff from spending the night on the loveseat. She'd never made it upstairs to the loft and her bed with the soft down comforter.

The phone still sat on the floor where it had fallen. She carefully picked it up, thinking if it really were a snake, it could strike at any time. She put it back in the cradle and made her way to the kitchen to put on some coffee.

Hoping that Zeke Hampton would be able to take her mind off everything else later that night.

Seven

—⚶—

"ARE YOU OKAY?" ZEKE ASKED WHEN JESSICA OPENED the door to him. She didn't look like he'd seen her on the other two occasions. Something was off.

"Yes, why?" she said, stepping back from the door so he could enter. He did, handing her the bottle of wine he'd brought. He kicked off his boots and took off his jacket and gloves, then put the gloves in the pocket and hung it all on one of the wooden pegs she had lining the walls of her mudroom.

"Nothing. You just seem...different."

She studied him, then walked down the hall to the main room of her A-frame. "You hardly know me well enough to know if I'm *different*."

This was not going how Zeke had hoped. On the drive to Eagle Harbor, he'd had a semi the whole way just thinking about finally seeing Jessica Chapman naked. All that smooth, pale skin and flaming red hair. And he wanted to try to get to know her a little bit better, too. See if there was something more than the lust that rushed through his body every time he looked at her full pink mouth and blue eyes.

"Jessica," he said when they were both in the main room. He used his military voice, and it worked, getting her to stop and turn toward him. "I'm here to have sex with you."

She blinked several times and then swallowed, letting Zeke know that even if it was only a healthy dose of lust he was feeling, it was reciprocated.

"And you think that's enough for you to gauge if I'm okay or not?" she asked. It wasn't in a bitchy way, almost playful, though there wasn't even a hint of a smile on her pretty face.

"Not always, no," he said. Sadly, that was the truth. He'd been with many women who he had absolutely no idea what was going on with, nor been able to tell if anything was amiss. Nor care even if it was, sadly.

But…

"Are you? Okay?" he asked again.

She searched his face, and though he wasn't sure what she was looking for, he tried to convey understanding and openness. It was odd that he'd press like this when it would have been so easy to take her hand and head up to the loft and her bed.

But he found he desperately wanted her to find in him whatever she was looking for.

Her shoulders slumped, and she looked down at the floor to her toes, encased in bright green wool socks sticking out from her jeans. The socks were the same bright jade as her V-neck sweater. She looked at her hand holding the bottle of wine as if she couldn't remember how it'd gotten there.

He took the few steps toward her, putting his hand out toward the bottle when she tensed. "How 'bout I pour us each a glass?" he said.

"I told you that you didn't need to bring anything," she said, but handed him the bottle, led him to the kitchen, and took two wine glasses from a white glass-front cabinet.

The kitchen was to the side of the great room and still had a lakefront window. It also had a large window along the side of building, right where a small table with comfortable-looking black chairs sat. The kitchen was done in gray and white with some black thrown in. Clean, expensive, and unadorned. Zeke thought of his mother's kitchen, cluttered with handmade items that he and Lizzie had made for her years ago. Trinkets that she'd picked up on family vacations through the years. Recipe cards jammed into the corner of a spice rack on the counter. Scarred cutting boards leaning against the faded backsplash.

Or Lizzie's kitchen in Finn's farmhouse. Overflowing with Sam's bottles and baby food jars, snacks that Clea had made in an always-full cookie jar. Annie's backpack slung over the back of one of the chairs.

This kitchen, Jessica's kitchen, could have been torn out of a design magazine after a staged photo shoot. But there were no signs of her in it.

No personal items, no handmade potholders, no dish towels with funny sayings on them.

Nothing that gave Zeke any clue about who Jessica Chapman was.

Maybe he was searching for something that just wasn't there?

She handed him a corkscrew and set the empty glasses on top of the black marble island.

"I didn't bring a meal, like you said, but I thought a bottle of wine might be nice. I hope this is okay?" He showed her the label. He didn't know anything about wine, being mostly a beer drinker, with an occasional scotch thrown in. He'd heard her order a Merlot at the Commodore last night, so he'd asked one of the workers at Jim's Foodmart—which had one of the best beer and wine selections in the Copper Country—for a recommendation.

"It's fine, I'm sure," she said. "I'm not picky."

He *really* couldn't pin her down. She hiked through Isle Royale all summer, and yet lived in this beautiful home with high-end finishes and furniture.

She seemed to want a down-and-dirty fuck, but balked when he asked if she was okay.

He was becoming more and more interested in Jessica Chapman even as he became more and more convinced that that was the last thing she wanted from him.

She took a sip of the wine after he poured, and nodded her approval. She smiled at him, but it was small and forced, and once again he got the feeling she was not at ease. Was it he? Did she regret inviting him?

"Umm…you didn't happen to call me last night, did you?" she asked.

He shook his head. "No. I don't have your number."

"Right. Yeah, I figured…"

"But I'd be happy to take your number," he said with a hint of teasing in his voice. She smiled again, this one almost real. But she didn't offer up her digits. She took another sip of the wine and placed it back on the island. Her hands stayed on the marble, so white against the black, veined stone. "You got a call you weren't expecting?" he said. She kept her head down, looking at her hands, but responded with a small nod. "No caller ID?"

"Unknown caller," she said.

He was going to say something about a telemarketer or wrong number, but Jessica was no dummy. She lived out here by herself with seemingly no qualms. If she was concerned about an unknown caller, there was a reason.

"Shall we take these upstairs?" she said, lifting her glass from the counter and stepping away from the island.

"Sure," he said. He let her pass him and was happy to fall in line and follow her and her spectacular ass to wherever she wanted to take him. But a heaviness weighed down on him, and he found himself reaching out and placing a hand on her hip and guiding her away from the steps to the loft—and bed—and over to a large couch that, with a loveseat, made up the seating area in front of a fireplace. "Or why don't we enjoy our wine down here," he said. "First," he added, making sure he still retained the option of a night in Jessica's bed.

She looked torn, even glancing up at the loft longingly. Oh, he understood that gesture. He wanted to get up those stairs too, but he got the impression hers was more a look of an escape attempt dashed.

"Umm…"

Which made Zeke all the more determined that they have a small conversation and a glass of wine before they tried to break that big bed of hers. "Here," he said, taking her hand and pulling her onto the couch with him.

She tucked her legs under herself and reached to the coffee table in front. Picking up a remote, she turned the fireplace on. Yes. This was good. A cozy chat in front of a fireplace.

Zeke took a sip of his wine, then set the glass on the coffee table. Slouching low in the soft couch, he stretched his legs out, crossing them at the ankles. Crossing his arms across his chest, he looked over at her.

"So, Jessica, want to tell me why the phone call made you jumpy?"

"Jumpy?"

He nodded.

She stretched an arm along the back of the couch, looking anything but jumpy. Still, he stood by it. "You know me so well. Because you're here to have sex and all."

He flicked a hand in dismissal of her throwing his words back at him.

"You might as well call me Jess." It was an olive branch, a small one, but Zeke reached out for it, though he didn't move an inch across the couch. He wanted to, but he kept still.

"So, *Jess*, what's up with the crank call? It *seems* to have made you jumpy."

She tried to hide a smile, but one played across her mouth.

"It did have me freaked out a little bit. It's just so unusual to even have it ring at all, then for it to be two dead-air calls so close together..."

He uncrossed his arms but stayed sitting where he was. "Two? It was two calls?"

"Didn't I say that?"

He shook his head. "Negative. And you heard nothing on the other line, no clicks, nothing mechanical?"

"No. No breathing, either. I mean, they were short calls."

He didn't like it. Not so much the fact that she got two calls in a row. Because that could be explained away with a robocall gone haywire. But the fact that she thought it was a big deal was enough for him to uncross his ankles and turn so he faced her, one knee up on the couch, his arm going across the back, his hand not quite touching hers.

"Do you think it was your ex-husband?" She looked away from him, toward the fire, and he knew he'd guessed correctly. "Are you hiding from him, Jess?" He leaned forward enough that his hand could reach hers on the back of the couch, and he grazed the back of her knuckles with his finger. She didn't flinch at the touch, but she didn't open her hand to his, either. "Are you in danger from him?"

"No, it's nothing like that. Or not exactly that, anyway." She took a long breath and let it out slowly. "This wasn't what this night was supposed to be. Telling each other our war stories."

"This night can be whatever we want it to be. And right now, I'd like to hear all about your war."

She tucked her hair behind her ear, looking back to the fireplace. Zeke wondered if maybe he'd lost her. If she'd forgo the story of why a phone call would freak her out and they'd end up in her bed in minutes.

Not that that would be a bad thing.

But Zeke found himself wishing that the trip upstairs would be postponed for a few hours.

"I started working at James's firm in Chicago right after I got my degree."

"Law firm?" Zeke asked, settling back into the couch, ready for her story.

"Finance. Hedge funds, mostly. Family biz for me. My dad was into finance, too."

"So you followed in his footsteps."

She chuckled, but it wasn't a warm sound. "Yeah, it turned out I did. When I was a kid, I was fascinated with wolves and then all wildlife. I thought maybe I'd be a vet or something. Somewhere along the line, that fell away…" She shook her head, as if trying to dislodge a memory. "I'm not really sure when.

I suppose when my parents finally split up. Anyway, I got the finance bug while at University of Chicago. My father got me a couple of prestigious internships, one of which led to a job at James's firm after graduation."

"Not working with your father?"

"No," she said firmly. Zeke didn't push it because he wanted her to go on, but he filed it away. "I went to work at one of his rivals' firms." Yeah, he'd definitely circle around to *that*.

"I met James, who owned the firm, at a social function after being with the company a few months. He was older, sophisticated…dazzling. And he pursued me with a full-court press. He'd been divorced a couple of years, had a daughter who was five at the time. That's her picture up in the loft." She looked from the fire down to the hand in her lap, her fingers ticking off on her thumb. "Five. We were married five months after we started dating."

"Whirlwind romance," he said. *Daddy issues*, he thought.

"More like mergers and acquisitions," she said. "I liked the stability of an older man. Every guy I'd dated to that point was still figuring out what they wanted to be when they grew up. James knew." Her voice turned emotionless when she added, "James knew everything."

"And you stayed on, working for him?" Zeke asked.

"For a while. But it got weird at the office. People thought I was either a gold digger or had a daddy complex, or both."

Zeke took a sip of his wine, swallowing hard to hide that he'd wondered the same thing. At least about the daddy issues. The beautiful home could signal gold digger. But the way she lived her life now, the simplicity of her profession? A woman who sat in a freezing plane with binoculars to observe wolves was no gold digger.

"I had some money and a couple of clients. I did some investing from my home office. James had just purchased a new apartment, and it had to be 'done' to the standards he held." She'd done the finger-quote thing, and there was an edge to her voice that hadn't been there before.

"Pretty demanding guy?" he asked, though he already knew the answer.

"In the most passive-aggressive way imaginable. It got so I questioned every piece of clothing I owned, every bit of furnishing for the apartment." She scoffed. "I spent two damn hours in the linen section at Neiman Marcus debating on peach or blush towels for the second guest bathroom."

"What is the difference between peach and blush?" he asked.

"Not damn much," she said, and they both chuckled. It felt good to share this with her. It might even be good for her to purge a little.

She unwound her legs from beneath her, letting one fall to the floor and bending the other in a mirror image of Zeke's posture. More open. To him.

"It went downhill from there, though the marriage lasted another five years. I built my own portfolio, kept those few clients, but was always able to be available to James when he'd travel. I made that penthouse a showpiece."

Penthouse. He knew they were talking major money. A Chicago penthouse was more major than Zeke had assumed.

"I stayed mostly for Cassie, his daughter. We didn't have her full time; he shared custody with his ex. I loved that little girl. But then…" She breathed deeply and shook her head.

"Then?"

"When we'd first gotten married, James had assured me he'd want more children. He never did. He wouldn't even discuss it after the first couple of years."

"And you did? Want children?"

She shrugged. "Not desperately. At least not in my mid-twenties. But yeah, I thought I would someday."

"And he never came around on that?" But Zeke knew the answer to that. Still, he wanted to hear it from her, get a sense of how much she would have liked children of her own.

He didn't let himself land on the thought of why that would

matter so much to him. Just circle that target for now. *Do not engage.*

"No. Never came around. In fact, the day his ex-wife *let* slip that James had had a vasectomy was the day I left him."

"Ouch. How long ago had he had one?"

She snorted at that. "Since before I met him. Can you believe that? When I confronted him about it, he said he knew that I'd love our life together so much that I wouldn't want to be tied down with young kids. So, he never thought I'd need to know that little fact."

"Wow."

"Yeah," she said, shaking her head. "The trust was completely gone. But I almost fell for it. That's the charm of him. So charismatic, so tuned in to someone, you know? That's what made him so great at what he did. I almost went back. Even did so for a weekend. For Cassie."

He was afraid to ask what had happened that weekend.

"I knew I could never stay when I went into that guest bathroom and the peach towels had been replaced."

"No," he said. He wanted to laugh but held it inside. But when she looked at him, she was smiling, and he let it out.

"Yes. Blush towels."

"I can see why you left him," he said, chuckling as he did. The chuckle turned into a full laugh as she pantomimed drying her hands on a nonexistent towel, only to pull it off the imaginary rack and hold it up to her eyes in disbelief.

"I couldn't believe it. It just solidified for me that I would never be what James wanted. And, frankly, that I didn't even want to try. Without trust, there was nothing to build on, you know?"

"So you left. Again."

She put the phantom towel back on the rack, straightening the air as if it were a wrinkled towel. "Yes. Again. He tried for a while, said he'd make the divorce difficult, and he did. But I didn't want anything from him, so it was easy to just walk away. From *him*, anyway."

He looked around the wooden A-frame and the tasteful, and likely expensive, furnishings, noticing for the first time the photos of wildlife and animals framed on the walls and wondering if Jessica had taken them. They were a nice touch on a gorgeous home. But the home wasn't all that cost money. A lot on Lake Superior and a cottage were a hell of a lot cheaper than a Chicago penthouse, but they still weren't free.

Following his gaze, she said, "It wasn't from him. I made my own money. Yes, my living expenses for seven years were covered by James, which allowed me to save what I made. But—"

He held up his hands. "No judgment from me. You did your time. You tried to make it work. The guy lied to you from day one about wanting a child. I say take him to the cleaners."

"I didn't want to do that. For one thing, it would have kept everything tied up so much longer. And I'd always feel like he had some kind of hold on me. I needed to be completely free."

He nodded, understanding. In a weird way, it was how he'd felt about leaving the Navy. It had served him as much as he had done his duty, but he wanted a different kind of life now. One of his own, no missions he didn't feel one hundred percent positive about doing. No regrets.

He had to make his own calls.

"I get it," he said. She studied him, as if weighing his words, then gave a slight nod. She leaned forward, took a sip of wine from her glass, then returned it to the table.

"He didn't let go gracefully. But he had no hold on me, other than cutting me off from Cassie, which he'd already done. Still, I wanted a fresh start. I know he knows where I am. A letter arrived last summer. It was a halfhearted attempt at an apology, but it was addressed to me here and came from him directly. Everything else had gone through my lawyer. I think as much as anything else, it was a way to let me know that he knew where I was. That he could always find me."

"That was the last you heard from him?" Zeke asked, and she nodded.

"I don't think he's dangerous or anything, but I don't want to antagonize him at all. I'm not on social media or anything like that. I don't rub my new life in his face in any way he'd be aware of. I just don't want to look up one day and see him standing there."

"The phone calls last night."

"Which were probably nothing. I mean, that was nearly seven months ago. He probably has a new trophy wife lined up by now, anyway."

"You weren't a trophy wife," Zeke said.

"Thanks a lot," she said, but she laughed.

He snorted and then waved a hand, indicating all that was Jess. "Of course you're a *trophy*. Or trophy material. But you're nobody's prize."

"Again, thanks a lot." They shared a laugh, and he shook his head.

"I'm usually much smoother than this."

"Really?"

He reached out, wrapped his hand around her calf, and pulled it across his thigh. He gave it a playful squeeze. It felt odd, and yet also right. "I'll have you know my call sign was Magnet."

"Your what?"

"My call sign."

She brought her other leg up from the floor and draped it over him with. Sinking her back into the arm of the couch, she said, "I have no idea what that is."

"A call sign? Navy pilots? Like Goose and Maverick?"

She sat back up, her legs sliding across his in a way that caused some—but definitely not enough—friction of denim on denim. "Are you telling me you were a Navy pilot?"

"Until about three months ago."

"For how long?"

"Fourteen years." Now her legs completely left his, returning to the floor as she leaned up and toward him.

"So, when we said we were going to swap war stories, you

have, like, literal *war* stories?"

"From thirty thousand feet up, yes."

She looked around the room, as if she were confused. Then those cool blue eyes settled on him, and it was as if she was seeing him for the first time.

"Okay, flyboy, your turn. Spill."

Yes, they were planning on having sex tonight, but maybe, just maybe, they were actually letting each other in.

Eight

—⁓—

JESS GOT COMFY, SLIDING DEEPER INTO THE BACK OF the couch, grateful for the spotlight to be off her and on Zeke.

Zeke the Navy pilot.

A memory from the night before came back at her. "Your sister, or maybe it was Alison, mentioned you were training for OCS. That's Officer Candidate School right? That's an *Officer and a Gentleman* thing?"

He chuckled, burrowing deeper into his side of the large couch, his long legs beside hers, his feet coming nearly to her hip. "Not quite so dramatic, but yeah. Though Petey does his best 'I got nowhere else to go' Gere impression all the time."

She laughed, thinking about the giant she'd met last night. "I can totally see that."

"So yeah, when I graduated from Tech, I went to OCS and was commissioned as an officer in the Navy. Then flight school. After I got my wings, I was stationed in Jacksonville, Florida for a while, then Oceana after they moved the squadrons out of Jax. I flew F/A-18 Super Hornets. My last squadron, the Gunslingers, was based in Oceana and flew off the USS *Truman*."

The pride he took in it all was evident. Which raised the question: "How long did you say you were in?"

He started to answer but stopped. "We don't have to do this, you know."

"I told you mine—"

He held up a hand. "And I'm happy to hear any and all details about Jessica Chapman that you're willing to share, but it doesn't have to be a two-way street."

She sat up a little straighter. "Why wouldn't I want it to be?"

He shrugged, plucked his wine glass from the coffee table, took a sip, and then placed it back on the table. "You just don't have to. I mean, you've had plenty of chances to ask me about myself, Jess. You haven't shown any interest before."

That was true. Before she could come up with some excuse, he added, "And that's okay. I know that wasn't what you were looking for that day we met. When you invited me back here the first time. In fact, I'm guessing that's why you asked me to leave. That necklace and the photo of your stepdaughter? It got real for you, yeah?"

She nodded, both relieved and hating that he saw her so clearly. "But I—"

"All I'm saying is that it's cool. It can be one-sided. I don't need to spill my war stories in order to be happy to be here with you." He stretched his arms, the one along the couch reaching even further in her direction. "I'm good."

She watched him, waiting for him to prod her, or go on, but he didn't. He really was content to just sit on the couch with her.

Which, dammit, made her really *want* to know more about him.

Nudging his side with her foot, she said, "You're right. I didn't show much interest before, but it wasn't for *lack* of interest."

"I know," he said, and flashed her a cocky grin, which made her smile.

"So go on. Now I *have* to know the saga of Zeke Hampton. Or should I say Magnet?"

He rolled his eyes. "I should clarify that many call signs are chosen for irony."

"So, no chick magnet? A monk, then?" She found that very hard to believe, with his good looks and self-confidence. And yet he was not a showboat. Not nearly as cocky as she imagined a fighter pilot could be.

Except for that grin.

"I didn't say *that*," he said.

"But not a girl in every port?"

He sighed. "See, that's the thing. Being a pilot is different. We don't necessarily *do* ports like regular Navy. Like sailors. Our squadron is stationed on land for long periods of time. Then we're on cruise for six-month stretches, give or take, on carriers. Even there, we're pretty segregated from the regular crew. We have quarters closer to the deck, so we can get there quickly if needed. Our squadron ready room is a combination of living room, office, conference room, and movie theater after the last launch of the night. It becomes our everything, that room, for these long stretches, except when we sleep or fly."

The way he said the last, when he spoke about flying, was wistful, and prompted Jess to ask, "Was it worth all the other stuff? Just to be up there in the air?"

He looked past her, beyond her home, and into the night, black once more. He nodded slowly. "Yeah, it was."

She did the math in her head. "Fourteen years, you said?" He nodded. "So, you got in not long after 9/11?"

"I'd actually committed to doing OCS before that, not knowing what was going to be happening in a few years. But those early years, that's when I really felt like I was doing something, you know?"

She nodded, though she couldn't imagine what he'd gone through. "Early on, we were flying a lot of support missions. No 'strategic targets' like they had at the onset of Desert Storm. No factories spewing out chemical and biological weapons. Our enemy was more unseen, blending with the local populace. Usually we launched off the carrier for CAS—close air support—of troops on the ground. Nineteen-year-old riflemen, from Kansas or Texas or maybe Hancock, Michigan, pinned down by insurgents, who needed a little help from above. And you *knew* you were making a difference.

"I mean, I got in because I wanted to fly, and if I was going to fly, I wanted it to be fighter jets. But to have all that training, to spend all that time in flight school, be entrusted with a seventy-million-dollar jet, and then be able to help our troops out? It just was the most delicious frosting on the best cake ever made, you know?

"As I told Petey, 'Imagine the excitement of playing in the Stanley Cup finals, while saving a hundred American lives. And you're wielding the most high-tech hockey stick in the world, which most people wouldn't comprehend, *if* they were cleared for that information, which no civilian is.'"

She nodded again, but knew she'd never felt anything close to the sense of accomplishment Zeke Hampton had felt in his life.

Sure, she was proud of what she'd done for herself—and her clients—in the investment field. And she beamed every time she walked into the home where they now lounged. But flying support missions to help out the troops? Yeah, that was something she'd never feel.

"And yet it's different, too, being a pilot. Being above it all. Having your target be twenty thousand feet below you, not staring you down with a gun pointed at you. Or a long dirt road ahead of you with the possibility of an IED exploding any second. You're in it, but not really in it."

"Islanders," she said.

"Huh? People who live on islands?"

She shook her head. "No. I mean, yes, but in this sense it's used as sort of a state of mind that people get into. Living in isolation for large chunks of time. Feeling a oneness, whether it be with nature or whatever. It's a term the rangers use to describe a sense of self."

He looked out the window again, as if he was mentally trying on the label. One that Jess knew fit her well, and she was guessing it fit Zeke too. He nodded and took another sip of wine.

"Yeah, pilots have islander mentality," he said. "Or at least I did. I'm guessing the reason I'm sticking around here, thinking about buying Bobby's business even, is that I'm tired of that mindset."

"No man is an island and all that?"

He chuckled. "Yeah, something like that."

"Wasn't there a way to stay in the Navy and be less of an island? Isn't staying in for twenty years a big deal?"

"Yeah, it is. Full retirement benefits. Everybody thought I was nuts to get out after fourteen. My buddies all said I should just gut it out the next six."

Though she had no doubt that Zeke was tough enough to gut anything out, he didn't seem like the type to do something he didn't want to do. "And?"

He gave both a sigh and shrug, then folded his arms. "Not my style. I was done. My XO had been bugging me about 'punching tickets,' polishing my résumé, so to speak, to look good for the command screening board— the anointed ones who determine who gets to be a squadron commander. He insisted I attend a war college, or accept a non-flying joint tour, or both, to be marketable. I knew I'd either have to piss or get off the pot."

"You got off the pot."

"Yep. I had a lot of respect for most of my squadron COs. Though some were complete assholes. A few were just kiss-asses trying to move up the chain."

"Guess what? That's how it works in the private sector too," she said, laughing, thinking of some of the dicks she'd worked with in the world of finance. There probably would have been more if she hadn't been James' girlfriend and then wife.

"Yeah, I suppose it does. I just didn't want to take that next step. Plus, the drones are doing so much of the stuff now that we used to do. It was time." He took a deep breath and let it out. "Yeah, it was time."

She sensed there was more to the story, and the haunted look that came over his face all but assured her that Zeke was running from more than just the lack of desire to fly less and lead more.

But even though she could admit to him—and herself—that

she wanted to know more about Zeke, she also knew that she didn't want to know everything.

Let him keep his ghosts, his secrets. She couldn't feel for him what he deserved.

Her eyes grew heavy while she felt him staring out the window, and her last thoughts were ones of regret that she would never get to know Zeke's whole story.

Nine

—⚓—

IT WAS THE SECOND MORNING IN A ROW JESS WOKE up in her living room instead of her loft bedroom. At least this morning she was on the more spacious couch rather than the cramped loveseat.

And she didn't have her phone staring at her from the floor either.

But the couch was cramped in a different way—sharing it with a six-two, solidly built former Navy lieutenant commander.

She had sorely underestimated Zeke Hampton the day she'd first met him and invited him home with her.

His good looks (that damn cleft chin!) were undeniable, but what she'd liked enough about him to ask him back to her place for sex was the air about him of just a guy flying his plane and nothing beyond that.

She hadn't thought he was dumb, per se, but uncomplicated, and that was what she needed for one night. Just one night. It had been so long, and she wasn't about to start up anything that she couldn't see through. When deadly handsome Zeke flew into her sights, she figured he was just what the doctor ordered.

Except, after last night, she realized there was nothing uncomplicated and simple about Zeke Hampton.

Fourteen years he'd been a naval officer. He'd served his country from the air, providing cover for troops and air strikes on enemies.

Not to mention landing and taking off from a carrier. That alone scared the breath out of Jess just thinking about it.

She'd wondered if she was in good hands when she'd filled in for Ralph observing the wolves. Now she knew she couldn't have been taken care of any better.

Watching his chest rise and fall with the grumble of a soft snore, she eased herself off the couch. When they'd nodded off, she was on the one end and he on the other. Thankfully, when she awakened, only their legs had entwined during the night.

She put the throw that had fallen off her onto him and stepped away from the couch.

Lying on her couch with morning stubble and a quiet snore, he was strikingly attractive. Mentally putting him in dress whites would be dangerous—

Too late. She could see it easily. A taller Tom Cruise from *Top Gun*. A less smarmy Richard Gere from *An Officer and a Gentleman*.

She took a few more steps away from the couch as those two movies flashed through her mind. Gere carrying Debra Winger out of the factory. Cruise showing up at the bar where he met Kelly McGillis.

That would not be her. Could not be her. First, she didn't need a man to save her.

Second, she'd fallen once for a man of power and confidence. James had been the commander of his own fleet and had been distinguished and handsome, even if he wore pinstripes and not dress whites.

Dazzling. Zeke would be dazzling in his uniform. Or in a flight suit, walking across the tarmac declaring his need for speed.

And Jess had done dazzling.

It'd bitten her right in the ass.

It was time to go into *Julie of the Wolves* mode and self-protect. Join the pack to survive, but never forget who she was.

"Seems like some really deep thoughts for so early in the morning." Zeke's scratchy voice caused her to jump. "Sorry," he said, sitting up on the couch, tossing the throw to the back.

"It's okay," she said, backing away even further, pushing back thoughts of him placing his white Navy cap on her head as he swept her up in his arms. "I was just thinking about all I need to get done today."

He looked at his watch and seemed surprised. "Shit. It's already oh eight hundred."

She nodded, but he didn't see her, already up from the couch and moving toward the bathroom. "I've got a thing I can't be late for," he said before he shut the door behind him.

After a flush and the running of the sink, the door opened again, and Zeke stood with one of her towels (deep green—no blush or peach in sight) in his hands, which he dragged across his water-splashed face and then put back in the bathroom.

As he neared her, she could see the water had gone into his hair, creating tiny little clumps of the brown strands, making them look as black as his twin sister's hair.

"Sorry for conking out like that," he said. "I know you didn't intend for me to spend the night."

She waved a hand. "It's fine. I fell asleep too."

He looked over at the now-empty couch. "So, you're saying we slept together?" Teasing in his voice coaxed a small smile from her, and she nodded even as she rolled her eyes. "Excellent."

He moved past her, not touching her, and Jess dismissed the brief feeling of disappointment. He went to the island of her kitchen and took the pen and pad she kept there, looking at her for permission to use them, which she granted with a nod.

"Listen," he said, as he scribbled something down, tore the piece of paper from the pad, and placed it at the edge of the counter. "I don't know if you saying you have a lot to do today was a way to get me out of here or not..." She opened her mouth to reaffirm her claim, but stopped. The truth was she didn't have a lot to do today. It was Saturday, and the island wasn't open yet. She'd planned a lazy day of reading and a snowshoe hike later on. Heaven.

"Either way," Zeke continued, "I have something I *have* to do today. But I'd love for you to join me. I've got to be there in an hour, so I'm leaving now. If you want to take your time and come down to Hancock, that would be great. I'd love the company, and when I'm done, I'll buy you a burger as a thanks for helping out."

She was already shaking her head, but he held up a hand. "I know, I know. You don't date. This isn't a date, believe me. It's me asking a…*new* friend for some help and then rewarding her with food afterward."

"What is it exactly I'd be helping you with?" she asked. Visions whizzed past her standing next to a plane while Zeke yelled for tools like a doctor asked for surgical instruments. Not entirely unpleasant, and probably ultimately interesting, but not as enticing as a good book and a long hike. Or a long book and a good hike.

"I'm no dummy. If I tell you what it is, I'm gonna lose you. I figure the curiosity might be enough to get you away from this gorgeous fortress."

"I…I'm not—"

"Think about it," he said. Nodding at the piece of paper, he added, "I'm there until at least five today. Show up anytime and you'll earn yourself a burger. Dress code is very, very casual. In fact, you could come right now if you wanted." He indicated her in the clothes she'd just slept in. And the hair that was stuck to the side of her face. And the unbrushed teeth.

"Uh, no. I have to shower and change before—"

"Great. Take your time. I'll see you whenever you're ready." He was coming out of the mudroom, boots on, jacket in hand, by the time she realized she'd just been played. His smile stopped her from calling him out on it.

Dazzling.

Damn.

"Thank you for last night," he said, his hand on the knob of the door.

"Nothing happened," she said.

His smile faded, and he looked at her with a slightly furrowed brow. "Jess, a *lot* happened last night. Just not sex."

He was gone before she could respond, which was probably just as well, since she didn't have an answer.

Mainly because he was right—a lot *had* happened last night.

That was the problem.

Ten

—⚬—

"BABYSITTING? YOU ASKED ME TO HELP YOU BABYSIT?" Jess said to him as he answered the door to his parents' house three hours later, little Peaches Luna settled on his hip.

"Not what you expected, right?" he said, carefully moving back to let her in, but knowing his nephew Sam was back behind him somewhere. He didn't want to knock the little dude over, but more importantly, he didn't want him making a dash for the door. Sam loved the snow and dove for it every chance he got, even if he was only in his socks and onesie.

Which he was now, because Peaches had demanded to be held while Zeke was trying to change Sam and getting him redressed.

"Eek," said Sam from behind Zeke, pointing up.

"Yeah, you got that right, kid," Jess said, walking into the foyer and kicking her boots off onto the rug. "'Eek' is exactly what I would have said if I'd known the assignment."

"He's talking to me," Zeke said. "Doesn't quite have that Z down yet."

"I got that," Jess said, rolling her eyes at him, making Sam laugh. "That Zeke is so silly, isn't he?" She unzipped her coat and took it off. After Zeke nodded to the wooden hooks, she hung it up.

"Eek," Sam said, again pointing to Zeke. Then, as if his uncle's genes were bursting through his brain, he studied Jess, his little head turning this way and that. Then he wobbled the few steps to her and stretched up his arms toward her. "Up," he demanded, and Jess bent down and swept the toddler into her arms, cradling him close.

Lucky little shit.

"The little guy you're holding is my nephew, Samuel *Ezekiel* Robbins. And this pretty lady is Peaches Luna." He leaned Peaches over toward Jess and Sam, making the baby giggle and Sam reach out for his friend.

"Peaches?" Jess asked, causing the little girl to bounce in Zeke's arms at hearing her name.

"Yeah. She's got a real name, but I can't remember what it is." At Jess's look, he clarified, "She was born a year ago when I was on cruise. I've got the email somewhere with the official announcement, but for some reason, she's always just been called Peaches."

"Is she a niece too? Do you have more than one sister?"

He waved Jess and Sam ahead of him into the living room that was littered with brightly colored toys, play mats, a portable crib, and an assortment of bottles, diaper paraphernalia, and other baby accessories. "Just Lizzie. Only sibling. Peaches' mother is Lizzie and Al's other best friend, Katie Luna. She and her husband spend half their time here and half in Florida and out on the PGA Tour. Her husband's a golfer."

"Kind of picking the wrong time to not be in Florida," Jess said, motioning to the big bay windows in the living room that showed a steady fall of soft, heavy snowflakes. Not uncommon in the Copper Country winters.

Zeke had missed the four seasons when he'd been stationed at Oceana and out on cruise, so he didn't mind a later winter. But he knew the locals would be nearing cabin fever levels by now, and a good thaw would be welcomed.

"I love these old homes in this neighborhood," Jess said, taking in the living room of the Victorian he'd grown up in. "Is this Lizzie's home?" She settled herself and Sam on the couch, but the kid was off her lap and onto the floor the minute she stopped moving. Jess put some of the toys onto the top of the coffee table next to where she sat, and Sam scrambled to grab them all up.

"No," Zeke said, sitting on the couch next to Jess, placing Peaches on his lap, her chubby little legs flopping over his knees. He kept an arm around her belly and let her lean over to get one of the toys Sam hadn't staked his claim to. "This is my parents' home. Where Lizzie and I grew up."

"It's beautiful," she said.

Zeke looked around the living room that he knew like the back of his hand. His mom had redecorated over the years, but the same basic layout of two chairs, loveseat, couch, and coffee table remained. He and Lizzie had spent most of their time as kids in either their own rooms or in the less formal family room at the back of the house. Being in the living room reminded him of having company over and holidays.

It had been designated baby central since Lizzie had Sam, even though Zeke's dad had also put a full crib and changing table in Lizzie's old bedroom upstairs.

They hadn't touched Zeke's room—which was both reassuring and slightly creepy now that he was back in it.

"I'm staying here for now," he said, gauging her reaction. Would she think he was some loser who had to live with his parents until he could find a job?

"Because you're not sure if you're staying in the area?" she asked. "That's smart."

Was that hope he heard in her voice? Was the idea that he might not be staying in the area appealing to her?

He'd told her last night about Bobby's offer to buy out his charter company. And about potential employment with commercial airlines. He didn't remember her commenting either way on those options, but that would have been about the time he nodded off, so maybe she'd already been half-asleep herself.

Damn, he could kick himself for falling asleep last night when he could have done a lot less talking and a lot more moving on up to that loft of hers.

But he had liked that she'd opened up to him about her marriage. Even if it had fried his ass to hear about the controlling, lying fuckwad that she'd married.

Who didn't tell their potential bride that they'd had a vasectomy?

Somebody who knows they'd lose a woman like Jess if they told her everything.

Still. This James guy sounded like a complete and utter tool.

"So it's girls' day out, and Uncle Zeke got roped into babysitting, is that it?"

He nodded. "Yeah, something like that."

"And then I got roped into it too," she said.

The thoughts about her dick ex-husband fresh in his mind, he sighed. "Yeah, sorry about that. I should have told you what I had going today. If you want to take—"

"Does the offer of a burger afterward stand?"

"Absolutely," he said. Peaches giggled and clapped her hands, picking up on Zeke's excitement.

"Then okay, deal. Next time, just give me a heads-up?"

"Roger that," he said, trying to keep his cool at her use of the words "next time."

"What exactly does girls' day entail?"

"Today they're all getting massages together. My niece Annie got to go along this time—her first. My mother would normally take the babies—happily—but she and my father are in Wisconsin this weekend visiting my aunt."

She found Sam's clothes on the end of the couch where Zeke had left them, and started wrestling his nephew into his shirt and overalls. Sam was putty in her hands, allowing her to move his arms this way and that, becoming completely docile at Jess's voice and touch.

Yeah, buddy, Zeke silently said with a look at his nephew, *I know exactly how you feel.*

"It's probably the last time they'll get to do it because Katie will be heading out on tour with Darío in a couple of weeks until she's not able to travel anymore." At Jess's questioning look, he added, "She's pregnant."

"Ah," she said. "Wait, Katie is Peaches' mother too?"

Zeke laughed. "Yep. Irish twins."

"She's going to be busy." Jess had Sam dressed and set him down within the confines of her spread legs, able to get back to the toys, but not all over. Good move. He'd have to remember that one.

But then he thought about Jess's spread legs and… Yeah, better not to go there with a couple of curious toddlers underfoot.

"Lizzie said Katie was kind of freaked when she found out, but only for a second. She struggled with infertility in her first marriage and assumed she couldn't have children." He lifted Peaches up, making her squeal and Sam clap his hands. "This one was a bit of a surprise to her—but she was thrilled. So another shock to be pregnant again, and so soon, but also thrilled again."

Jess smiled at Peaches, making a face that caused the baby, now back on Zeke's lap, to bounce up and down. "You said in her first marriage? So Peaches' father is her second husband, then?"

"Yep. It was a whole scandal a couple of years ago. Katie's husband got some girl pregnant and left the marriage. Katie had a one-night stand while she and Lizzie were in Texas at a golf tournament. Peaches is cooking in the oven, and Katie and Darío get together, get married. In fact, Lizzie went into labor with Sam during their reception."

"Oh my God," she said. "That must have been quite a night."

"Yeah," he said. "I heard it was. I was out on a cruise at the time. Couldn't make it."

"You missed a lot while you served," she said. Her head was down, and she handed a toy to Sam that he promptly stuck in his mouth. When Zeke didn't answer right away, she tipped her chin up, the layers of cinnamon hair falling back. Her blue eyes were steady on his. They weren't pitying, but he thought she understood how he'd felt being so far away when his friends and family had such milestones.

"Every man and woman who serves does. I was no different," he said.

She nodded. "You're right. But I thank you for your service."

He'd been told that thousands of times, in airports, grocery stores—basically anytime he was out in public in uniform. It made him both burst with pride that he was able to serve the country he loved and also feel woefully inadequate. And uncomfortable.

That was what he felt now with Jess's gaze still lasered in on him.

He was ready to come back with his standard "It was an honor to serve. I only wished I could do more." It was true. Had been true for fourteen years. But instead, he said nothing and looked at his watch.

"Naptime for you, beautiful," he said to Peaches. She understood that word well enough, seeing as her little rosebud mouth pouted. Of course, she didn't want to miss out on any of the fun Sam was having. "Don't worry—naptime for Sammy, too."

"Did you hear that?" Jess said, scooping Sam up in her arms. "Naptime." The little dude scrambled in her arms, wanting to get back to the floor where he could make a run for it.

"He has a crib upstairs in Lizzie's old room. They tried having Peaches' portable crib in with him, but you can imagine how that went. So now she sleeps down here and he's upstairs."

"Should I take him up or do you want to switch?" Jess asked.

"You don't mind putting one of them down? I was just going to ask you to watch Peaches while I put Sam down."

"I've got to earn my burger, don't I?"

Zeke chuckled. She hadn't seemed real jokey on the plane trip to Isle Royale. And the subject matter last night wasn't giggle material, so it was nice to see her crack a small joke. And her smile when she did? It made Zeke wonder just how scarred little Peaches would be if she had to watch Zeke and Jess make out on the couch while she drifted off to sleep.

Keep it in your pants. At least until the second watch arrives.

"Instead of shuffling them around, why don't I take Sam up and put him down? That is, unless you prefer I didn't go upstairs."

In the back of his mind, when he'd thrown out his plea for her to come down to Hancock that morning, Zeke had known his parents would be in Wisconsin overnight. He most definitely wanted Jess to see the upstairs of his home, entangled in the arms of a man. Just later, with the arms not belonging to eighteen-month-old Sam.

He waved to the oak staircase. "It's the one with the big white crib in it—can't miss it."

"I think I can figure that out. Does he go down with anything? A pacifier? Special blanket?"

She said her stepdaughter had been five when she'd married her ex. For a woman with no children and no desire to have any, she seemed to be in tune with the needs of a baby. Or was that every female and Zeke was just clueless with that stuff?

But learning fast. "There's a little Red Wings blanket hanging somewhere in there—on the crib, or the rocker, or changing table. That goes in the crib with him. No pacifier."

"Red Wings blanket?"

Zeke smiled. "A present from Petey when he was born. The kid loves it. Won't sleep without it. Lizzie finally got another one so she had one here and at her place."

She nodded. "Got it. Be back as soon as he looks settled." Jess made her way to the stairs, and Zeke watched as she cooed in Sam's ear while holding him close. Sam's little head slumped onto her shoulder, his dark hair resembling Zeke's more than Lizzie's. The sight stirred something in Zeke, something primitive, something he should be much too evolved to admit. He liked imagining a woman holding his child.

No. Scratch that. He liked imagining *that* woman holding his child.

Then she started up the stairs, her hips swaying, her jeans pulling across her awesome ass with every step, and something entirely different stirred within him.

Eleven

—⚋—

IT PROBABLY DIDN'T NEED TO TAKE AS LONG AS IT DID
to get baby Sam to sleep, but Jess enjoyed the weight of his body
against her as she rocked him for a bit before putting him into
the crib.

She didn't hear Peaches anymore and assumed Zeke had
gotten the little girl to go down. As she stood over Sam's crib, she
put her hand on his back, watching with awe as it rose with his
breathing. The kid was out, and yet she felt she could stay here for
hours, watching his little hand lodged under his chin, as if he were
some mini Rodin's *Thinker*.

"Everything okay?" Zeke said softly from the doorway.

She looked up, slightly embarrassed to be caught gazing at a
baby, but only nodded and made out that she was straightening
Sam's perfectly straight Red Wings blanket.

She walked out of the room and past Zeke, stopping at the
top of the stairs when he touched her elbow. "I wasn't checking
up on you or anything. I just wanted to make sure you didn't need
help but didn't want to yell because of hopefully sleeping babies."

"Right. No, it's fine. We just rocked for a little bit." She
didn't add that Sam had fallen asleep in her arms right away but
she continued to rock, lulled herself by the muted sounds of Zeke
speaking soft nonsense to Peaches downstairs.

She went down the stairs, noticing a large wooden curio at
the bottom that she'd failed to notice when going up the stairs

with a wriggling Sam in her arms.

What struck her was not the piece of furniture itself—though it was an older, polished wood that bespoke generations of ownership—but the framed photos that took up every available inch of shelf space within the glass doors.

"Oooh, family pictures," she said, stepping closer to the glass while Zeke groaned from behind her.

"Jesus," he mumbled. "Can't we just pretend you missed this?"

She smiled at him over her shoulder but then quickly turned back to begin her perusal of the Hampton family photos. "Not on your life," she said.

It was easy to see that Lizzie's new family was taking up the most real estate. The photos were newer, no fading, and near the front glass on all shelves, as though Mrs. Hampton had just put them in and pushed the older photos to the back. But Jess was able to get some glimpses of twins Lizzie and Zeke on their first day of school, holding hands and with big smiles on their faces. Also at their high school graduation—no hand holding, but still big smiles. There were others too, with their parents on family vacations, fishing, boating, even downhill skiing on what looked like Mont Ripley. A pang went through Jess as she remembered the family vacations she'd had before her parents split up, and the uncomfortable, taxing ones she'd had with either of her parents afterward. Where they'd try to outdo each other with the luxury places they'd take Jess, but then not spend any time with her once they arrived, either on the phone to his office in her father's case, or with a new lover in her mother's.

She knew that was part of the reason she allowed herself to be swept off her feet by James—he was the stability she craved.

And he was. But then the stability turned into a cage. Gilded, of course, but a cage nonetheless.

There were photos from what looked to be Lizzie and Zeke's late twenties, where Lizzie was much heavier than she was now, but always had the bright smile, just like she had the night Jess had met her at the Commodore.

And then there was Zeke in all his military fineness. Yes, in the dress whites. Yes, in the flight suit. Even one with him sitting in the cockpit of a Navy jet.

Dazzling. No other word for it.

The feeling of envy over the happy, younger Hampton family surged into desire as she stared at the man in the pictures, so heroic, so handsome, while feeling his presence just behind her. Having watched him moments ago with Peaches and Sam, goofy and tender, far removed from the hotshot Navy pilot.

But certainly no less attractive.

"Okay, okay, you've had your fill," he said, taking her hand and guiding her away from the stairwell, past the living room where Peaches lay in her porta-crib, her little butt in the air as she slept, and through to the kitchen, where he waved Jess to a seat at a large oak table.

"Coffee?" he asked, already moving toward the coffee maker and grabbing the carafe.

"Please," she said, settling into one of the chairs. She noticed a baby monitor in the middle of the table, right next to a basket that held pinecones. Fresh ones, based on the scent they were giving off. "Is this on in the nursery?" she asked, pointing to the monitor.

Zeke nodded, picking it up and turning it on, then setting it back on the table, nearer to where Jess sat. She heard Sam's soft breathing. They'd probably hear him if he cried out, but having the monitor near made her feel better.

She didn't want anything to happen on her watch.

Her watch. She shook her head, not really believing that she was sitting in the Hamptons' kitchen having coffee with a dashing fighter pilot with two sleeping babies only a couple of rooms away.

It wasn't part of her under-the-radar, become-one-with-nature life she'd been living for the past few years.

But it felt right, natural.

"Cream or sugar?" Zeke asked as he took two mugs from a

weathered cabinet.

"Black," she replied. He set the two mugs down on the table, then returned to the counter, where the coffee was beginning to sputter out into the carafe. He stood with a hip wedged into the corner of the counter, ankles crossed, arms folded over his wide chest. He was wearing a black zipped sweater, and it made his hair look more black than dark brown. His jeans fit him perfectly, and Jess had to look away before she asked him for something other than coffee.

His gaze told her he was willing to give her just that—wanted it too—but he didn't move. After the debacle of the night they met, she didn't blame him for being cautious. Last night didn't help, with her falling asleep while they talked.

"There are babies sleeping in the house," he said. It felt like it was as much a warning to himself as it was an explanation to her.

"Right," she said, then had to clear the frog out of her throat. Which made him smile, his chin dent becoming pronounced and his straight white teeth almost blinding her.

God, the Navy sure had missed an opportunity by not using him on their recruiting posters.

"But their mothers will be picking them up in a few hours," he said, promise in his voice.

A promise that, this time, she was determined to take him up on.

Twelve

"STILL NOT A DATE, RIGHT?" JESS ASKED WHEN THEY were seated near the fireplace at the Indian River Steak House.

"Nope. Just a burger to say thank you for helping me out today," Zeke said. She took off her toque and shook her hair out, the firelight catching strands, making the mass of hair look like an extension of the nearby flame.

She was stunning. Even with what looked to be like a bit of Peaches' lunch stuck to the shoulder of her sweater.

"Seems like you had it well in hand," she said as she picked up her menu. "I'm not sure I was really needed."

He leaned forward, forearms on the wooden table. Careful not to take her hand in his, though he wanted to, he clasped his together to fight the urge. "Needed? Maybe not. Appreciated? Definitely."

"Thus the burger," she said.

He nodded, then sat back in his chair, also wooden and made out of logs to go with the ski-chalet motif in the bar side of the restaurant. "Thus the burger."

She pulled the wine list out of the holder at the edge of the table. "And do my babysitting skills earn me a glass of wine also?"

"You saw how much my nephew adored you. Order the bottle."

She laughed, and he relaxed. He thought she might bail when Lizzie, Katie, Alison, and Annie had shown up after their day out.

She'd seemed a little overwhelmed by the hurricane Zeke's sister and her BFFs could create when together, choosing to stay out of the conversation and even physically distancing herself from the rest as they all hung out in the kitchen while Lizzie and Katie went about getting their children ready for the cold air.

Jess was polite with all the women. But not one of the group—not wanting to be.

Which was fine with Zeke. He didn't know where things were headed with Jess. She certainly showed no signs of wanting a relationship. Which was also just fine with Zeke. He didn't know where he was going to end up, so starting something serious was probably a bad idea.

But dear God, he wanted to sleep with her. Maybe more than he'd ever wanted to be with another woman. And they'd already established that she was not comfortable with a quick hookup with someone she didn't know well.

In that mode, it just made sense to get to know her so that she *wanted* to sleep with him.

There was a line, though, and he knew it. A tightrope of getting to care and connect with each other enough to want to sleep together, and yet not enough that he wouldn't be able to walk away and she wouldn't feel her freedom was at risk.

Because it had become very clear to him in the past forty-eight hours that Jessica Chapman was a woman who valued her freedom. Had worked hard to have it, was comfortable with it, and would not lose it.

Not even for some world-class sex.

"Probably not the bottle," she said as the waitress approached. "I'll have a glass of Merlot," she told her. Zeke ordered a beer and pretended to study the menu while sneaking glances at Jess. She bit her lower lip while looking over the choices, in either indecision or anticipation. White teeth biting down on the pink of her lips. He imagined biting those lips himself. Just a soft nip and then he'd lick away the pain.

He sighed. Yeah, it was a fucking tightrope for him, too.

When their drinks arrived, they both ordered burgers. He raised his glass. "To babysitting," he said. She smiled, clinked his glass, and then took a small sip from hers.

"I know you said your mom watches Sam for Lizzie most of the time, but you seemed pretty natural with him for having been in the Navy all those years. Do you see him a lot?"

He chuckled, thinking of the machinations his twin had gone to since he'd been home. "As much as Lizzie can manage." At Jess's questioning look, he continued, "She thinks that if I spend enough time with Sam that it'll be too hard to leave and I'll end up buying Bobby's business. Or, if not that, at least settle up here permanently."

"Oh," she said, sitting back in her chair. "Is her plan working?"

He couldn't decipher the look on her face. Did she *want* Zeke to stay in town? Two days ago, he would have guessed not. That was part of the draw for her—he was not sticking around, no threat to her new life. Her lone-wolf status.

"Hard to say. I love the kid, but I've always loved my friends and family and the time I've spent up here with them. Didn't mean I couldn't leave if I needed to."

She seemed to relax, and it pinged a little bit of guilt in him. He liked her. A lot. He should be honest with her, or at least as honest as he'd been with himself.

"But her plan has worked in a different way. One I feel like I should talk about." He took a drink of beer, liking how the condensation on the outside of the glass felt on his hands. It was still cold outside—snowing, in fact—but that feeling always felt like summer to him.

"Okay," she said. The relaxation was gone, and her guard, if not up, was at least put in place. Which only confirmed to him that he needed to be honest with her.

"Being with Sam, before that, honestly, has made me realize that I want what Lizzie has with Finn. What Katie and Darío have. What my friend Twain Beck and his wife, Liv, have. A family. It's part of the reason I got out of the Navy. It can be done, and is, by some amazing people. But I was ready to walk away from that life to one of hands-on dad, helping with dinner every night, doing homework. It's what I want. A wife. Kids. All of it."

He let out a breath at the end of declaring his wishes. A long, deep breath that was probably years in the making. One that he'd probably started holding when he was at Lizzie and Finn's wedding two years ago and saw how at peace his sister was.

They had a deep bond, he and Lizzie. Not the I-broke-a-bone-and-he-felt-it-in-Topeka kind of bond some identical twins had. But it was there, and it had him off kilter for the past two years, knowing Lizzie was living a life of contentment and happiness that Zeke hadn't even realized he was missing.

But now he'd said it aloud. Had given voice to the thoughts that he wrestled with during the past two years. It shouldn't have been so odd—most people had families without giving it the deep analysis he had, but Zeke had thought he'd be in the Navy his entire career and be too busy, and not really want anything else.

But it had changed. He'd changed. Lizzie finding her happiness had been the start of it.

Five months ago had been the end.

No. Now was the end. Saying it to someone else. Admitting to himself that the next phase of his life would be one spent with a partner and their children.

Now he just had to find the woman.

The one sitting directly across from him quickly took herself out of the running.

"That's great. To know what you want out of life. It took me the last three years to really figure it out. Longer, I guess, if you factor in my marriage."

"Yeah, thanks," he said. "It feels weird to say it to someone else. But...yeah...I guess good in a way, too."

She nodded, took another sip of her drink, then sat back in her chair. He knew what was coming. He'd seen it on her face when he'd made his little confession.

"And I don't want to presume you have me in mind for

the title of mother of your children or anything like that." She chuckled as if making a joke. It should be a joke. That two people who just met a couple of weeks ago, who'd only spent a few evenings together, should have each other on their short list for possible life partners.

And yet…

"It's okay," he said, waving for her to continue, smiling like he was in on the joke. He was, and yet in a way it didn't seem so funny to have Jess's name on the list.

Possibly at the top.

Shit, who was he kidding? It was a list of one at this point.

"But if you *were* thinking of me as someone who, you know, *way* in the future, after getting to know each other…" She rolled her eyes, as if knowing they'd known each other too short a time to even be thinking about talking about all of this.

And yet…

"I just want you to know I don't want that. I think it's great you do, but I don't."

He nodded, but didn't say anything, wanting her to go on, to possibly find some flawed logic in what she was saying, to sway her, change her mind.

But no, that was wrong.

"I just don't want that. I thought I did once. And finding out that the choice of children had been taken away from me unknowingly by the man I trusted most in the world was a huge blow. But as the wounds healed, I found that I wasn't desperate for children. If I were, I would have found other means to have a child in the past three years." She was still, no sign of discomfort in the words she was saying, no trying to sell it.

If there was one thing Zeke had learned about Jess in the short time he'd known her, it was that she was a straight shooter. No nonsense. Get to the point.

He liked that about her. A lot. But in this instance, a little doubt creeping in would have been a nice bone to toss him.

"I've found a peace up here. In the solitude. I like living

alone. I just want to be really clear with you."

Yeah, not a shred of doubt. She didn't want what he did. She was thirty-two. He was thirty-eight. They were old enough—and had both been around the block enough—to know what they did and did not want out of life. But they weren't young enough to spend a few years messing around together to see if either one changed their mind.

Well, shit.

"So this leaves us where?" Jess said after they'd finished their burgers and split a brownie sundae for dessert.

"What do you mean?" Zeke asked.

"I want a purely physical relationship for a short period of time, but I can't seem to bring myself to go there with someone I don't know. The two times you've been to my place bear that out.

"To get to know you better, we'd fall into something that I don't want or need. You need to get started on the life you want, not spend time with me when it's not going anywhere."

"Wow, I guess…I guess…"

"That I summed it up perfectly?" she said. She wasn't proud of the fact that she'd so succinctly stated the totality of their non-relationship. "I was an analyst, after all," she added.

"And I'm guessing a damn good one," he said.

"I was."

They watched each other over the table, knowing that she spoke the truth, as much as he didn't want to face it. "I guess there's only one thing left to say," he said.

"What's that?"

He raised a hand. "Check, please."

Thirteen

ZEKE PULLED HIS TRUCK UP TO THE PLOWED DRIVEWAY at his parents' place, behind Jess's Range Rover. He killed the engine, but made no move to leave the warm cab. It seemed like there were more words to say, and yet he couldn't put them together in any way that satisfied what he was feeling.

Maybe because he couldn't define exactly what it was he was feeling.

It was like a small sense of loss, but for something unknown, unseen. Unpromised.

Yes, it was the unknown of what might have been with Jessica Chapman.

"So…" he said, still sitting tight, but not being able to stand the silence any longer, wondering if she felt the same thing. Was a feeling of regret going through her or was it one of relief?

"So," she repeated. "I guess this is it, then."

"Yeah," he said, turning to look at her. She was staring straight ahead, toward the garage door. Putting his arm across the back seat, he pulled a knee up until it hit the console. "I guess that's it. Pity. My parents are out of town. I've got that whole big house to myself."

She smiled and turned to him, mimicking his movements with her knee up and arm along the back, her hand resting close to his. But not touching.

It had only been two weeks and a handful of meetings, but

Zeke could sum up his feelings about Jess in exactly that way—
almost touching, but not quite.

"You sound like you're sixteen years old," she said, her smile
still playing on her porcelain face.

He chuckled. "Believe me, since we've met, I've felt like a
sixteen-year-old often."

"I bring out the immaturity in you?" she teased.

"You bring out the horny little teenager in me."

She smiled wider, and it nearly took his breath away. She
wasn't one who walked around smiling and laughing, like his
sister did, but dear God, when she did, it was like the heavens
opening up and sunshine beating down after a long Copper
Country winter.

"Do I say 'I'm sorry' or 'thank you' to that?" she asked.

He reached out then, grazing her hand with the back of his
fingers. It felt so natural for her to turn her hand over and let
him slide his across hers, entwining their bare fingers, creating a
steeple.

He wasn't sure where her gloves were, and was ecstatic
that he'd forgotten his own. Cool and smooth, her fingers were
long, those of a pianist, and he remembered noticing them as
she pointed to the wolves from the cockpit of Clint's plane. He'd
wanted for those fingers to be all over him—his face, his mouth,
wrapped around his cock—from that second on. The past two
weeks had not diminished that feeling.

But today had extinguished his chances of ever having it.

"I wish we'd met some other time—at some other point in
our lives," she said.

The thought sobered him. Would he have been ready for a
woman like Jess five years ago? Ten? No. That was probably why
he'd limited himself to party girls, ones who weren't looking for
anything more than to hang with a pilot for a few nights or weeks.
Anybody with marriage on their mind, Zeke had done a quick
flyby.

But if one of them had been Jess?

"It doesn't matter now, I guess," she added when he didn't answer her.

"No, I guess not," he said. And then, because he couldn't *not* say the words to her, he added, "I wasn't ready before. I didn't want this before. But I'd like to think that if we'd met, my mind would have been changed."

He felt her hand loosen, as if to pull away, but he squeezed, hanging on.

"Are you saying I should change my mind? That because I've met you—someone who, yes, I'm very attracted to—I should forgo all the plans I've made? Change the course that it took me thirty-two years to get to?"

She was mad, and he didn't blame her. That was exactly what it sounded like he wanted her to do. And maybe it was, even though he knew that wasn't fair.

"I'm not asking for anything that you don't want to give," he said. He rubbed his thumb along the inside of her palm, feeling the lines. Which one was the love line? The one he traced now, that seemed to end much too quickly?

She sighed heavily, and he braced for what was to come next. After she'd laid it out so plainly at dinner, it was all just aftermath anyway.

"I've got nothing to give to you, Zeke. Even a casual hookup at this point would feel wrong, you know? Knowing that you want a relationship with someone, want something more."

He nodded. He wanted to push her. Every fighter-pilot aggressive instinct in him said to win her over, to woo her, to seduce her, to make her crazy about him. Top Gun doctrine taught pilots the "conservative-aggressive" mindset. Be very choosy before entering the fray; stay high and keep your knots up. But once you've dropped the anchor, engage with total fangs-out ferocity.

But then what? Make her *need* something she was very honest about not at all wanting?

He genuinely liked her too much to do that.

He throttled back emotionally and only nodded to her, disentangling their hands.

"It was good to spend time with you, Jess," he said.

She nodded. "Good luck with whatever you decide, Zeke. Whether it's staying up here and buying that charter flight business or elsewhere."

"Thank you. And to you as well. Really, Jess, I hope the life you've created for yourself here is exactly what you want."

She nodded but didn't move. Their hands were free from each other, but still inches apart.

He had to taste her. That was all. Nothing more. No trying to convince her to come inside with him, but he knew not kissing Jessica Chapman would haunt him.

He leaned forward over the console, and halle-fucking-lujah, she met him halfway. She didn't want what he did, but she wanted this, small and insignificant as it was.

But it wasn't small, though the kiss, when he finally touched his lips to hers, was soft and gentle.

And it most certainly was not insignificant.

Her lips had the faintest taste of chocolate and coffee from their shared dessert, and he pressed deeper, needing to see if she tasted of more.

Her lips softened and expanded under his, and he swept his tongue across her plump pink bottom lip and then into the warmth of her mouth, her tongue meeting his.

He took the seatback and held the back of her head, leaning as far as he could without crossing the console, deepening the kiss, wanting her to know what she'd be missing.

Wanting to know himself what could not be.

She didn't pull away, instead meeting him halfway in the push and pull of tongues and lips. Her head tilted, and a soft sigh whispered out of her. Her hand fell to his arm, stroking up his bicep.

Fucking console. Why'd he ever get a truck and not a comfy sedan with a large bench seat that reclined?

She broke away, as if he'd said the words aloud. From the dazed look in her blue eyes, she might not have heard the words in his head, but she was thinking along the same line.

Her eyes darted to the house. The big, empty, many-bedroomed house. He kept still, silent, letting her make up her mind. Using all his self-control not to tempt her more.

"Goodbye, Zeke," she said, sliding away from him. Grabbing her bag from the cab floor, she opened the truck door and slid down. Looking back at him, she kept those beautiful eyes down, addressing his boots. "Thank you for…" There was nothing to thank him for, and she obviously realized it, not finishing her sentence.

"Jess—"

He didn't know what he was about to say, but it was just as well that she didn't hear him over her shutting the truck door on him.

He waited in the truck until she'd gotten in the Range Rover and backed out of his parents' driveway.

Zeke sat in his truck longer, still feeling odder than he had in years.

Fourteen

—m—

Damn, why wasn't she built for casual sex? If she were, she would have slept with Zeke Hampton the night she'd met him over a month ago. And perhaps a second time three weeks ago, when she'd helped him babysit.

And she certainly wouldn't have spent the last three weeks wondering about what it would have been like to go back inside his parents' house that night instead of getting in her car and making the trek back to Eagle Harbor.

It wasn't the only thing she'd thought about, but wondering about Zeke Hampton's big body under that sweater had carved out ample time in Jess's day-to-day activities.

But enough. She'd just shake those thoughts from her mind (again!) and take a look at the small home in Dollar Bay that she'd driven into town to take a look at.

The idea of buying and renovating a home had come to her gradually. She'd felt a sense of accomplishment at what she'd done with her A-frame and a profound hole when she'd finished.

Even after fitting it out exactly as she wanted with fixtures and furnishings, she had plenty of savings in the bank and her investment portfolio was healthy. She still dabbled in finance, but only with her own money, and only when she wanted to, which was less and less while she'd been working with the construction crew on her house.

Funny, she'd never thought herself one to toss away

spreadsheets and commodities for sheets of drywall and commodes, but there she sat, in front of an open house.

Paint job. New roof. Major landscaping. Two of the three she could do herself once the weather became stable. No sense planting flower beds in mid-April—too risky in the Copper Country. She left her Range Rover and made her way up the stairs of the small home. These cookie-cutter homes, originally used for mining families, were all over the small burgs of Houghton and Hancock. Close to the road for less shoveling, the little houses were no-nonsense. Jess had been in some that had been beautifully restored, so she saw the potential of this one. Fix it up and make it attractive for a couple just starting out, a single person, or even a couple of Tech students who didn't want to live on campus.

She'd mentioned the idea of it to Reilly, one of her ranger colleagues who was also part time. He had some background in construction, and they talked about working together.

After working for James at his firm, Jess wasn't so sure about partnering up with anyone, but maybe she could just hire Reilly out for a job here or there.

But first she'd have to see the house and determine if it was a lost cause or a soul waiting to be saved.

The realtor met her at the door and waved her in, though she was on the phone and made a "one sec" motion to Jess.

It was as tiny inside as it looked from the outside, but Jess was already thinking of ideas to turn tiny into cozy.

"And you could take this wall out," she heard a woman say from the next room. A male grunt. Then the woman again, "Or maybe not. It's kind of neat to keep the original style of these houses."

Jess silently agreed just as she was thinking the voice seemed vaguely familiar.

"Jesus, Lizard, enough with the hard sell. You got me here, that's enough. Keep the rest of your opinions to yourself."

Oh, that voice she definitely knew. It had been haunting her thoughts for the past three weeks. No. Longer than that. Since he'd flown her around Isle Royale with his quiet confidence.

And the dimple in his chin.

She thought about running. Turning around and walking out of the house. But the realtor was in front of the door chatting about square footage to someone, and Zeke and Lizzie were fast approaching the kitchen, where Jess stood like a deer caught in headlights.

A woman caught in Zeke Hampton's throaty voice. Just as mesmerizing.

Dazzling.

"Okay, but you have to admit— Jessica!" Lizzie said upon rounding the corner and seeing Jess in the kitchen. Zeke was right behind her, and his head swiveled from looking at the ceiling to following his sister's gaze.

Jess recovered first, though seeing him, so tall and broad and fighter pilot-esque, made the small room even tinier, as if someone had sucked all the air out of the kitchen. She fought the urge to take a few calming breaths. "Hi, Lizzie. Zeke."

"Hi, Jess," he said. His voice had none of the irritated tone that he'd just had with his twin. Instead, it was soft and low and almost floated in the air between them like a current rushing back and forth.

"What are you doing here?" he asked. "I mean, are you interested in this house?"

She shrugged and moved deeper into the kitchen, noticing their jackets on the back of a chair set up in the corner in the otherwise empty room. "I was thinking about some renovation opportunities. It's early stages yet. This is actually the first house I've looked at. But if you're thinking about it…"

Lizzie sighed. "No. He won't even—"

"I might be," Zeke said, drawing Lizzie's surprise and Jess's attention. "This is the first one I've looked at, but the price is right for just a place to crash for now."

Jess nodded. It was a bargain, less than a new car. But it would be a lot of work. And she hadn't even gotten past the kitchen.

His thinking was obviously news to his sister, who continued to stare at him and then looked back to Jess with a twinkle in her eyes.

No. Don't go there. She tried to convey the thought to Lizzie as well as herself. She would not—could not—be the reason Zeke Hampton bought a house and stayed in town.

"So you bought the charter business, then?" she asked, moving into the room, kicking off her boots, then placing them beside those of the Hampton twins. She removed her parka and placed it on the chair over theirs. No other choice, but she didn't like the visual of her parka linked with Zeke's fleece. It conjured too many other thoughts. Other clothing being thrown aside. Other body parts linking.

Lizzie again was shaking her head as Zeke's words contradicted her. "We're getting closer," he said. Lizzie's brows rose and she moved toward the realtor, who was just getting off her call.

"I'm so sorry to keep you waiting. I'm Susan—"

"Susan, show me the basement, will you? Let's see what's down there," Lizzie said, taking the realtor by the arm and leading her through a small door that led to the basement.

"My sister was never known for her subtlety," Zeke said, smiling as his eyes followed the door that Lizzie closed behind herself and Susan.

"No," Jess said, and moved past Zeke and around the corner to the living room. Tiny, with orange carpeting that was circa early seventies. But Jess looked beyond that. She'd worked with a blank canvas on her own home, but liked the thought of restoring, renovating, or perhaps, in this case, completely gutting somebody else's original vision. The bones looked good, with no obvious structural shifts or water damage. She started moving things around in her head—walls, windows, doorways—much like she used to shift columns of spreadsheets in her head during her finance days.

Exploit what works, walk away from what doesn't. Don't get emotional. The same basic theory would do well for her if she really pursued house renovation projects.

All of this assessing would be much easier if she wasn't aware of Zeke's big body behind her. She stopped at a window, taking in the swollen edges, knowing they'd need to be replaced. Wishing Zeke would pass by, but no, he stopped too. A little too close.

"I can't stop thinking about you," he said, nearly a whisper. She almost felt his breath next to her ear.

She needed to move away, get out of the house. She could come back some other time, or send Reilly. Or just forget house flipping altogether.

"Neither can I," she said, her voice as soft as his, her brain not believing that she'd let the words get past her lips.

But it was the truth. They'd been so brutally honest with each other so far that there didn't seem much reason to start playing games now.

"What are we going to do about that?" he said. He made no move to get closer, did not hem her in, which would have made her feel trapped and wanting to escape.

She did not want to escape Zeke Hampton.

And yet she could not be what he wanted, either.

Turning from the window, she faced him, tilting her head up slightly to watch his brown eyes looking down at her. "Nothing's changed, Zeke," she said.

"I know." He took a step back. "Or maybe it has." At her puzzled look, he continued, "You were right that night over burgers. I want to settle down, start a family, be a business owner. Stop having islander mentality."

She nodded. One only had to see Zeke with his sister and their friends to know that he was not someone who wanted to live a life of isolation. Up in the sky? Yes. Maybe that was just enough time for Zeke to ground himself, to recalibrate. Once back on terra firma, he was a man who wanted connection.

"But you might be off about my timetable. It doesn't *all* have to happen for me right now."

He was either placating her or himself. Sighing, she moved

from the window and started walking through the rest of the rooms, taking photos on her phone and trying to grasp what would be needed to make this house habitable, without pricing it out of the market.

"I'm buying Bobby's business," he said from behind her. Coming to her side, he pointed her phone to the banister while he wobbled the rungs. She snapped a couple of shots. That would be short work for Reilly.

"And that's going to take a lot of my time—moving the operations to Hancock, rebranding, all of that stuff."

She nodded and walked up the stairs to the second floor, aware that Zeke's voice trailed off as she did. She put a little extra sway in her step, and he laughed, knowing her game.

Startling thought, that she liked playing games with Zeke Hampton. Nice, flirty games, not the horrifying head games James used to play with her. On her.

"And, obviously, I'm looking for a house, too. That's taking time, and when I find something, I'll have to go get all my stuff out of storage in Virginia Beach and move it up here."

They entered one of the three tiny bedrooms and Jess switched her camera to video and did a slow circle, getting in the whole room. She'd probably knock down a wall to make an actual master bedroom and then just have the spare one as a guest room or office.

Yes, she started to see how it could come together. She could not see how Zeke's plan—whatever it would end up being— would overcome her initial objections to them being a couple.

"Could be just two bedrooms up here, eh? Knock out one of these walls," he said. She only nodded and moved on to the next bedroom, sweeping it with her camera as she'd done with the first.

"Anyway," he said, "when I *finally* get around to finding the right woman, I want to have those two things firmly worked out, you know? Give all my attention to it."

"Lucky unknown woman," she said, rolling her eyes at him and moving on to the cramped bathroom.

"You know what I mean. All I'm saying is, yes, I want all the things you don't, but I don't have to have them *all* right now. Let me just get my business off the ground, find a place to live, and get my shit from Virginia."

"Sounds like a plan," she said, moving into the bathroom and zooming in her camera on the claw-foot tub. Well, now. That could be something. The rest of the bathroom was a dump, but with some cool tiling? Maybe that retro white with black diamond mosaic highlighting the tub.

"The tub's a keeper," Zeke said. She turned and sat down on the edge of it, facing him.

"What exactly are you trying to say, Zeke? I'm sort of working here." She wasn't, or at least not anything that she couldn't do with him talking, but she didn't like the feeling being with him brought out in her. Like she had to be on guard or a riptide would pull her under at any second. And that she might actually enjoy going under. Didn't she read once that drowning gave one a pleasurable feeling?

"Let's hang out. Nothing more. For as long as it takes for me to get my feet on the ground."

"Until you're ready to start wife-hunting," she added.

He shrugged and looked embarrassed. "I've got time. No biological clock." Jess winced, but Zeke went on. "I hate to be so cold-blooded about it. And it would serve me right if, when I do start looking, I can't find Mrs. Zeke Hampton anywhere."

"It would absolutely serve you right." But it wouldn't happen. As soon as Zeke sent up the flare that he was husband material, every sane woman in a five-county radius would be lining up at his door.

But until then…

She eyed him suspiciously. "No trying to change my mind? No getting lazy and thinking, 'Yeah, Jess is already around, why bother signing up for YooperMatch.com?'"

"Is there a YooperMatch.com?" he asked.

She sighed and pushed off the bathtub, pleased at how sturdy it was. She tried to brush by Zeke, but he took her hand. "Jess, seriously. I listened to you. I heard you. I know we want different things. But I think we also would love to take things further between us, if only for a little while."

He moved closer, and her hand slid deeper into his. Lacing her fingers into his, he bent his head down and whispered, "You call all the shots. And you say when it's over. I just… I just don't want to walk away from you yet."

She didn't want that either. She tried to gauge if she felt like he was trapping her. If he was saying what she wanted to hear. If it was James saying he wanted children with her all over again.

She didn't think so. She'd like to think her bullshit meter had improved after the honing that her marriage had given it.

"We're not a couple. No dating. Just—"

"Whatever you say. Put whatever label—or non-label on it that you want."

"No family dinners. I liked your sister and friends a lot, but I don't want to become attached."

He waved a hand. "No worries. When we're through, Lizzie will assume it was my fault and keep you in the circle and toss me out."

"Still, I—"

"No family dinners. Got it. I mean, there will be times if we're… It is a small town, you know."

She took a step closer to him, brushing against his broad chest. It could totally be a trap, but damn, she was going to enjoy the bait. "You've got a deal."

He smiled, and then his lips were on hers. Suddenly, the tiny bathroom seemed cavernous, and all she wanted to do was get closer to Zeke. Twining her arms around his neck, she let out a soft sigh, which was answered by his breath hitching and his arms wrapping tightly around her.

Her lips parted and their tongues danced while Zeke's hand slid down her back and cupped her ass through her jeans. Lifting her leg, she eased closer yet to him. She was half wondering if the rickety vanity would hold her when a loud throat-clearing from the hallway forced her back to reality.

She was making out with Zeke Hampton in a bathroom at a Dollar Bay open house.

"I think I can find my way, Susan," Lizzie said loudly from the hallway. "I'm sure Zeke just wanted a second look at the upstairs."

Loud—very loud—footsteps from the hall to the bathroom forced Jess out of Zeke's warm embrace, and she stepped back into the bathroom.

Lizzie's head peeked in from the doorway. "All clear in here?" she asked, looking at Jess and then Zeke. She studied her twin, then started smiling.

Yeah, Jess had called it right in not wanting to spend too much time with Zeke's family. They could see right through him. And probably Jess too, if the blush creeping up her neck was visible, which she knew it was.

"We're good," Zeke said, leaving the bathroom and waiting for Jess in the hallway.

"Yeah, you are," Lizzie said to her brother in a singsong voice. Jess expected her to burst out with "Zeke and Jess sittin' in a tree…"

"Zip it, Lizard," Zeke said, pulling on his sister's hair.

"Okay, okay. I was just rounding you up because I need to get going. Finn has to be at some meeting in Chassell. One that Sam would not be welcome at."

Zeke nodded and turned to Jess. "So? Your terms. Name a time and place."

She went through her mental calendar for the coming week. Ranger stuff, meeting with Reilly to talk about house stuff. It was actually kind of busy. Then she looked at Zeke's face, at the desire in his eyes, and the mouth that she'd just kissed.

"What works for you?"

"I have to be in the Harbor on Thursday. I'm flying the plane up there to dock it for the season."

"How did you plan on getting back to town?" she asked.

He shrugged. "I hadn't worked that out yet. Petey or somebody, I guess."

Jess looked behind him and saw that Lizzie was down the stairs and out of view. Still, she stepped closer to Zeke and softened her voice as she said, "How about if I pick you up at the marina? You tell me when. And then I can bring you back to town." He was nodding, but his head stilled when she added, "Friday morning."

The dimple in his chin almost caved in on itself, his grin was so wide. "Five at the marina? We can grab something at the Seafarer. First."

"Thursday at five," she said.

He nodded, turned, and sauntered down the steps. At the bottom, he looked back at her. "Oh, and if you're interested in this house, go for it. It needs more work than I'm willing to put into it right now."

"Home renovations not your thing?" she asked.

"Not really. I'd rather do turn-key, with all I have going on." He grinned again. "And all I *hope* to have going on." He waved over his shoulder and was gone from her sight.

She stayed upstairs for another ten minutes, making sure that Lizzie and Zeke would be gone when she went downstairs.

"What do you think?" Susan asked Jess in the kitchen.

"I think I'm in deep, deep trouble."

Fifteen

"SO, WHAT? YOU CHANGE HER MIND, BE IRRESISTIBLE, and win her over, and then she's in a place she's been very clear about not wanting to be? That seems pretty douchey, Zeke," Lizzie said to Zeke later that same evening.

They were at the ice arena, Lizzie joining him, Petey, Annie, and Sam, though it was still only Petey and Annie doing the skating. Although Annie was the only one on the ice at the moment. Petey must have sensed there was a reason Lizzie tagged along, so he had peeled off and joined Lizzie and Zeke in the bleachers as soon as Annie's friends had arrived.

"I would have thought you'd be all for me winning Jess over," Zeke said to his sister. She was standing at the side of the bleachers where she could let Sam climb, and her head was level with Zeke's where he and Petey sat on the wooden stands. "You know, love wins and all that."

"Yes, love wins, but not at the cost of someone's wishes. Then you've got resentment building up. That's not going to work in the long run."

"Resentment? She wouldn't resent me." He leaned over to his pal and mock-whispered, "I'd keep her waaaay too happy for resentment."

"Got that right," Petey said, and stuck his fist out for Zeke to bump.

"Oh my God. When you two get together, you revert to high

school seniors," Lizzie said.

"You loved us then," Petey said.

Lizzie snorted, causing Sam to look up at his mother. "Hardly. And if I did, it was only because I was immature too."

"Did she just call us immature?" Petey asked Zeke.

Zeke nodded, looking from his best friend to his sister. "That she did. Can you believe that shit?" Sam's little head whipped from his mother to his uncle. "Sorry, little man. Don't listen to Uncle Zeke."

"Eek," Sam chirped, pointing up, then lifting his arms. Zeke bent over the railing, grasped his giggling nephew, and hauled him up to sit on the seat between Zeke and Petey.

"Wave to Annie," Petey said to Sam as Annie skated by. Sam did as he was told and then began climbing on the former NHL defenseman. Like a bug climbing Everest.

"What if it's you who resents her?" Lizzie said, her eyes away from Zeke, toward the ice, watching her stepdaughter skate.

"How would that happen?" Zeke asked. He sat up on the hard wood, draping his arms across his knees, his pose much more casual than he felt inside.

"Say you fall hard for her and stay together. You said she didn't want kids, right? And you do, right?"

"Yeah, I do," he said. Spending time with Lizzie's kids had only reinforced that feeling.

"So what happens if she holds to that? You won't resent her later for not giving you children?"

He didn't like the feelings her "what ifs" were bringing up. "She wanted kids once. That's why her marriage fell apart."

"From what you said, it fell apart because he lied to her about something very, very important. The trust was gone."

"Yeah, and he was a controlling bastard, right?" Petey chimed in.

Zeke had to start remembering to keep his mouth shut around these two. They shared everything and remembered even more.

"People change," Lizzie said. "She might have wanted children in her mid-twenties, but losing the relationship with her stepdaughter in the divorce would have, could have, made her change her mind."

She turned to Zeke, draping an arm over the side railing, putting her face close to his. "I've only been married to Finn for two years, but if for some reason we split up and I lost Annie and Stevie—and was not allowed to have contact with them? I...I..." Tears were starting to well in his sister's eyes, and Zeke felt like shit for ever telling his twin about Jess's relationship with her stepdaughter.

"That will never happen," Petey said.

"That's just my point," Lizzie said. "You can't put 'never happen' on anything. *Anything* can happen." She waved her arm between the three of them, then out to the ice, encompassing Annie. "We have no clue what life is going to throw at us." She pointed at Petey. "A year and a half ago, would you have guessed you and Al would be married?"

"Nope," Petey said. He leaned back on the seat behind him, putting his arms behind his head, letting Sam hop on his big chest. A smile slashed across his face. "Wasn't anywhere on my radar."

"Exactly," Lizzie said. "So, no, I have no plans for Finn and I to *ever* separate, but shit happens. And all I'm saying is if I lost my relationship with those two kids, it would seriously change my view on life."

"But see, that's not going to happen here," Zeke said. "That's why we put ground rules in place today at that house. We're just going to hang out while I get the business going, find a house, do all that boring stuff. When it's time to get serious about the next step, I respect her wishes and back off. Start the wife hunting, as she called it." Zeke glanced at first Petey, then Lizzie, expecting looks of admiration for the adult way he and Jess had worked things out. They both looked at him, but not with admiration. Then they looked past him and to each other, and they both— damn them—started cracking up.

"Yeah, good luck with that plan, buddy," Petey said.

"Nobody knows better than I do how plans can backfire on you," Lizzie said.

He dismissed them both with a wave of his hand. "You guys don't know shit. I've got this."

They only laughed harder.

Sixteen

—ɷ—

"THAT TUB LOOKS COOL," REILLY TURKONEN SAID TO Jess three days later when she showed him the photos she'd taken at the Dollar Bay house.

"It was. Really special," she said, remembering not only the claw-foot tub but also the kiss she shared with Zeke in the little bathroom.

"So you're seriously considering this? Doing business together?" he asked her. He handed her back her phone and took a drink of beer from his bottle.

They were at the bar of the Seafarer in Copper Harbor. Reilly and his girlfriend, Paula, were with Jess discussing the house in Dollar Bay.

He put her phone down on the bar and looked at Paula, who gave him a nod. "Yeah, I'm in. Let's do this."

Heat flooded through Jess, and she realized how much she wanted this—to flip a house. To create something of purpose and substance, a place that would be as special to someone as her home was to her. Not just buying and selling, columns of profits and loss on paper.

Something in which you could put down a couch and spend your life.

Though, given the size of the house in Dollar Bay, it would be more like a loveseat than a large couch.

Still, when she and Reilly were done with it, it'd be perfect for a single person with a home office or small guest room.

Paula nudged Reilly's arm, and he looked at her and then remembered what Paula obviously wanted him to say. "Oh, right. Yeah. So, how are we going to do this? I mean, partners and all? I don't really have the capital right now..."

"Why don't we do this house as a trial basis? I'll pay for the house and all the materials. Both our labor will be *donated*, though yours will be more, obviously." Reilly would do the electrical and the plumbing, something he knew well, growing up as the son of a contractor. He had several brothers who had taken over the family business, which seemed to be fine with Reilly, who spent his summers as a park ranger, mostly on Isle Royale.

But Jess wouldn't be any slouch either. She could do drywall, and had even helped lay the flooring of her place. And she'd loved it. Getting her hands dirty was as enjoyable to her as checking on campers along the various sites on the island.

God, if her coworkers at James' firm could see her now.

"When we sell the house, we'll split the profits fifty-fifty."

"If it's all profit, meaning you'd be paid back for the price of the house and the materials, shouldn't the percentage be higher for Reilly? He'd be doing the bulk of the work?" Paula asked. Reilly seemed embarrassed but looked at Jess, waiting for her to answer.

"That's true, but I'll be taking the bulk of the risk. All Reilly is potentially wasting is his time. I could be out thousands of dollars if we don't find a buyer."

"Time he could be working elsewhere, so potentially lost wages," Paula countered.

"Hey, Paula," Reilly said.

"No, she has a point," Jess said. She looked past Reilly and to the true decision maker of the pair. "But that's my offer. If we like what we're doing, make a profit, and want to keep on, I'm more than willing to work out a legal partnership where we both have equal monetary input and risk. Or an agreement where Reilly is just paid like any contractor and I own everything outright. In fact, that may be—"

"No, I like this plan," Reilly said. When Paula was about to pipe in, he placed a hand on her arm. "Let's try it with this house and see if we can make it work."

Jess nodded, not looking at Paula, then put her hand out for Reilly to shake, which he did. When Paula made a move to be included, Jess reached for her glass of wine.

It wasn't that she didn't like her friend's girlfriend. Okay, she didn't. But there was nothing really wrong with Paula. It was just that Reilly was such a different person when she wasn't around. Fun and caring, Reilly was great as a ranger, especially with the families who were camping on the island. Jess had learned a lot from him the previous summer, her first full season as a ranger. But where he was on sure ground in the outdoors, he was quiet with Paula, allowing her to make all the decisions for them as a couple.

Jess knew that all couples functioned differently, and if things worked, that was all that mattered. But there was something about Reilly and Paula's relationship that reminded her of her marriage to James, with the roles reversed.

Just as well, though, because with his curly blond hair and puppy-dog eyes, Reilly was adorable, and she didn't need a partner who was a good ranger, so, so cute, *and* single.

Not that she was attracted to Reilly. Now that she thought on it, he was exactly what she first thought Zeke Hampton was. Simple, uncomplicated, laid-back. Not an alpha bone in his body. That was why she'd thought Zeke had great booty-call potential that first night—not her type.

But that was not Zeke. Frickin' Navy pilot was not the job tree huggers sought out.

She sighed and picked up her menu, looking for something light, since she'd be seeing Zeke later that night for dinner. Right there at the Seafarer.

ZEKE STEPPED OFF THE DOCK where he'd just parked the Cessna 206 seaplane and felt a rush of pride zip through him.

It was no Super Hornet, but the plane was now his. Almost his. There were still titles to transfer and tax shit to do, but he was now docking Bobby's Cessna in the Copper Harbor marina and starting his business for real. He had a maintenance engineer hired, and Lizzie's PR team was putting the finishing touches on his rollout (their words) with the new website, logo—the whole enchilada.

His sister was very good at what she did, and her (free!) help at getting Hampton Air Charters off the ground (she loved using that pun) was invaluable to Zeke.

It would still be several weeks before Isle Royale was officially open, but he wanted a chance to do some solo flights, landing at the island's harbors and some of the inland lakes. The island opened mid-April, but the charters didn't start until the beginning of May.

He'd done all the quals he needed for the amphibious plane, and everything was signed off. But a period of empty flights was welcomed.

He figured if he could land an F/A-18 on the deck of a carrier in roiling Indian Ocean storms, he could manage a few people wanting to fish in the heart of the island.

"Looks good, sitting there. Just what we needed for a little variety up here." Zeke turned to see two men waiting for him at the base of the long docking area. One was Frank Belson, whom Zeke had met two weeks ago when he'd come to the marina and put down his deposit on his docking fee.

Frank was in his sixties and had the weathered look of a man who spent his life in the outdoors—and those outdoors being the ravaging Copper Country.

The other man was Jim Peterson, whom Zeke had met last summer.

Probably in his early fifties, Jim was a handsome man who had the look of money about him. His chinos, Sperrys, and polo were all expensive, as was the *Mina*, Jim's boat, which the men were standing by.

"But how loud is that thing going to be in the mornings?" Frank asked as Zeke drew even with the two men.

"Loud," Zeke said. "But it'll be loudest away from the marina and out on the lake before takeoff."

"Isn't Lake Superior going to be too rough for takeoffs up here?" Jim asked.

"Could be. I've got dock space reserved in Hancock, too, just in case I need to fly in and out of there. This is easier, though, if lake conditions are good."

"Jim Peterson, Zeke Hampton. Until about five months ago, Lieutenant Commander Zeke Hampton."

"We've met," Zeke said. "You probably don't remember, Jim, but I was part of a sunset cruise you did last summer."

"I remember," Jim said. "You were friends with Huck's brother Twain, right? We all went to the Seafarer afterward."

Zeke nodded. It had been a large group, and Zeke hadn't been sitting close to Jim, so was slightly surprised he remembered. The man must have had a lot of different faces on his boat over the course of the season. Still, he probably didn't go out afterward with most of them.

"She's looking good," Zeke said, pointing at the *Mina*. Jim nodded, and the three men stared at the boat in front of them. Zeke noticed the look of pride on Jim's face and assumed that the *Mina* was a fairly new purchase. He couldn't remember what Jim's story was from last summer. Was he new to chartering? Yeah, that might have been why Huck had worked for him. Something like that. All Petey had said was that Twain had mentioned that his little brother Huck was working a boat in the Harbor and Petey wanted to take a sunset cruise to mess with him. Lizzie and Finn, Petey and Alison, and Zeke had all gone on the cruise along the lakeshore. They'd gone to the Seafarer afterward, with Jim, Huck, and Huck's wife Kelsey joining them. In fact, it was the first time that Zeke had told Petey and Lizzie that he was getting out of the Navy.

That was nearly a year ago, and he couldn't believe how

different his life was. Different and better.

Yeah, there were things he missed about the Navy. The camaraderie with the guys, for one. But he had Petey for that. Not to mention Katie's husband Darío, and Twain and other guys in the area that Zeke had known all his life.

And the flying. He missed the jets. The speed, the power, the high-tech weaponry. The F/A-18 Hornet was a much nimbler fighter than its predecessor, the F-14 Tomcat, and a more precise bomber than the A-6 Intruder, both of which required a crew of two. Zeke was a one-man-band when he crossed the beach into bad guy territory. Throw in a wingman similarly equipped, and they could devastate an entire nation-state.

But when he was in the Cessna, a different sort of feeling overtook him. Still that of oneness with the sky and the earth below him. But also a peacefulness that wasn't prevalent when going Mach two.

So, maybe he didn't miss all that much after all. Oceana had lots of beautiful women, but it didn't have Jessica Chapman. Not that Zeke really did either, but he had her tonight. And for the foreseeable future.

Until you start wife-hunting.

He could drag this out. The season was going to be crazy, getting his grounding with the business. Hopefully they'd both frequently be in town or also on the island at the same time.

Once the season came to an end, he could really settle into a place to live. That could take a while. He'd need to go to Oceana and get his stuff out of storage and move it all up here. Maybe Jess would even go with him to—

"Zeke?"

Shit. Frank was asking him something, and Zeke was totally zoning out.

But if you were going to zone out thinking about something, it might as well be a sexy redhead.

"Sorry, Frank. Mind was back on the plane." He nodded over to the Cessna, but the sly grin on Frank's face told him he hadn't fooled the old man.

"I asked when your first charter is."

"May second," Zeke answered. "A day after the charter boats and planes officially start." The two men nodded, and they continued talking about various charters they had coming up, staffing, and other issues that interested Zeke. But not as much as thinking about his date later that evening.

As if she was reading his mind, his phone chirped in his pocket, and he saw it was said sexy redhead calling him.

"Don't move an inch," Jim said, laughing. "If you're getting a cell signal strong enough to answer a call, stay right where you are."

Zeke knew cell coverage was spotty in the Harbor, so he quickly answered before he lost Jess. "Hey, what's up? I'm in the Harbor already, so I'm not sure how long I'll have the connection."

"Okay, I'll be fast. Well, maybe not. That's the thing. I was at the Harbor earlier, at the Seafarer even, and now I'm running late."

"Are you at your place?" She must be, because he was pretty sure the number she gave him was her landline.

"Yes," she said. "I have a couple of things I need to do. A call to— Never mind all that. Just can we push a little bit?"

"Are you sure you even want to come back in to the Harbor? Why don't I pick up some dinner somewhere and bring it to you?"

Frank and Jim had walked down the dock of the *Mina*, giving him some privacy. Frank was pointing out something on the boat, and Jim was nodding and then pointing at something different.

"Would you mind doing that? That would be great."

"No worries. And hey, this makes it seem even less like a date, so you should be happy."

She laughed, and the sound made his stomach heavier than pulling six Gs in a Hornet.

"See you in an hour or two?" she said.

"Roger that," he said.

"I'm looking forward to it," she said.

Frank and Jim were now walking back toward him, so he couldn't really tell her how much he was looking forward to the night to come or about all the things he'd been dreaming about doing with Jess for the past week. Longer.

"Me too. See you soon, Jessica," he said, trying to drag out her name, sexy-like. She only laughed and hung up.

"Jessica?" Frank asked. They were back to where Zeke stood.

"Yeah. My girl," Zeke said. Well, she was tonight. And for as long as he could milk this getting-his-life-together shit.

Jim was watching him carefully, waiting for more. Or maybe realizing Zeke was just wishfully thinking when it came to Jess being his girl. "Jessica Chapman. Know her?"

Jim's hand froze halfway to his face, then dropped to his side. Frank was shaking his head. "Nope. Can't say I do."

"She's a ranger with the park service. Isle Royale mostly."

"So she takes the *Ranger* out to the island. Doesn't mess around with the charter riffraff," Frank said, chuckling.

"Yeah, probably," Zeke said. Jim still hadn't said anything, but his face had gone pale, so Zeke pointedly said, "Do you know Jess, Jim?"

As if shaking himself from a dream, Jim focused on Zeke. "Um...I'm not sure. I think maybe we met, but I don't... Oh, there's Bonnie. I need to talk to her about something. Good to see you guys."

Jim brushed past Zeke and headed toward the marina offices to speak with Bonnie Brinanen, who ran the place. "See ya," Frank said to Jim's back.

Zeke found Jim's reaction odd and would have liked to ask him more, but Jim was gone before Zeke could. He must be thinking of someone else. Because if Jim had indeed met Jess, there was no way he would forget it.

Zeke had tried—desperately—and failed.

Seventeen

—w—

GOD, HE WAS SO GOOD LOOKING. JESS WAS SURE SHE'D
done nothing but stare at Zeke Hampton across her kitchen table
throughout the whole meal.

He'd been telling her about all he'd been doing since they'd
seen each other at the open house in Dollar Bay. She told him
about meeting with Reilly earlier and making the call to Susan to
make an offer on the little house.

The Little House That Could, as she'd begun thinking of it.

So, yes, she had held up her side of the conversation, but
really, all her mind had comprehended were things like how his
hair was growing out from the military cut he'd worn. She knew
from the pictures in his mother's curio cabinet that it hadn't been
a buzzcut, but a little longer on top.

And how, as his hair grew in, she noticed a little bit of wave,
different from the straight hair of his sister.

Now there was just enough on the top for her to run her
fingers through when they—

"Oh, yeah, I ran into someone today in the Harbor you
might know. Or who thinks you may have met. He's got a boat—"

"Do you want to go upstairs?" she blurted out, unable to
keep her hands to herself after waiting all week (six weeks since
she'd first met him on that flight to observe the wolves) to be up
in her loft with a naked Zeke Hampton.

The cleft in his chin deepened as he grinned at her, and their conversation, such as it was, faded away. It was just Zeke and Jess, staring at each other across her table. Wanting each other. Desperately.

"Desperately," he said, and she laughed, nervous energy forced out of her.

She stood, taking her wine glass and the bottle and walking away from him. The screech of his chair pushing back was immediate. She heard the glass of his beer bottle being dragged from the table, then his footsteps behind her on the stairs up to the loft.

It was dark outside, but the lights from the kitchen below were enough for her to see her way to the bedside table, where she put down her wine and lit a candle that she'd placed there earlier.

Zeke stood along the railing to the downstairs, watching her, one leg crossed over his ankle, his arms crossed over his broad chest, his beer bottle dangling from a loose hold.

She skidded against the end of the bed, staring at him as she made her way to the other side and lit the candle on that table. He smiled at her, knowing just the sight of him made her bump into the furniture.

"Don't be so cocky, flyboy," she said once she was back at the foot of the bed, a mere seven feet away from him and the railing to the main floor below. A distance she'd decided on with her contractor. Right now, it seemed both too far away and way too close.

"Who, me?" he said.

"Yeah, you," she said. "Throw out all that fighter hero bullshit. I can't handle all that tonight."

Another grin, this one wider, brighter. Dazzling.

"Oh, Jess, I'm sure you can handle anything I throw at you."

It had been three years since she'd been with a man. And the last year of her marriage had been tense, the sex filled with anger, recriminations, and desperation.

None of which she felt with Zeke.

None of which she ever wanted to feel again.

Zeke was light and fun and sweet. And so, so hot.

It was the hot part that had her sitting down on the edge of the bed, afraid her legs would start knocking together. Not exactly the sign of sexual confidence she wanted to exude.

"Jess?" he said, coming closer, going down on his haunches in front of her, placing his beer bottle on the rug and taking her hands in his. "Hey, are you shaking?"

Was she? She shook her head. "No. I mean, I don't want to be."

"If you don't want to do this, that's fine. Let's just go back downstairs and—"

She snorted out a half laugh/half groan. "God, how many times am I going to invite you to my home and then chicken out?"

He ran a hand down her calf in a comforting way. "As many times as you want. You *never* have to say anything more than 'no' to me. You know that, right?"

She did. She absolutely did.

"But here's the thing. I really, *really* want to say yes to you. I did that first night, but I just couldn't with a stranger. And I wanted to the night we talked about my marriage."

"But we fell asleep," he said.

"And I really want to now," she said.

"But?" His hands were on her knees, and she took hers from the bed and placed them on top of his.

"No buts. I just need you to know that it's been a long time for me. And even then, it was…not great for the last while."

"So, no pressure or anything," he said, chuckling. "Just make it great."

She joined him in the laugh. "You joke, but that's exactly it. No pressure on *you* at all," she said.

"There's no pressure on you either. Do whatever feels right."

She shook her head. "It's different. Anything, any touch at all, is going to feel wonderful to me. I've really missed it, being touched, being held."

"Kissing? Have you missed kissing?" he asked. She met his eyes, and her breath caught at the desire, and yes, playfulness, beaming out at her. Weird to think of those two things so entwined, but she realized that was how her feelings for Zeke worked—desire and lightness.

"Yes, kissing," she whispered, his lips nearly on hers. He rose from his haunches into a squat to be level with her and leaned forward, his mouth brushing across hers. Opening her lips, she slid out her tongue to meet his. He tasted of beer, and though she was a wine drinker, she fleetingly thought that nothing had ever tasted as good as a Bud on Zeke Hampton's full, firm lips.

He rose further, taking her in his arms and pulling her up, all the while never breaking their deepening kiss.

"Hugging? Have you missed hugging?" he asked, ending their kiss, enveloping her in his strong arms, his hands sliding up and down her back.

"Yes. But not as much as kissing," she said, smiling up at him.

He laughed, then dipped his head and kissed her again, taking from her, but giving too. Definitely giving.

Their tongues twisted and collided, dancing, finding each other. Warm hands skimmed up and down her back, almost making her purr from the perfect sensation. She gave as good as she got, her fingers sliding over strong arms and up his firm back, feeling the shift of his muscles as he moved. As they moved. Together.

"Touching," he said.

"Wha?" was all she could get out, dazed as she was becoming.

"Another thing you missed," he said. He pulled away from her and placed his large hand at the center of her chest, his fingertips brushing the chain of her greenstone necklace. She'd decided to wear it today, wanting to exorcise any negative feelings from a necklace she loved. The greenstone was below her heavy knit top, hidden when she'd met with Reilly and Paula earlier. Hidden from Zeke, but probably not for long.

"Yes. Touching," she said. He smiled at her and pushed her back to the bed with that big hand, sliding it down her body as she sank to the mattress, ending with a grip on her ankle.

"Good. Because I plan on doing a *lot* of touching, Jess." He slid that hand up her leg, his other one joined in his crusade, and they came together at the button at the top of her jeans. He quickly undid the button and fly, and she shimmied and lifted while he peeled her jeans down and off her legs. Next came her socks, joining her jeans on the floor. She lifted her arms up for Zeke to join her down on the bed, but he shook his head. Those strong hands—hands that held controls steady while experiencing strong G-force—began to knead her feet. His thumb digging into the sole made her roll her head back on the bed.

"Oh my God, that feels so good."

"Good touching?"

"Very good touching."

"I know other good touches," he said.

She snorted and her eyes closed, the back of her skull digging into the comforter as his foot massage encompassed her toes and heels. "I'll just bet you do."

He gave her other foot the same treatment, and the promise of sex seemed like just a cherry on the sundae of the best foot massage she'd ever had. A thought went through her head that it was too bad she and Zeke would be over before too long. She could really use this when she was spending days hiking and on her feet.

But she couldn't think about that. Not about the future and Zeke Hampton out in the wilds wife-hunting. Tonight, he was here, making her feel relaxed and helping her forget that it had been so long since she'd been with a man.

"Incredible legs," he said as his hands slid from her feet down her calves.

"All that hiking," she said. "Snowshoeing in the winter."

"It shows," he said.

She loved what the past three years of being outside and all the physical activity had done to her body. Though her clothes size was about the same from her hedge-fund days, her limbs were strong and toned, her stomach flat and hard. She loved how powerful her body made her feel. And not in a sexual way.

Except tonight. Definitely feeling her body in a sexual way tonight. She liked how Zeke's hands traced the muscles of her legs, his thumbs following the line of toned thigh. Instead of reaching for the edge of her panties, he took the hem of her shirt and lifted it up her stomach, his hand flat on her, pulling the material, his thumb trailing behind on her bare skin.

She put those ab muscles to use, lifting in a crunch while he pulled the shirt over her head, then tossed it to join her jeans and socks. She was in her bra and panties, both a deep emerald-green satin with cream lace trim at the edges.

"Holy wah," he whispered. She'd heard the Yooperism before, of course, but never whispered with such awe and desire.

He stood over her, looking down. It might have made her feel intimidated. James would have used it as a power pose. And Zeke was absolute power. Yet she felt they were in it together.

She flicked a hand up and down, indicating his shirt, and he obliged her by peeling his fleece then tee over his head, throwing them on the ever-growing pile of their clothes.

"Holy wah yourself," she said, admiring him.

"I've kind of let myself go since getting out," he said.

"If that's letting yourself go…"

He chuckled and flexed, kissing his biceps. "Like the gun show, darling?"

She laughed. "I did. Until you did that."

Smiling, he bent down, placing both hands on either side of her head, his "guns" right next to her, but not touching.

"About that good touching you bragged about," she said. "Or do you only do feet? Not that I'm complaining."

His fingers bracketed her head, thumbs and fingers gently massaging her scalp. "Oh, I do more than feet."

"Prove it," she said breathily, the words coming out with a

sigh from his magic fingers now on the nape of her neck.

She spread her legs, dangling them from the side of the bed, allowing him to lower himself onto her, which he gently did, while his fingers moved down her neck to the straps of her bra on her shoulders.

"Beautiful as this is, let's get it the hell off you," he said, peeling the straps down, the cups following until they uncovered her breasts, which stopped him.

His brown eyes focused, and she could feel the heat of his gaze all over her skin. "It cannot be overstated. Holy fucking wah."

His thumb brushed over a nipple, which instantly hardened and pebbled at his touch. She watched the top of his head as he ducked down, his tongue coming out and tracing the satin of her bra, tucked under her breast, and then up her warming flesh, to finally—finally!—take her nipple in his mouth.

"Zeke," she said, her hands going to his head, weaving her fingers into the soft, longer waves on top, the shorter sides growing in.

One hand gently massaged her left breast while his mouth taunted and teased at her right. As her breath became more ragged, his touch turned firm and his sucking became more insistent, causing her to arch her back, giving him more. Wanting to give him all.

No, not all. She held a little part of herself back, determined never to give everything over to any man ever again. It had destroyed her once.

But even with that tiny nugget held back, she could enjoy this. Enjoy what Zeke was making her feel. Things she'd forgotten she liked, things that her little mechanical buddy in the nightstand drawer was not capable of.

Heat. Pressure. Wetness. Zeke.

He moved to her other breast, reaching around and undoing her bra, sliding it from her body, and then feasting once again. "God, that feels so good," she said, running her hands from his hair down his neck and to his broad shoulders, loving how his strength shifted and rippled under her fingers.

"Tastes pretty fucking good, too," he said, then sucked her deep into his mouth, making her cry out. She rolled her hips under his body, needing more of him. Needing him other places. Needing him everywhere.

He knew what she needed, and left her breasts, placing one last kiss on the tip of each nipple before trailing his tongue down her stomach. As he did, he slid from on top of her and went to his knees on the floor, pulling her closer to the edge.

After kissing along the seam of her panty line, he scooped up the back of her thighs, raised them in the air, and pulled her panties down her joined legs, off her toes. Then released her so her legs spread around him once again. Not a move of amateurs or those without the strength that Zeke possessed.

It should bother her that Zeke was so more experienced than she was, but it didn't. She could hold her own, she knew, and it looked like she might pick up a new trick or two.

He stroked up and down her thighs, pushing them farther apart with each pass. "I figured you were a natural redhead," he said, staring down at her with amusement—and heat—in his eyes. "But nice to have it confirmed."

She would have been embarrassed, but she found those feelings didn't come up with Zeke. He was playful enough that she was completely relaxed, so she spread wider for him. And intense enough that she knew he'd be seeing how wet he'd made her.

His arms once again hooked under her thighs, this time bringing her legs up to hook her knees over his shoulders. Then he proceeded to kiss down the inside of her thigh. Closer, closer, but just when she thought he would put his mouth on her, his head popped up and he looked at her with a grin. "Hey, you know what's good about fighter pilots?"

"No, what?"

"We're very good at finding our target."

She barked a laugh and dropped her head back onto the bed. "Yeah, but no fancy technology here to help you."

He slid his tongue along the crease at the top of her thigh. Who knew she'd be so sensitive there? "That's true. But even though we have all that 'fancy technology,' as you say, the best pilots depend most on their instincts."

"And what are your instincts telling you?"

His hand moved from her thighs to the heat of her, spreading her wide, sliding into the wetness. "My instincts say I am approaching my target, and I am ready to engage."

Engage he did, with tongue and a warm mouth. The man knew his target. Jess arched and dug her heels into Zeke's back, praying the sensation could go on just a little longer, but knowing it had been so long that she was able to come at any—

"Hey," she said when he pulled back, taking the pressure away and just nuzzling his nose into her thigh, pressing soft kisses on her thigh. Which was nice, of course, but…her *leg*? Now?

"The other thing we pilots will do, you know, when we're in a real dogfight? Back off when we're too close to the target. Because maybe it's not the right time. Maybe it's better to disengage and then re-engage." More kisses down her thigh, and this time he nearly got to her knee. The wrong damn direction.

"Why on earth would you want to do that?" Her hands were in his hair again, urging him up, but he was strong and wasn't going to go anywhere he didn't want to. Until he wanted to.

"Because sometimes if you pull off your target, they get disoriented, wondering when, and where, the next attack will come from." His mouth returned to her, and by the time she'd finished sighing with relief, she was gasping from new sensations as he slid one finger inside her, then another. "You see." His thumb was added at her clit, taking up the stroking that his tongue had started. "Always keep the target off guard if you can." Her hips rose to meet his fingers as they easily glided through the wetness, curling up, and he… Oh, yes, he definitely found her target.

"Zeke," she moaned, shattering with the exquisite shuddering that soared through her body. Colors flashed behind her closed eyes, though she wasn't aware if it was the candlelight or just the electric current that flowed through her.

"That's it, Jess. Detonate. Total destruction of the target." His fingers curled again, scraping against her most sensitive spot, and she clenched her legs together, her knees at the side of Zeke's head.

"Oh, shit, that's good," she managed, though she wasn't sure how she got the words out.

"Fuck yeah, it's good," he said, then kissed her just above her red curls as his fingers and thumb continued their strike upon her.

She trembled as another wave washed over her, making it last, with tiny aftershocks as Zeke slowed his pace, gauging her release. Her hands dropped from his head to the bed beside her. Her legs loosened, falling against his shoulders, every muscle in her body spent like she'd just run five miles. In snowshoes.

Gently letting her legs down from his shoulders, Zeke stood and reached into the back pocket of his jeans, pulling out a condom. Barely coherent, she had enough thought process left to say, "I bought a box. They're in the nightstand."

He smiled as he tore open the package, then tore open the fly on his jeans with just as much urgency. "Good. Let's use 'em all."

"It's a big box," she said.

"Mission accepted," he said, and she laughed. A laugh that left her body when he dropped his jeans and black boxer briefs and she finally saw all of Zeke Hampton.

He was sporting an impressive heat-seeking missile, and it was all for her.

"Do they give out medals for something like that?" she said, then scooted up the bed, peeling the comforter and sheet back and climbing underneath. But she didn't pull them up over her. That would mean covering up Zeke, and that body was much too magnificent to cover.

"If they don't, they damn sure should," he said, stroking himself a few times, then rolling the condom on. He tossed the empty package onto the nightstand and crawled onto the bed, then up her body, nuzzling and kissing as he went.

"Purple throbbing heart?"

"Oh, it's throbbing all right." He took her hand and placed it on himself, proving his point. She would play more with his medal later—or missile, or whatever other military dirty talk they came up with. Right now, she needed it seeking her heat.

Which he did, sliding into her easily. Well, not easily, since he was medal-sized and it had been a long time for her. But any discomfort was quickly gone when he began to move inside her, and she wrapped her arms around his neck.

He buried his face in her shoulder, kissing her, gently nipping at her skin, then tasting her with his tongue. "I'm not going to last long." She was nodding when he added, "This time." The promise of a round two in the throatiness of his voice as he pumped inside her sent waves through her again, and she felt herself tighten around his cock.

"Jesus, Jess, that feels fantastic. Tighten up on me. Yeah, just like that."

She loved the words, the meaning, the feeling, and did all that he suggested, letting it all rush through her again, his hips grinding into hers, their arms around each other.

He lifted his head from her shoulder and held her face in his hands. "Here we go," he said as he quickened his pace just as she'd been starting to come back down. He took her back up, sky-high, drifting into the clouds.

His eyes stayed on hers, and she couldn't look away. Loved watching his face as he reached for it. Pumped one last time and put on the afterburners.

Target completely, totally destroyed.

Eighteen

—~~—

ZEKE FIDDLED WITH THE NECKLACE ON JESS'S CHEST, his hand brushing against the top of the sheet that covered her. Covered that glorious body and all the creamy, delectable skin.

"I love this greenstone against your skin. It's a shame you don't wear it out for everyone to see."

She shrugged, and the necklace fell from his fingers and onto his chest where she laid her head. He pulled back her red hair, wanting to see her face as she spoke. There was something about the necklace that had jolted her the first night he'd been up in the loft. But she was wearing it now, so maybe she'd moved past whatever it was and just liked a beautiful piece of jewelry.

Besides, it hadn't been only the necklace that night, but also the picture of her former stepdaughter.

"It'd cause too much hassle," she said. "When it's on the mirror on my vanity, I actually see it more, enjoy it more, than wearing it under my top."

"Makes sense." He trailed a finger up her arm while she traced the hair on his chest. Nice. Comfortable. That was the thing with Jess—even that first day in the plane when she was wolf observing, and it had been uncomfortable, it was still... comfortable. He knew that didn't make sense, but wanting to spend more time with a woman who didn't want to get serious didn't make much sense either. And yet there he was. Happily.

After he and Jess had come down from their explosion and

blood had returned to his brain, he'd disposed of the condom, brought her a warm, wet washcloth from the bathroom, then gone downstairs and brought them back two bottles of water. They'd each taken a few sips, then burrowed under the covers of Jess's fluffy down comforter, wrapping their arms around each other.

"That was really lovely, Zeke," she said softly.

He snorted. "Lovely? That's the word? Lovely?"

He felt her smile against his chest. "What word would you use?"

"Something a little more hardcore than lovely. Fan-fucking-tastic comes to mind."

She rolled closer into him, her amazing tits smashing against his side. "It was that, too. Intense. Physical. Intoxicating."

"Damn right."

She giggled, a sound he hadn't heard from her, softer and gentler than her regular laugh. "All of those. But also really lovely. And just what I needed."

"Right back at ya," he said. They lay in silence, and he wondered if she had drifted off to sleep, but her breathing didn't change.

"It's a weird kind of betrayal, what I went through with James," she said. "No other women, no out-and-out abuse, or keeping of money, or anything like that. And yet it felt like a physical blow, a hurt like I'd never felt."

"When you found out about the vasectomy?"

She nodded, the silkiness of her hair gliding along his chest. "I'm sorry. I'm sure you don't want to talk about my ex-husband. Not with all those fabulous adjectives I just threw out hanging in the air."

He put a finger under her chin and lifted it up so she'd look at him. Those blue eyes of hers would be the death of him, he knew, but what a way to go. "I want to hear you talk about whatever you want to talk about. I'm guessing something made you think of him."

She nodded, giving the tip of his finger a kiss, then setting her head back on his chest. "I was just thinking about how different this was from the last time I had sex."

"And how much better, of course."

Another small giggle. "Of course." He slid a hand from her arm down to pat her hip, then kept it there, liking how his big hand curved around her so easily. Perfect fit. In many ways. "But seriously, I was thinking about how I've only known you six weeks, and I'd been married to James for seven years, and how much more open, trusting I was with you just now."

"Because I didn't betray you like he did." He wanted to add that he never would. That if he had a woman like Jess in his life permanently, he wouldn't be a big enough idiot to lie to her about something so huge.

He kept that to himself, knowing she didn't want to hear about Zeke's feelings. That was part of their deal, and he meant to abide by it.

"Yeah, probably. By that time, I think we both knew it was over, even if we kept trying to hang on."

"Why did you? Try to hang on, that is? I know why he tried to hang on to you." That was as close as he'd let himself get to telling her about his growing feelings.

"Cassie. His daughter."

The picture on her makeup table. "Right," he said, trying to sound understanding on a subject with which he had no experience.

"I mean, we didn't have her all the time, and not when we were traveling for business, but I really loved her. James's relationship with Cassie's mother wasn't the best, so it was tricky at first, but we really formed our own relationship. He'd been divorced for two years when we met. Cassie was five when James and I married and twelve when our marriage was falling apart. So, I'd really watched her grow from a kid to a young lady. And it crushed me to think of my time with her going away if I left James."

"And you're not in touch with her? At all?"

She stilled in his arms, and he regretted the question. He

hadn't meant it to sound accusatory; he knew Jess would have wanted to do whatever was best for Cassie.

"That's just it. As an ex-stepmother, there are really no rights, you know? I mean, there is no reason for me to see her, because I'm not living with her father. I reached out to her mother to try to keep my relationship with Cassie, but she was not a fan of mine anyway, so that wasn't going to fly." She took a deep breath and slowly let it out. "James was punishing me, so he wouldn't let me see Cassie when she was with him. Or he'd let me see her, but only if I went to dinner with the both of them or something. And, of course, Cassie has her own phone and everything, so she started contacting me. When Elsbeth—that's James's ex—found out, she went nuts.

"Finally, I realized that Cassie was being put in the middle of all of our garbage, and the kindest thing I could do for her was cut off contact. So, I wrote her a long letter—a text, actually, since I didn't trust she'd actually get a letter I sent—about how I'd always love her and be there for her if she needed me, but for now, it was best that we didn't communicate."

"God, that must have been hard for you."

"Hardest thing I ever had to do. She lashed out, said I was dumping her like all the adults in her life did."

"She was hurt. I'm sure she didn't mean it. Plus, she's a kid."

"Yeah, I know all that intellectually. But still…"

She slid her hand over his chest and wrapped around his side as she rolled even closer to him. He wanted to offer words of comfort, but they all sounded hollow in his head. So, he just held her to him.

"She stopped texting after a couple that I didn't respond to. Then I got a new phone and moved anyway. Got off all social media because of James, which I don't miss, but that was one way to kind of see how Cassie was doing, what she was into.

"But I was thinking that maybe I could reach out in a few years, when she's eighteen, and away at college or something."

"I'm sure she'd like that," he said, not at all knowing that to be true.

"Maybe. Or maybe that would just mess her up. It's probably selfish of me to do that, just when she's starting her own life."

"You could reach out. Whether she wants a relationship would be up to her."

"Yeah. We'll see. It got so ugly at the end with James, it was almost a relief that he'd had a vasectomy. I couldn't imagine having children with him now. He'd use them for leverage, just like he did with Cassie. I don't want to do anything remotely like that."

"You wouldn't. You never could." Of that, he was absolutely certain.

"Hmm," she said, obviously not as certain. She looked at him. They were both lying on their sides, facing each other, their legs entwined below the knees, each with a hand on the other's hip. "Sorry to be such a downer."

"Not a downer," he said, then squeezed her hip before curving his hand over her ass and pulling her closer.

"Still. Not what you signed up for. We're supposed to keep this light, casual, right?"

"We can make it up as we go along," he said. He felt her stiffen just the tiniest bit and knew she thought he was going to push for more, that he wouldn't respect her boundaries. Shit, after he'd been with Jess only one time, he wasn't sure anymore himself.

He was no longer an officer. Could he stop being a gentleman too and pursue Jess beyond a summer fling?

He'd think about that later, not tonight, when she was so soft and warm and the scent of their lovemaking still hung in the air around them like a canopy. He tucked her under him and rolled so he was on top of her, pleased when her legs quickly spread beneath him, giving him full access to her body.

"But for now, why don't we just work on making a dent in that box in your nightstand?"

She smiled at him, taking his breath away, and ran her hands down his arms and to his cock, which was standing at attention.

"Yes. Let's make a dent in that box."

Nineteen

—∞—

ANOTHER TWO BOXES WERE PURCHASED OVER THE NEXT three weeks. Jess figured she'd just go ahead and buy in bulk, but then she stopped with her hand hovering over the 1-Click button on Amazon.

This could all go away at any time.

For all she knew, Zeke was somewhere out there right now meeting the future Mrs. Ezekiel Hampton, mother of his children. And in theory, she encouraged that.

In practice, however, she couldn't wait until he showed up on her doorstep later that evening, packed to spend the weekend with her at her place.

She'd definitely made up for her lack of sex over the last three years. There had only been two days over the past three weeks when she and Zeke hadn't found a chance to be together. Most times he came to Eagle Harbor, while also checking in at the Copper Harbor marina and his plane. But there were days she needed to be in Houghton for ranger stuff, so they found places to be together there, too. Which was trickier, since Zeke was still staying at his parents' place.

This included a rather chilly experience in the cab of his truck while he showed her where he used to take girls to make out while in high school.

The seller of the house in Dollar Bay had accepted her bid, so she would be in town even more frequently in the coming weeks, once she had her schedule for the island finalized.

Isle Royale would be officially opening in two weeks, so both of their schedules were about to get a lot busier.

She started prepping for the dinner she wanted to make for Zeke, even though he'd offered to bring something up with him, like he had on other occasions.

But tonight, the first time he *officially* spent the night—with a packed bag and plans for the next day being the only difference—she wanted to cook.

She'd been very particular about her kitchen when working with the architect and then the contractor. Not "peach versus blush towels" particular, but she knew what she wanted.

She hadn't cooked much when she was married to James. They spent most of their evenings out with clients or movers and shakers in Chicago. But when they had Cassie, Jess always made an effort in the kitchen, often times wrapping Cassie in an apron and insisting she help out. It had become a way they'd bonded in the beginning—over cracked eggs landing on the floor and chocolate chip cookies eaten straight from the baking pan.

She took a seat on a stool at the island and set down the ingredients she'd pulled from the refrigerator. The sadness that she felt when she thought of Cassie seeped through her. Doubt. Second thoughts. Everything crept in when she remembered putting together the text she'd sent her ex-stepdaughter.

Thankfully, she heard Zeke's truck in the back, and she shook the dark thoughts from her mind, determined to have a good evening.

He knocked, and she let him in. After a fairly lengthy welcome kiss against the wall of the mudroom, she resumed working on dinner, shooing him to the barstool with a beer when he offered to help.

"Oh, crap, I forgot," he said, getting off the stool and moving to the area where she kept her landline. "Is it okay if I make a call? I meant to text Lizzie before I got this far north, but I forgot. I can't get any bars here."

"Help yourself," she said, returning to the glaze for the salmon she'd picked up that morning at the fish market.

"Hey, Lizard," Zeke said. "I'm going to have to wave off for Sunday skating this week." He paused, presumably while his twin spoke. "Yeah, I know, I know. But one of these days I'll surprise you and actually show up with skates." Another pause. "No, it's fine. I'm just going to be in the Harbor all day Sunday and don't think I'll be back in time for skating. Knowing you're your worrywart mother's daughter, I just didn't want you freaking out if I wasn't there." A deep laugh from Zeke, which made Jess smile as she dabbed the glaze onto the salmon. "No, I haven't checked email since noon. Okay, I'll take a look, thanks. I'm sure what you put together is great. Seriously, Lizard, thanks for everything." Pause. "Yeah, you too. I'll check in with you on Monday, yeah? Okay. See ya."

Moments later, he was behind Jess, wrapping a strong arm around her waist, resting his chin on her shoulder. "That looks amazing."

"New recipe," she said. "Could be a disaster."

"Well, it'll be an amazing-looking disaster."

She smiled, though he couldn't see. His hand flattened against her stomach, sending a wave of heat through her. "Will anything explode or become inedible if you just let it sit like that for ten minutes?" he asked.

His hand moved south, inside the waistband of her jeans, below her panties, making her gasp. "No. Nothing will perish. But is ten minutes all you need?" she said, barely getting out the words as his fingers found her, spread her, then slid down and inside.

"No, Jess. *I* need all night long, and I'm going to get it. But, judging by how wet you just got all around my fingers, I'm guessing *you* only need ten minutes." She rolled her head back onto his chest, and he kissed the side of her neck. "Maybe less," he added, just as he added another finger and stroked the inside of her.

It took less.

"JESS, YOU NEED TO SEE THIS. Wake up, Jess," Zeke whispered in her ear.

"Everything okay?" she mumbled. "Need sleep. You wore me out." She curled deeper into the comforter, smiling as she heard Zeke chuckling from the other side of the bed. He was sitting up, and she felt him get out on the other side and heard his feet pad against the hardwood floor. Seven steps. He'd gone to the railing.

"Right back at ya. You took a toll on me too. But come and see what woke me up." There was wonder in his voice, but no panic or sense of alarm, so Jess didn't think there were armed bandits downstairs. Curiosity won over comfort, and she unwound herself from the burrito of bedding she'd made and got up.

She really didn't need to; the Northern Lights were bright enough that she could see them from the bed. She'd made sure the front window of her A-frame was high enough that she'd be able to see the lake view from her bed, but this sight was definitely worth getting out of bed.

"Holy wah," Zeke said as the natural glow shifted and moved on the horizon. "I've seen them before, but never this bright. Never this close."

She snagged his discarded Henley from the floor and slipped it over her head as she made her way to stand beside him at the railing. The soft knit shirt smelled of Zeke and hit her mid-thigh. She rolled the sleeve up a couple of times, liking the way she felt in the top.

"Holy wah is right," she said, taking in the whole panorama of color through the entire front triangle window of her home.

"Did you have this in mind when you designed the house?" he asked.

"I did," she said.

"Smart woman."

"I am." He chuckled and took her hand. They stood there for a half-hour, not saying anything, only touching where their hands were entwined.

When the glorious light show had faded, he led her back to bed. They took their time, touching each other everywhere, reaching plateaus, falling over peaks. Creating their own glorious show.

Twenty

SUNDAY MORNING, ZEKE WAS MAKING PANCAKES FOR breakfast when he heard Jess coming down the stairs. "Hope you don't mind, but I invaded your kitchen."

"With an aroma like that, you can invade anytime," she said as she rounded the corner of the island and swatted him on the ass as she made her way to the coffee maker.

He wanted to, God how he wanted to. Invade her kitchen. Her home.

Her heart.

Yeah, shit, even that. Though he knew it was a fool's mission, striving to invade Jess's heart. And one thing he'd learned when he became designated an airwing strike leader—never commit to a target, or bogey, without reasonable assurance of success.

No suicide bombers in the U.S. Navy.

So why did Zeke feel like he'd strapped on a vest made of explosives whenever he thought about the day when Jess would pull the pin and their interlude would implode?

"Although you invaded me plenty last night. In a non-rapey way," she said. He chuckled, going along with her lightness, as if his whole world hadn't shifted in the last three weeks spent with Jess.

She would cut him loose soon, send him off to commence his hunt for the woman who would become his partner in life.

When the only woman he could focus on was standing next

to him, waiting for her coffee to drip into her cup like it held her life's blood.

He flipped the pancakes in the skillet, happy they didn't fall off the spatula. He wasn't much in the kitchen, had never needed to be. But he found he liked the little bit he did do—basically pancakes and lasagna. A limited but potent load-out.

"Coffee?" she asked.

Zeke peeked in his cup and saw he had about half left. "I'm good, thanks."

She brought her cup over and stood next to him at the counter, her ass against the island. "Hey, I wanted to talk to you about something," she said, then took a sip from her mug, not meeting his eyes.

Not fucking meeting his eyes. Shit, this was it. They'd had a weekend-long fuckfest and she was giving him the boot.

The timing made sense. The season on the island would start in a couple of weeks and they'd begin their busy time. But he'd hoped that might mean as much or even more time together, since they'd be in same vicinity—the Harbor and Isle Royale—more frequently.

"Shoot," he said, managing to sound nonchalant. He flipped the pancakes once more to get the sides evened out. Inside, his heart was beating faster. He had to tell himself that he would survive being dumped by Jess and that he only had himself to blame by pursuing a woman who from the very start had told him there was no future together.

Petey would hoot an "I told you so."

"That call you made the other night? To Lizzie?"

"Yeah?" he said, hope starting to return. Maybe this wasn't a dumping?

"You cancelled on something for tonight, right?"

"Just weekly skating. I don't even skate. Petey takes Annie every week. Since I've been back, I bring Sam and we hang in the bleachers while they skate. Sometimes Lizzie goes, sometimes it's a chance for her and Finn to do couple shit."

"That's nice of you," she said, then took another sip of coffee. There were no lipstick stains on her white mug. Whatever lipstick she might have had on before Zeke had kissed off completely hours ago.

Days ago.

"It's nice of Petey, actually. It's his gig. I just sort of jumped on."

"Still. I just wanted to say, it won't bother me if you wanted to leave tonight and still make it. I know we said you'd stay the weekend, but we didn't really say what all that entailed. I mean, where the clock stops and all."

Okay, not a dumping, then. Or at least not entirely. Still, Jess was a woman who had lived alone for the past three years and enjoyed it. Reveled in it, from what she said. Maybe she just needed a little alone time after him being here since Friday night.

He'd lived alone for most of his career in the Navy, after having a roommate at one of his earlier apartments. But, of course, when on cruise, you were "housemates" with thousands. On his first cruise he'd quickly gotten over needing any alone time—there was simply none to be had.

So, how to approach this to give Jess what she needed? As long as what she needed wasn't an opening for a breakup.

"Actually, I could use a week off from skating. I'll hit next week, and then it'll probably be hit or miss during the season. You know, I'm not even sure if they do open skate during the summer. I'll ask Petey next time I see him."

There. That was convoluted enough that he might just get away with it.

He'd gone through training on what to do if he was shot down and captured, for Christ's sake. He should be able to pull off a little subterfuge with this one.

"Oh. I…" She looked at him, confusion in her eyes. "So…?"

"I'm skipping skating tonight."

She nodded and drank her coffee, then moved away, setting down her mug, getting plates, and gathering silverware.

Now was the time when he should add something like "But if you need some time alone, I can get out of your hair." Something light, and referencing only today, not their entire future.

But he didn't say it. He just loaded the pancakes onto the plates she held out and followed her around the island to the barstools.

He'd spend the rest of the day—and night—making sure she was glad he stayed.

ON MONDAY MORNING, Jess rolled over to him in bed, wrapping an arm around his waist. She slid down his body, wrapping her creamy white hand around his already hardening cock. She looked up at him, her eyes gleaming with mischief.

"I'm glad you didn't go to skating last night," she whispered.

"So am I, darlin'. So am I," he said—the last words he could manage before she took him in her mouth and gave him the best blowjob he ever had.

Twenty-One

THEY TOOK A SAUNA LATER THAT MORNING, AND HE showed Jess some interesting things that could be done with a loofah.

After they were showered and dressed, Zeke started packing up his things to head back to Hancock. Slowly.

"Okay, I guess that's everything," he said when he went downstairs with his duffel bag. Jess was on her couch reading a book, the view of a thawing Lake Superior behind her almost as breathtaking as the redhead.

"Well, it wasn't like you brought much," she said, and he nodded.

"What's on your schedule for this week?" he asked, setting the duffel on the floor by the fireplace and walking over to the couch.

She placed her book on the coffee table and sat up, pulling in her knees to make a place for him, which he took.

"Actually, I wanted to let you know I'd be on the island for the week before opening day. Incommunicado."

"Isn't the whole island basically incommunicado?"

"Pretty much. But I'm going camping. I did it last year right before the season started."

"You don't get enough of that during the summer? Like when the weather is good?"

"This is different. One of the other rangers told me about it, and I tried it last year. She hikes the whole island, from one end to the other. It takes five days, and it's just a way to, I don't know, set your compass. Get your head in the game."

"The whole island?" he said, impressed.

"Tip to tip, right down the center. The whole Greenstone Ridge trail. It's really amazing. Challenging. But amazing."

"So, you do it with other rangers?" She'd told him about some of the rangers she worked with, a few men, a few women. A guy named Reilly who would work on the Dollar Bay house with her. Given that the rangers typically worked in separate areas on any given day, it wasn't the same as sharing cubicle space with coworkers. His former squadron being similar, Zeke understood. They were people you relied on to get your job done and saw from time to time, but you were also on your own a lot.

She shook her head. "No, though I think Rayna—that's who told me about it—will most likely be doing it too, though I don't expect to run into her or anything. Maybe see her dust on the trail, that kind of thing. But it's a solitary thing. For just me."

"But late April? You could freeze your ass off."

She laughed. "Very likely. But I'm prepared. It's my job to give advice so people don't freeze their asses off. And weather reports are for some rain, but temps won't be truly awful. Rayna said she's had snow during her hike in past years."

"Well, yeah, we can get snow until mid-May," he said. But they'd had a fairly mellow spring in the Copper Country, and there was only snow on the ground in the woods under dense tree cover where the sun took a little longer to thaw it all out.

"I'm sure there'll be snow in some places on the island still, but I've got good equipment for the nights."

He wanted to volunteer to go with her. He knew she could handle herself—it was her job. But his instinct to protect came out hard, and he had to fight it. Mainly because she would be more likely to protect him from the wilds of Isle Royale than the other way around. And also because he just didn't want to be away from her for five days.

He kept his mouth shut. Until he remembered something that might keep him closer to her for a little while longer.

"I wanted to go to Minnesota before the season started, introduce myself to the folks around Grand Portage. I don't see getting too much business from that area, but you never know. I'd like to familiarize myself with the harbor at the very least, in case I need to take people there from the island."

"Okay…"

"So, why don't I fly you to the island on my way? Drop you off and then go on to Minnesota. I don't know if I'll be there the whole time, but I can plan to pick you up whenever you say you'll be ready."

"I was just going to ride the *Ranger* over with other staff. The people who will be working in the lodge and the shops. They'll all be going over before the season."

"Come on, let me fly you over. You already know I'm a good pilot."

"I don't have a lot to compare you to, as far as little planes flying into Isle Royale. I've always taken a boat over."

"This would be so much faster and not nearly so cold as the deck of a boat in the Lake Superior winds."

She nodded. "You got it, flyboy. Thanks."

"No problem. Like I said, I'm going over anyway. You'll be good company."

"I wasn't very good company the day we looked for the wolves."

He remembered how little she'd said that day. He'd thought her aloof. She hadn't been aloof in his arms last night.

Or that morning.

"You were just taking the wolf thing seriously. Since you were filling in for Ralph."

She raised a cinnamon eyebrow at him, knowing he was giving her a pass. "Okay," he said, "you were hot for me from the minute you saw me and just couldn't handle being so up close and personal with me. You could barely see those damn wolves as caught up in your lust for me as you were."

She nudged his hip with her foot, which he grabbed and pulled onto his lap. "You wish," she said, sounding like an eighth grader who'd just been busted.

"Oh, I know," he said, then pulled her other leg up too, which led to her sliding onto his lap.

Which led to him getting a much later start back to Hancock than he'd thought.

When he was finally at the door saying goodbye, she buried her head into his fleece jacket, breathing him in. He thought his heart might burst, the gesture was so sweet.

"So, I'll pick you up on Thursday morning? We'll grab some breakfast in the Harbor and then fly over?" he asked. She nodded, her head moving against him, her hands finally loosening the hold she had on his jacket.

"Thanks for this weekend," he said.

"Thank *you*," she said, looking up at him. He kissed her softly, not wanting to end up back in the bed. Well, yes, he wanted to end up exactly there, but knew he needed to get to Hancock this evening.

"Bye," he said after one more taste of her.

"Bye." He turned for the door but stopped when she whispered, "You were right."

"Huh?" he said, still facing the door. It seemed to give her some courage, because she cleared her throat and said, "That day on the plane. I wanted you from the moment I saw you."

He started to turn around, but her hand on his back pushed him toward the door, so he kept going. He wasn't even sure she heard the "Ditto" he said as the door closed behind him.

Twenty-Two

THE SIGN ON BOB'S MOBIL AS ZEKE DROVE UP THE street to his parents' house read, *He who finds a wife finds what is good and receives favor from the Lord.*

He tried not to read too much into that and Jess's upcoming hiking trip as he walked into the kitchen, seeing Lizzie at his mother's table with her laptop in front of her. His mother was at another chair with Sam on her lap.

"Oh, good, you're home," Lizzie said. "I was just about to print this out to leave for you with my notes, but now I'll go over it with you in person. I emailed you a copy of everything."

"What, more tweaks to my marketing plan?" he said, teasing. But by the look on his sister's face, that was exactly what it was. "Okay, give me a second to dump my stuff and I'm all yours."

He gave his mother a kiss on the cheek, his nephew a raspberry on the top of the head, which caused Sam to squeal in delight, and then went through the house and up the stairs to his room.

"Hey, son," his father called to him as he passed his parents' bedroom. "Got a second?"

"Sure," Zeke said. He threw his duffel into his room and then doubled back to join his father, who was putting clothes from a laundry basket into his dresser.

Some clothes. Others Hugh Hampton was setting next to an open suitcase on the bed where Zeke went to sit.

"Don't tell me you're leaving Mom," Zeke said, then laughed at the look his father shot at him.

"Bite your tongue," his dad said. "That woman's the best thing that's ever happened to me. I'd be a fool to ever give her up."

"Damn straight," Zeke said, stretching out on the bed, pulling a pillow from his father's side of the bed and stuffing it behind his head. "So why the packing?"

"It appears you've had a lot on your mind lately. Did you forget your mother and I are leaving this week for vacation?"

"Yeah, I completely forgot. Sorry. Need me to do anything while you're gone?"

Hugh placed two pairs of dress socks in his suitcase and the rest of the socks from the laundry basket into his dresser drawer. Then he shut it and faced Zeke. "I think your mother is leaving a list of anything that needs doing, but no, not really. I'm guessing she's just doing it so you'll feel useful and stay longer."

Zeke laughed. "Yeah, that sounds about right."

"Not that you've been around much lately anyway." His father watched him until finally Zeke could stand it no longer.

"When am I ever going to be able to outlast that stare of yours? When I'm forty? Fifty?"

His father chuckled, then went about taking some golf shirts from the closet and removing them from the hangers. "Never. That's how parenting works."

"Sheesh." Zeke watched his father continue to pack before he finally settled on just how much intel he was willing to share. He'd told his parents he was spending the weekend in the Harbor—he just hadn't said anything about with whom. Lizzie had undoubtedly filled their mother in on Jess. Or maybe not. His sister could keep a secret if she felt it was important. And maybe she figured Jess would be over so quickly that it wasn't worth it to get Doris's hopes up that her son may have finally found the one.

And that was the problem.

"I think I found the one," he said, shocked he'd said the words aloud. To his father, no less. Hugh had his back to Zeke and had frozen at the declaration, but then just continued on, selecting pants from his closet. Waiting for Zeke to continue.

"But she doesn't want anything serious. She was very upfront about that. Right from the start. And I want to respect that."

His father brought the pants to the bed and meticulously folded them before placing them in the suitcase. "Sounds like there might be a 'but' at the end of that sentence."

Zeke covered his face with the pillow, wanting to scream into it. Instead, he set it to the side and jackknifed into a sitting position. His father joined him, sitting on the other side of the bed, the big suitcase between them.

"That's just it. I don't really have the right to a 'but,' do I? She told me what she wanted, and I said I was okay with it. It feels like it'd be really shitty to push her on it now."

"It would be, and I don't think you're the kind of man who is shitty to women."

Oh, there were probably some women out there who might disagree, but for the most part, Zeke had been upfront with any woman he'd dated. None had ever been surprised when he broke things off. Disappointed? Sometimes. But he'd never walked away feeling shitty about the break.

"I don't think I am," he said. His father nodded, then slapped his hands on his knees in a gesture Zeke had known since he'd been three. He tried to mimic his father, slapping his own knees before getting up.

"Well, my boy, you're just going to have to hope that you become the one for her."

"But she's already had her one. 'One and done' were her exact words about long-term relationships."

"So the question is, knowing that, are you doing yourself any favors continuing on with her? Getting yourself in deeper?"

No, of course not. He'd been just thinking that over the weekend.

"But then again," his father added, "you were never one to take the easy way out."

Zeke sighed and continued to sit on the bed as his father packed around him. The easy thing would be to say goodbye to Jess at the island after he dropped her off. Spend the time in Minnesota getting his head on straight, then come back and start looking for someone who wanted a future with him.

He let out another sigh, knowing there was no way in hell he'd go through with that plan.

His father only laughed at Zeke's sighs as he zipped up his suitcase. Zeke pulled the pillow back over his face. "Fuck," he whispered into the soft down.

"You can say that again," Hugh said, chuckling some more.

Twenty-Three

—ᴍ—

THE BLUE OF LAKE SUPERIOR GLISTENED WITH SUNLIGHT below them, as if the big lake was ecstatic to finally be rid of all the ice and snow and was able to shimmer again.

Jess felt the same way, though she wasn't sure it was from spring finally arriving in the Copper Country (in late April!) or because she was with Zeke again after four days of being apart.

Just as she knew the shimmering lake was deadly cold, she felt the bottom drop out of her euphoria while riding next to the man she'd spent the last four weeks sleeping with.

Too long, she knew, the coldness zapping some of her shimmer. Not wise. For her or him. He needed to be looking elsewhere, and she needed to not be looking, well, for him.

Still, she was going to be away from him for days—away from everyone for days. And that, coupled with the four days they'd just spent apart seeing to their various commitments, should be enough for her to put this all in perspective.

She was sleeping with Zeke Hampton because she was wildly attracted to him, he was good in bed (okay, exceptional), and she was coming off a world-class dry spell.

Nothing more to it.

"I really missed you these past few days. I'm sorry we couldn't figure something out for a dinner, at least."

There, that should be the warning she needed. He, the man who should be out trying to meet his future baby mama, was missing her while their schedules were incompatible. And as if that weren't enough, he didn't say he wished they could have hooked up or found time for a quickie. No, he was sorry they hadn't been able to even squeeze in a dinner. Like it was her company he missed and not her body.

She didn't know whether to be complimented or offended.

Warned. Warned was what she should be.

"Me too," she said, damning herself for the honest words that slipped past her lips. It would have been the perfect time for a "Yeah, but we both have pretty tight schedules now, so…" A warning to him. An opening for a break. Something.

He reached from the yoke over to her knee and squeezed, and she looked to him and smiled. She couldn't help it. Not when he was smiling at her, that damn cleft chin dimpled deliciously, his Aviator-style sunglasses sitting rakishly on his straight Roman nose, his hair even longer now. Not long, but no military cut any longer, not that she'd minded it.

Good grief, when would her days of solitude and centering herself begin? Could she Zen Zeke right out of her system? Would the flora and fauna make her not crave the things he did to her body?

The island was beautiful and all, but come on… There was no chance it could compete with shattering apart with those strong arms wrapped around her and his husky whispering in her ear about how hard she made him, how wet he made her.

"How much further?" she asked, and he laughed, as if he could read her dirty mind. Yeah, he probably could.

He pointed, and she saw Isle Royale in the distance. Right past his long fingers. Fingers that had—

"Enjoy the ride. Think of us as one of those movie couples in the planes. *Out of Africa* or *The English Patient* or something. Of course, in those movies, you'd be sitting behind me, not next to me. You've come a long way, baby."

She snorted and took her eyes from his hand as he dropped it back down to the wheel. Wait. "Didn't someone die in each of those movies? And weren't there horrifying crashes in both?"

He thought for a second, as did she, trying to remember.

"Okay, scratch that. Just enjoy the ride."

She did. She particularly liked the parts when Zeke reached over to touch her leg, her arm, her hair.

The flora and fauna better be fucking fantastic.

THE LANDING WAS SMOOTH, which shouldn't have surprised Jess. Zeke had landed jets on a carrier in rough waters. But she knew he hadn't flown the seaplane all that long. He had them tied up at the dock and Jess off the plane in no time.

"You're going to be very good at this," she said, and he beamed with pride.

Dazzling.

"I really think I'm going to like it. We'll see when I have to start dealing with any dickhead passengers, but for now, yeah... I'm glad I did it."

It was part of his plan. Business. Home. Family. Part one was checked off, though his business would be growing for a while. Home would come easily if his sister continued to drag him to open houses. It was the last that had Jess swinging her pack over her shoulder, even though Zeke tried to take it from her, and quickly walking up to the lodge where she'd store some of the other things she'd brought but wouldn't take hiking with her.

"Wait up," he said. She continued on, but his long legs had him easily catching up. "At least let me take this," he said, reaching for her other bag, a duffel she carried by the handles. She would repack at the lodge, adding in fresh water and dry food, before starting out on Greenstone Ridge that afternoon. After letting him take her second bag, she slowed as she climbed the steps up to the lodge, which looked out over the harbor. She stopped on the porch of the lodge, swung her pack off her back, and set it next to the wall. "You can just put it there. I'm going to repack after I go in to say hi and get a couple of things from the store." The little area of Rock Harbor was on the side of the island where boaters came from Michigan, from either Hancock or Copper Harbor. On the other side of the island, where she would hike to, was Windigo, the marina where campers from Minnesota and Canada docked. At Rock Harbor, there was the marina, and the lodge, which also had several cabins besides the main building.

"Okay. So, I'll see you in five days, then," Zeke said, clearly taking her cue that she'd go it alone from there.

If only she felt as confident about that decision. She nodded. "And if you book a charter for that day, don't worry about me. Just leave word at the Windigo Visitor Center. I can get back to Copper Harbor a bunch of different ways."

Not a bunch, but enough to give Zeke an out if his business dictated it. Or if he wanted it.

He didn't want it, if she was reading his glower correctly. He looked away from her, up to the sky and hills that were inland. Probably wishing he were far above it all in his plane again, away from her attempts to passive-aggressively push him away.

Half-assed attempts, because she really didn't want to push Zeke away. But she couldn't keep him, either.

"I'll be here," he said. Firm. Authoritative. He had said he hadn't wanted to be a squadron commanding officer—didn't want to be pulled out of the sky—but he would have been a good one.

"Okay," she said. "Thank you for bringing me. It really was a nice trip."

He nodded and looked at her mouth like he was going to kiss her, but he didn't. Instead, he touched her hand with just his fingertips. It was so soft, so fleeting, that it was almost more intimate than if he'd bent her over and kissed the life out of her. "Be safe. Be mindful. Or whatever it is that you call it."

She gave him a small smile. It wasn't goodbye—he'd be there to meet her in five days—and yet it felt as if something was shifting, giving way, as though she were hiking on a rocky cliff and one wrong step would create a rockslide of epic proportions.

She watched as he retreated down the wooden steps. Three steps down, he stopped and turned around.

"You know, flying is great. You're up there by yourself or with a copilot. It's just you and sky. It seems limitless, like you could go on forever."

She wasn't sure where he was going, but gave him a quick nod.

"But then, sometimes, the sky seems too vast, too big, more than you want to handle on your own, and you start looking."

She didn't want to ask, didn't want to go where he was no doubt trying to lead her. "For what?" she said, her voice more breathless than she'd intended.

"You look for a soft place to land."

She didn't gasp aloud, she had that much presence of mind, but her heart hitched, and it felt like Zeke saw into the very soul of her. A soul she had tried hard to protect and hide while living her life the way she wanted.

"I can be that for you, Jess," he added. "A soft place to land."

Before she could answer or nod, or hell, burst out crying, he turned and continued down the wide wooden steps, back to the marina and his plane.

Where he would take flight once more. But eventually come in for a landing.

Could she be that for him?

HE'D TOTALLY MESSED THAT UP. Fuck. He'd done nothing for the past four days except tell himself he'd be cool when he saw Jess again. That the desperation he'd felt while away from her wouldn't creep through, that he'd do nothing to scare her off.

He'd almost made it. Seconds from a clean getaway.

And then he had to go and spout some bullshit metaphor about flying and landing and how that somehow equated to commitment.

A commitment she'd been pretty upfront about not wanting. A commitment she'd trusted him not to pressure her for.

A woman with trust issues from a disastrous marriage.

Fuck.

He took off in the Cessna from Rock Harbor, bringing the plane around so he could fly right down the center of the island, passing over Greenstone Ridge and the path that Jess would be taking. He'd never been into camping—six-month cruises on carriers was as much roughing it as he wanted to do—but he wished he were down there, getting his gear ready, lacing up some hiking boots, ready to hit the trail behind Jess. Yeah, definitely walking behind her.

Most of the trees were still bare below him, not much different than when he'd first flown Jess to the island two months ago. Except the snow was gone and greenery was trying to make its appearance. The pines were still thick in places, and Zeke wondered if the two wolves were down there right now, wondering what that strange, loud, metallic bird in the sky was.

I can be your soft place to land.

God, what an idiot. Way to drop something like that on her as she was about to embark on a five-day hike with nothing but time to replay his needy, clingy, commitment-seeking words in her head.

Okay, enough. Enough with the self-flagellation. If he learned nothing else the past fourteen years in the Navy, he learned that when a mission went bad, you debriefed, did a "lessons learned," and then put it from your mind and moved on to the next mission. And he'd been able to do that.

Mostly.

A flash of one of his last missions went through his mind, and he quickly refocused his thoughts. Red hair. Glorious pale skin. A greenstone pendant dangling around her long, graceful neck.

Yeah, better.

He didn't need a five-day hike to "get centered." All he needed to do was think about Jess, and the cobwebs—and ghosts—all cleared away.

For now. But she wouldn't always be there.

Five days. Would she greet him at the docks with a

welcoming hug, his heavy words forgotten the minute she'd started communing with nature? Or would she greet him with a sad look and a conversation that started along the lines of "We need to talk"?

Either way, he'd survive. It'd be a blow if she was ending it now because of his last words to her, but he found that he could live with that. He'd failed in missions before, some life-altering for both him and others. If he failed at getting Jess to think about him as something more than a diversion to enjoy until he was ready to wife-hunt, so be it.

God, he hoped he hadn't.

He veered off, as if wanting to give her the space she wanted, and headed toward Minnesota, hoping they had a good bar or two in Grand Portage.

Twenty-Four

—ππ—

JESS WOKE UP WEARY AND TIRED ON HER FIFTH MORNING.
Her hike today would be a little less than the daily eight or nine
miles she'd been doing. From the Island Mine campsite where
she'd stayed last night to the Windigo area where she would meet
Zeke was around six miles.

She turned over in her sleeping bag, moving her feet back
and forth, trying to get warm. It was the last day of April, and Jess
knew the temps could have been a lot worse the past four days.

She'd run across a couple of other rangers on her trek, but
they'd only stopped, chatted for a few minutes, and then gone
their separate ways, wanting to make the journey alone.

Like a pilgrimage to Mecca.

Only with moose.

She'd been fortunate enough to see a few moose along the
way, and had taken some great photos. She also took some photos
of plants that were new to her, though not everything on the
island was in full bloom yet, the long winter seeing to that.

She stretched her arms over her head, cringing when they
came out of her light, but effective, sleeping bag. She burrowed
back in, mentally checking her body for any new aches and pains.
Nope. Just a little sore from all the miles walked over uneven
terrain.

Snowshoeing this winter had paid off. Last year when she'd
done this, she could barely get out of her bag the last morning,

and for most of the day had sworn she'd never do it again.

Having the whole day ahead of her, she turned over again and snuggled deeply, allowing herself to go back to sleep if she wanted.

But sleep wouldn't come, and she knew why. She'd be seeing Zeke again today. After four days apart, the hours they spent flying to the island weren't enough. And now another five away from him—

Stop. Don't go there.

This was exactly what she wanted. Great sex with somebody she really liked, knowing it would go no further.

Yeah, there was a lot to unpack in that thought.

Great sex. Yeah, definitely. Beyond definitely.

Really liked. Of course, she liked Zeke, but she knew her feelings had slipped past *like* and into something much deeper. Which would be fine, considering…

It would go no further.

She'd been clear about that with him. More than once. And he'd said he could live with that. That he just wanted to be with her until he had his ducks in a row with his business and where he was living.

Until he started looking for the mother of his children.

The thought of him out there looking for Mrs. Zeke Hampton sent a stab through her that made her feel small and petty.

Had he met her in Minnesota? A cute, fertile, dying-to-be-married honey who worked at the marina in Grand Portage?

Or perhaps he'd bumped into an old flame from high school at the grocery store.

Gah!

She shouldn't care. She *couldn't* care.

And honestly, she cared about Zeke enough to want those things for him—a partner, a mother for his kids, someone to grow old with. She just wanted him for a little while longer, that was all. And she thought he was cool with that.

I'm just looking for a soft place to land.

Damn it, why'd he have to go and say such a great line to her? While walking down the stairs, gorgeous Lake Superior shimmering beyond him. That damn dimple nearly reflecting the sun to blind her.

Okay, it hadn't been that blinding, but the whole scene of him standing there and dropping lines that made her want to drop her panties? Yeah…dazzling.

She'd been lulled by dazzling before. And even before her disastrous marriage.

When her father had started his own company and they'd moved to Winnetka, she'd been dazzled at first by their new life.

And that had crumbled around her, leaving her with a workaholic father who forgot most of the weekends he was supposed to have Jess, and a bitter mother who tried to first drink away her loneliness and then marry it away—multiple times.

It had led Jess into the sure arms of James much too young, craving the stability he offered. On some level, trying to fix her parents' shattered marriage by making a success of her own, to a man just like her father.

It had also led her to be estranged from her parents now. Her mother had only met Cassie once, being in Europe with husband number three (or was it four?) during most of Jess and James's married life. Jess's father had only met Cassie twice.

Neither of her parents had been invited to her wedding, with James whisking her off to be married in the Bahamas, just the two of them.

She'd thought it terribly romantic that he didn't want any of their friends or family there, when really it should have been just another red flag.

But she was too dazzled—and too hungry for something she thought would make her whole—to see the warning signs.

And here she was, years later, estranged from them all. For the most part, she was okay with that. The pangs of missing the parents she'd known as a child came to her at odd times, but she knew that family didn't exist any longer, if it ever really had. And she ached with pain when she thought about hurting Cassie, leaving her when she left James. She eased that pain by telling herself that Cassie was now a busy teenager who probably barely had time to spend with her two parents who lived apart, let alone with an ex-stepmother.

Sometimes it worked and the ache eased. Most times it didn't.

And soon she'd be estranged from Zeke, though with none of the dramatics of her past breakups.

She'd see Zeke from time to time, both being part of the Harbor and island crew. They'd be civil, of course, maybe even share a hug and a little small talk.

Maybe she'd even meet someone who was looking for what she wanted—a no-strings, no-future arrangement.

But he wouldn't be Zeke.

Yes, she'd survive. She'd survived worse. And it had brought her to this place in her life where she was happy, really, truly happy.

Could she be that happy with Zeke? Long term?

The what-ifs started pinging through her head, exhilarating her. And scaring her.

She knew trust was, at heart, the issue for her. From her parents' nasty divorce to James keeping his vasectomy from her, she'd taken a big hit in that department. A big enough hit that she wasn't sure she had it in her to let somebody in again. Not all the way in. Not as deep as you need to really make a lasting relationship work.

But what if it that "somebody" was Zeke?

The last what-if made her get out of the sleeping bag.

She would talk to Zeke about it. Today. Let him know her fears and concerns, but that—*maybe*—she might be thinking long term with him after all.

Maybe he *could* be her soft place to land.

As she started to pack up her gear, she heard rustling in the woods beyond the campsite. Expecting a squirrel or rabbit or even a moose, she slowly rose to stand and reached for her phone in her pocket, ready to snap some photos. She'd brought her actual camera for the good stuff, but that was at the bottom of her backpack, where she'd put it for safekeeping during the night.

From the cold. She didn't think Bullwinkle was going to steal her Nikon.

But it wasn't Bullwinkle staring at her on the edge of the woods. Nor Rocky, for that matter.

One of the two remaining wolves was watching her, its eyes darting between Jess and the clearing beyond.

"It's okay," Jess said in a low whisper, causing the wolf to take a few steps to the side. "I'll get out of your way. This island is much more yours than mine." She slid her pack slowly from the ground and up to her shoulder. The wolf had now come out into the clearing of the campsite, and Jess recognized it as the female of the two. She looked around for the wolf's companion, but didn't see any signs of the male wolf anywhere.

Maybe the wolf just needed some alone time. Jess could relate.

Maybe the wolf really needed to think through this whole procreation thing a little bit. Again, Jess could relate.

The female wolf walked across the campsite, careful to stay on the far side from Jess. Trying to move as little as possible, and stunned that the wolf was coming that close to her, she slowly pulled her phone out of her pocket and got it in camera mode.

The wolf stopped at the unnatural sound of the phone clicking when Jess unlocked it, and stood facing Jess, only fifteen yards away.

Jess knew she'd never get so close again. Her phone camera would get closer pictures at this distance than the big lens on her Nikon had ever gotten at the long distances she'd seen the wolves before.

And yet she didn't take any photos. Her hand went back to her pocket, depositing her phone as she simply watched the wolf.

The wolf had survived a hard winter, looking a little leaner than she had in the photographs Jess had seen before. Her brown coat was matted and patchy, but fuller in some spots from the winter. But survive she had. Just as Jess had.

And maybe that was all that was needed. Just surviving and taking what nature threw your way.

Nature had thrown Zeke Hampton in Jess's path. And damn, she wanted more with him than just to survive a long winter. She wanted spring. And summer. And fall.

She wanted it all.

She waited with the wolf until some other noise, or scent, or something else Jess couldn't hear or see, sent the wolf darting from the campsite.

Jess waited for a few moments to see if the male would come after her, but there was no sign of him. As she made her way out of the campsite and onto the trail headed for the Windigo harbor, she smiled, secure in the thought that her own male was following.

Twenty-Five

—◠◡◠—

BE COOL, MAN. DON'T BLOW THIS. KEEP ALL THOUGHTS *of landings and that bullshit to yourself.*

The hard truth was Zeke might have already blown it days ago. He'd received a text from Jess the night before he was due to fly back to the island, shocked that it had even gotten through from out there.

Don't know if you'll get this in time, or at all, but don't come until later. I'm picking up a shift for a sick ranger and won't be done until eight.

It could have been worse, he thought. It could have been a "don't come at all" message. Maybe she'd forgotten his parting words—his *pleading* parting words—on the five-day hike. All that nature may have helped him out and she'd been so distracted with the beauty around her that she'd forgotten about the way he'd begged for more just before he left her.

Christ, Petey would have had a field day with that. And he would have if Zeke had told him about it. But after a couple of days in Grand Portage, Zeke had steered clear of his friends back in Hancock. He'd immersed himself in his fledgling business, going over the marketing plan his sister's team had put together for him, booking a few early charters for the upcoming weeks, and trying to forget about Jess.

Because Jess was probably right then figuring out how to let him down gently.

And then he saw her, at the edge of the dock, addressing a small group of campers, in all her ranger glory.

He wasn't sure how she'd gotten a uniform, whether she'd packed one with her, or if they had them at the offices at this side of the island, or if it belonged to the sick ranger, but Zeke couldn't believe that her uniform had the effect on him that it did.

Probably just because it'd been five days since he'd seen her, that was all. Because, come on, who would ever think that dark olive-green slacks, a drab, lighter green shirt, a bulky fleece, and a Smokey Bear hat would be so damn sexy.

She wore it well. Or maybe it was because he knew the body beneath it so intimately. Either way, he needed to make some kind of move or soon he was going to be sporting wood and scaring off all the campers.

Leaving the dock area, he vaguely noticed a couple of large boats moored as well. Not a lot of activity on opening day, it being too cold for most. In fact, he was somewhat surprised that the group around Jess were campers. It looked to be a youngish couple, maybe in their late twenties, and then a family of five, with the parents and three kids, two boys and a girl, who were around the eight- to twelve-year-old range. The kids got out of school to go camping on Isle Royale in late April? Maybe it was their spring break?

Much as Zeke loved the area, he thought it a cruel trick for parents to bring their kids to the still-wintry Copper Country for camping during spring break. But the kids were listening to Jess with rapt attention, so what did he know?

One thing. He knew listening to Jess with rapt attention was no hardship.

As he approached, she made eye contact with him and smiled. That smile. The pink lips, even a bit pinker from the cold, the white, even teeth… God, he could look at her smile—at *her*—forever.

Wait. She was smiling at him. And giving him a "one second" finger waggle. That had to mean she was happy to see him, right?

That she wouldn't be giving him his walking papers tonight?

He was reading a lot into a little finger movement, but it gave him hope as he leaned against one of the wooden railings at the edge of where she had her little group assembled. He listened in. Because if he could watch her smile for the rest of his life, he could absolutely listen to her voice for all eternity. Even if it was spewing facts and figures about Isle Royale to listening campers.

"And remember, rock hunting is big here on the island, but you cannot keep the agates or the greenstones. You're not even to disturb them. A strict observe-only situation with the greenstones here. It's the same with plants, antlers, driftwood, and other natural items found. Fish, on the other hand, are legal to keep once caught, as long as you have the proper fishing licenses."

She continued, but Zeke's mind wandered to the memory of Jess's greenstone necklace when she wore it—and only it—for him in bed. How the green of the stone glinted in the candlelight against her skin. He wondered if perhaps she was wearing the necklace now, under her layers of warmth? She'd said she didn't like to wear it when it would show, since she was part of the "establishment."

"And that's it. So, stay warm, stay safe. The entire list of regulations is in the packet you'll get at the visitor center." She pointed behind her to the building where the campers would go to start their journey. The couple stayed and asked her a few more questions. Then they followed the family down the path to the visitor center, and Jess turned to him, her smile becoming even brighter.

No way in hell was he getting his walking papers tonight.

"Hey," she said as she neared him.

"Hey," he replied, still half leaning/half sitting on the dock railing. He spread his legs wide, and she walked into the space he created for her. If only it were that simple—Zeke creating space for her in his life and Jess so easily walking in. His part of that equation was no problem. Hers? Well, there was that smile she was still sporting. And she was wrapping her arms around his neck and pressing her body into his.

Maybe the hike had been life altering in some way for her? Could seeing a couple of moose do that?

Shit, seeing Jess Chapman spread out beneath him on her bed, whispering his name as she climaxed, had absolutely altered *his* life.

"Missed you," she whispered as she nuzzled into his neck.

"Missed you too," he said, nearly weeping at the beauty of the moment. His stupid-ass words when last he saw her hadn't wrecked everything. She was still his. Not forever, he knew that. Knew it wasn't what she wanted. But at least for now. At least for a while longer.

He didn't want to ruin it, knew he should just let sleeping dogs lie, but he had to let her know he wasn't going to push it. That he respected her wishes, that he *listened* to her. "I really want to—"

"Shhh," she said. She hugged him hard, then leaned back, her hands still around his neck, clasped together at the back of his head like she was hanging on for the ride. God, please let her be willing to hang on for the ride a little longer. "You don't need to explain the other day. Really."

"But I feel like—"

"Really, Zeke, it's fine. I appreciate that you were so honest. And it made me realize I need to be as honest with you as you were with me."

Shit. He'd been duped by the "missed you" and the hug. She really was backing off. But no, there was still the smile, and she was beaming right at him. And, as if she couldn't help herself, she leaned forward and kissed him.

He loved when she smiled, yes, but he loved it even more when she put her mouth to his and he felt the tingling coldness turn to heat. It was soft, and so, so sweet, and then she was gone, looking at him once again. Smiling once again.

"And it was time to be honest with myself, too," she said. Her smile turned tentative, and she took a deep breath. And, oh, holy shit, she was going to give them a chance. He could see it in her eyes. "And after I got over my fear of what being honest would mean, I—"

"Jessica? Is that you?" A voice from behind them, further down the dock, interrupted Jess. And by the way she froze in his arms, Zeke guessed she recognized the voice.

Once she stepped back, and Zeke could see beyond her, so did he. If not the voice, he recognized the man. Jim Peterson, boat captain. Zeke looked closer and realized one of the two boats docked was indeed the *Mina*, Jim's boat. And he seemed to remember that Jim was new to the area, had only been there a couple of years.

Jess stepped back, away from the end of the dock from which Jim was now approaching. Cautiously, with a hand out, like Jess was a small animal he didn't want to scare away. And by the shocked look in her eyes, Jim's movements of caution were warranted.

Jim. James. James?

Oh, fuck no. Zeke stepped in front of Jess, placing himself between her and Jim Peterson. Then, making sure she was safely behind him, he walked toward Peterson, trying to make himself as big and badass as he could. He was a pilot, for Chrissakes, not a SEAL, but he was a trained fighter, and he wasn't backing down from this dogfight.

"I don't want any trouble," Jim said to Zeke. "I only want to talk to you," he said to Jess. Zeke heard Jess's intake of breath and strode the remaining few steps to Peterson, placing a hand squarely on the older man's chest.

"She doesn't want to talk to you," he said.

"I'd like to hear that from her," Peterson said, looking first at Jess, then at Zeke.

"Jim. James. Are you James, motherfucker?" Zeke said, Peterson's rational voice bugging the shit out of him.

"What?" Peterson looked confused. "James is my real name, yes, but I—"

"Zeke, no," Jess said from closer behind Zeke than he would have liked. She must have followed him out onto the dock. "It's not what you think. It's okay—"

"What'd you do? Become a boat captain just to be near her?" By the look on Peterson's face, Zeke knew he'd hit the nail on the head. "You sick stalker—"

"No. Not like that. Not in a stalker way," Peterson said. He looked to Jess, who was now standing almost even with Zeke. "It wasn't like that, honestly."

Jess stared at the man and then nodded. Zeke felt the bottom drop out from under him. Shit, she was going to forgive her ex. Any chance he might have had—any chance *they* might have had—was floating away like the last chunks of ice on Lake Superior.

"No. Not after all the shitty things you did to her," Zeke said, getting a look of deep—and genuine, it seemed—regret from Peterson. And a look of confusion from Jess.

"How do you know what he's done to me?" she said.

"Are you kidding me?" Zeke said. "You mean there's more than trying to control you, make you feel inadequate about everything, and, oh yeah, lying about having a vasectomy?"

A gasp of disbelief came from Peterson, and Zeke spared him only a glance before returning his gaze to Jess.

"No. Zeke, you've got it wrong," Jess said. "He's not James. Not *my* James."

"No?" Zeke said, still not quite believing it. There was something deep at play here. She was too affected for it to be just running into someone she would rather not see. Was she covering for her ex because she thought Zeke might beat the shit out of him? Not a bad guess. "This isn't your ex-husband? Peterson wasn't your married name?"

She shook her head. That damn Smokey Bear hat that had seemed so sexy moments ago now seemed almost comical on top of her head, her eyes wide with emotion, her mouth open in amazement.

"No. I kept my married name after the divorce for professional reasons. I married James Chapman. Peterson is my maiden name."

His brain stalled, clogged by emotion because Jess was in distress. Zeke Hampton, who was calm, cool, and collected— intercepting bogeys at over a thousand miles per hour—wasn't computing any facts being dropped because his girlfriend was visibly upset.

"He. Wait. What?" His hand dropped from Peterson's chest, because even though he was just barely catching up, he instinctively got that Jim wasn't any threat to Jess.

"He's not my ex-husband, Zeke," Jess said. She took a deep breath, let it out, and said, "Jim Peterson is my father."

Twenty-Six

—∞—

JESS SAT IN ZEKE'S TRUCK, STUNNED. SPEECHLESS. JUST as she'd been since seeing her father on the docks of Isle Royale.

On the flight back to Copper Harbor, she replayed his words over in her mind, grateful that Zeke didn't press her to speak or even, other than one time, ask if she was okay.

Her father hadn't completely followed her to the Copper Country, but it was not just a coincidence that he'd bought a boat and started a charter company in the small community she'd claimed three years ago.

She still stood on the dock, the cold air biting into her as she listened to her father explain that he'd always wanted to buy a boat, to do what he was doing now. When he learned that Jess was in the Copper Country—where he'd brought their family years and years ago for a vacation—he decided that he'd finally live out his dream.

That he might be able to reconnect with his estranged daughter was only a bonus to him. He would leave it up to Jess how much—or how little—she wanted Jim in her life.

And she believed him. For if he'd been here two years and they hadn't run into each other before now, he obviously wasn't searching her out.

A lot of Jess's shifts were in Houghton at the visitor center or aboard the *Ranger* for the rides to Isle Royale, so it was no surprise that she wouldn't be acquainted with charter boat captains. She'd have no reason to interact with that segment of the tourist-serving community.

Her father had followed her to the isolated Copper Country because he wanted to reconnect with her. The thought blew her away. The absentee, always preoccupied even when they were together, all-business father of her teen years could not be any further from the man on the docks today. He was relaxed, casual. And even though he'd been sharply dressed for a charter boat captain, with his North Face fleece, khakis, and Sperrys, he was still dressed like...*a charter boat captain*. Gone were the impeccably tailored suits that she could remember from the time they'd moved to Winnetka and her parents' marriage had begun to unravel.

"Jess? Babe?" Zeke said from beside her. She looked up to see they had parked in her driveway. "Do you want to go somewhere else? Maybe get a drink somewhere?"

There wouldn't be much open this late at night in a tourist area that really wouldn't come alive for another month or so. Besides, she wanted the comfort of the home she'd built. The home she loved.

And she wanted the comfort of Zeke.

"No. I just want to go in."

"Oh, yeah. Okay. Well..."

A moment of panic rose from her gut at the thought that Zeke was just dropping her off. She didn't want to be alone tonight. And the truth was, she didn't want to be with anyone other than Zeke. "You can stay, can't you?" The words sounded like she felt—scattered and more than a little shook. "I mean, if you want to, that is."

He placed a hand on top of hers. "Of course I want to. I just wanted to give you space if you'd rather be alone."

That was all she'd asked from him: that he give her space. Not crowd her, not ask for more than she was willing to give. He'd done it, too. Never pushed her, not even now. He'd probably fought every alpha fighter pilot instinct he had to do it.

An ache rushed through her, one so pure and deep that she almost gasped at the physical sweetness of it.

She loved Zeke Hampton.

"I want you to come in," she said. They were the only words she trusted herself to say right then.

"Then let's do that," he said, cutting off the engine. He was out of his side and around to hers, helping her out, before she'd even been able to manage the thought of opening the door.

He held a hand out for her, which she took and hung on to, even when he reached into the back of his truck and grabbed her pack.

"It's going to be okay," he said as he swung the pack over his shoulder. He released her hand, but only so he could wrap his arm around her shoulder.

She wanted to believe his words, she really did, but the shock of seeing her father, on top of all the self-truths she'd faced on this long day, had her clinging to Zeke's strong body as they walked into the house.

"THAT'S AMAZING. DID YOU GET ANY PHOTOS?" Zeke said an hour later as he handed Jess a refilled glass of wine and settled back onto the couch beside her.

She shook her head, her loose hair catching the light from the fireplace that she'd turned on as soon as they entered her home. "No. I started to, but then she just stayed there, staring at me, and I…just stared back. I never got one picture."

Zeke shrugged and tapped his head. "It's up here. There's your picture." She smiled and nodded, and he brought her legs back to his lap, where they'd been for the past hour until he'd gotten up to refill their glasses.

When they'd come home, Jess had taken a long shower and then put on those sexy, tight, stretchy pants she wore around the house, a long knit top, rag-wool socks, and a green cardigan that hung loosely on her. Gone were the ranger uniform and the hat, though maybe, depending on how the night went, he could coax her into pulling the hat back out later—in bed.

If they got to bed, that was. He'd been careful not to push her about seeing her father, letting her set the topic of discussion, which so far had been solely about her hike and the various sights she'd seen. Including the lone wolf. But sooner or later, he assumed she'd get around to the elephant in the room.

Jim Peterson—*her father!*—lived in the Copper Country and wanted to be a part of her life. Zeke made a mental note to contact his friend Twain Beck and get the skinny on Jim, since Twain's brother Huck had worked for him part of last summer.

"Seven years," she said, bringing his mind back to the conversation.

"What?"

"It's been seven years since I've seen my father."

"Ah," he said. Apparently she was ready to talk about it now.

"He hated James. Hated that I married him. James was a few years older than my father and was a business rival."

"So not the 'married the father's best friend' scenario?"

She scoffed. "Hardly. Although it's probably fair to say that it was, in its own way, a bit of a 'fuck you' to my father, being with James. Though I didn't think it at the time. I truly was swept off my feet by him."

Yeah, until he dropped her on her ass by keeping that little fact about a vasectomy secret.

Enough about dipshit James.

"So, seven years ago…?"

She took a sip of wine, then handed her glass to Zeke, who put it on the table next to his. She pulled a pillow from the top of the couch and settled it behind her head, her red hair fanning over the taupe pillow like a delicate pattern. Burrowed deep into the couch, she took a deep breath and then looked away from him and to the fire as she spoke.

"So, we were a pretty normal family until I was around ten and my dad started his own financial firm. We quickly went from well off, to *really* well off. Then to super rich. And both my parents became slaves to it. My mother to the status, my father to the business. Nothing was ever enough for them, and it shattered their marriage. It got really ugly between them. Thankfully, they both just ignored me."

Her eyes were glassy, and Zeke wasn't sure if it was tears or just the reflection from the fire into those deep blue orbs. There was pain across her face, and he wanted to soothe the young Jess, whose childhood had been ripped apart by parents being vicious to each other. Probably better to be ignored than pulled into her parents' war, but being neglected was its own kind of pain.

No wonder she latched on to something as secure as an older, stable man like her ex.

And no wonder that she was so sour on the idea of marriage. It wasn't just her own, but her parents' divorce that shaped her view on the institution.

"So, seven years ago, for my birthday, we all went out. Tried to be adults about it all. James and me, my mom and her newest husband, my father and his second wife, and Cassie."

"Newest husband? Second wife?"

She nodded. "My mother's been through a bunch. With my dad's second, I'm not even sure how long that lasted. We were estranged when they divorced, so I'm not sure exactly when it was."

"And the dinner did not go well?"

"A shit show from start to finish. Everybody getting in any dig they could. My mother got drunk and threw a wine glass at my father. James lorded it over me for weeks. Said he wouldn't invite his daughter around my parents again. I didn't blame him, really. I didn't want Cassie around that either.

"I called my mother. She apologized, cried even, and I let her off the hook, though I still didn't see her often after that. When I left James, she gave me an 'I told you so' speech, and after that, I was done. We speak, I don't know, a couple times a year, I guess."

"And your father? Jim?"

She sighed, then looked from the fire to Zeke. "He called the day after too, but not with an apology. He went on and on about James and how he treated me, and that he couldn't believe I didn't see it too."

That was interesting. Not what Jess would have wanted to hear that day, surely, but Zeke filed away the information that Jim Peterson knew his daughter was not being treated the way she deserved to be.

"He told me that he'd support me if I left James, give me a job at his firm, but that it had to be then, not years from now, when kids were involved and it was…messy. I mean, who was he to tell me about messy?"

"I take it you didn't appreciate his offer?"

A snort. "Hardly. And it wasn't an offer so much as wanting a transfer of power. And yes, I was starting to see some of the things he was talking about with James—things I'd overlooked before."

"Because you were dazzled," he said.

A soft, sad smile played on her lips. "Exactly. Beware of dazzling."

"Dazzling has its place," he said, tweaking her toes through her thick, soft socks.

"That it does." She stretched her hands over her head, then laid them on top of her green sweater, the paleness of her fingers a stark contrast. "Obviously, enough of the dazzle was still there, because I told my father to go to hell and haven't spoken to him since."

"Until today," Zeke said softly, starting to massage her feet.

"Until today." She pushed her feet deeper into his grasp. "God, that feels amazing."

"I've got other ways to make you feel amazing," he said.

She studied him, then gave one short nod, sliding her feet from his grasp and rolling to get off the couch. Standing over him, she reached out a hand. "Come on, flyboy. Make me forget about today."

He wanted to remind her about their embrace at the docks, before Jim had come upon them. She'd been glad to see him, had seemed to want to say something to him, something important. He didn't want her to forget about that.

But then he looked at those fathomless blue eyes. Red hair and blue eyes was the rarest match. He'd looked it up, pussy-whipped fool that he was. And right then, her eyes held pain, the pain of the past catching up with her.

If he could help her erase that pain, he would do it. And then try to bring her back around to where they'd been on the dock.

Tomorrow.

Twenty-Seven

SHE WANTED TO RUSH, TO HAVE ZEKE QUICKLY BURIED deep inside her. When he peeled his clothes off and she hurriedly discarded hers, she quickly moved to the bed, holding her arms open to him.

He came to her, but not with the same urgency she felt. After peeling back the sheets, he moved her to the center of the bed and then hovered over her on all fours, staring down.

Her hands skimmed down his powerful chest, gliding over muscle and warm skin. Curling around his hard cock and stroking. He came down in a push-up move, his face close to hers. "Jess," he whispered. His brown eyes seemed to burn into her, and she was sorry she'd left the lights on.

There had been too many tumultuous emotions for her today. She needed a quick fuck to wipe it away. Some down-and-dirty screwing to take herself out of her head and back into her body.

"Okay. Let's see if you really are Top Gun," she said, trying to put on a sexy smile.

He watched her, not smiling back. "Jess," he whispered again.

Crap. He didn't want it down and dirty tonight. He wanted it slow and soulful. They'd done both—many times—and she loved it all. But what she needed right now was—

"Let me make love to you."

Not that. God, not that. Not today, when she'd decided to give them a chance, only to have the ghost of bad marriages past show up. To have her thoughts of what if doused with cold water like a jump into Lake Superior in March.

"Zeke, I—"

He dipped his head the few inches between them and kissed her, cutting off her words. And just like that, everything from the day was gone, and she was enveloped in Zeke's soft, deep kisses. He tasted of wine, and his tongue coaxed hers into a sweet dance. She slid her hands up his arms and met again behind his head, clasping together. Clasping Zeke to her.

He reached over to the nightstand and grabbed a condom, then quickly tore it open while her fingers played in his hair. She had a moment of madness where she almost—*almost*—told him not to bother with the condom.

Why? Why would she think that? It was their only form of birth control. Did she subconsciously want a decision about her future with Zeke to be taken out of her hands?

But then she wouldn't be Debra Winger from *Officer and a Gentleman*. She'd be the other one. The blonde with the bodacious set of tatas.

So why would such a life-altering—*irresponsible*—thought flitter through her responsible brain?

Because this was the last time. Their last night together.

She didn't want that to be true. But on some level, she knew it was.

Jess took the condom from his hands, took it out of the package, and rolled it on him. Then she put her hands back around his neck.

"Hold on," he said, and then slid his hands under her back and to her hips as he sat back, taking her with him so she sat in his lap. Her butt was on his rock-hard thighs, her legs dangling behind him. Gaining leverage, she scooted up, aided by his hands on her ass pulling her to him. His hands skimmed up and down her back, giving her the warmth she'd needed since she woke up in her sleeping bag that morning.

Her legs widened as he pulled her even closer, his hard cock pulsing against her. She was wet, and the glide as Zeke edged her hips toward him was smooth, silky, and delicious.

"Yes," she said on a gasp, the electric shock of contact racing through her. Zeke pulled her thighs even further apart, and one of his big, warm hands skimmed over her leg and to the center of her, sliding between her and his erection.

"So warm," he whispered. She tried to burrow her head in his neck, but he drew his head back, watching her. "Look at me." She did, her eyes melting into his as his devious fingers played below, opening her, gliding through the slickness, and finding her clit while one finger slid inside her.

She murmured her delight, wanting to drop her head back and close her eyes, but his steady gaze wouldn't allow it. Instead, she watched as little flecks of gold glittered in his intense and caring brown eyes.

Caring.

She leaned forward, and he parted his lips for her, but before she got to them, she slid her tongue along the cleft in his chin, trying to commit it all to memory.

For later.

He kissed her deeply while he stroked her, the heat rushing through her. The need. She rocked herself against his hand, wanting to hurry, wanting it all.

He broke from the kiss and looked at her as his fingers slowed. "We've got all night, baby," he whispered.

That was just it. That was *all* they had. He didn't know that, of course. Or, given the way he was staring at her with something close to pain in his eyes, perhaps he did.

"Zeke," she said softly, "I need you." She meant it in the "Get that glorious cock inside me *now*" way, but the words caught in her throat, the meaning becoming deeper as his brow furrowed and his breath hitched.

"I need you too," he said. Definitely not how she'd intended. His words were spoken softly, but solemnly, with intent that went beyond their coupling.

And that was when she absolutely knew that it would be their last time.

Reaching down between their bodies, she tangled her hand with his and stroked his cock while his finger circled her clit. Her thighs clenched, the muscles strained from their position and her days on the trail. It was an ache that felt good in so many ways.

His finger continued to circle her while another joined the one inside of her, slipping through to the core of her, curling up. Groaning at the sensuality of it, she arched her neck and his mouth, warm and soft, was on her, kissing and dragging his teeth across her sensitive skin. His hand played her. He knew the tune by heart. She tried to stroke him as skillfully, but her mind was hazy, and her hand slowed down.

"It's okay," he said, as if he sensed her desire, if not her ability, to make him feel as good as she did. "You get yours. Come for me, Jess. Fuck my hand."

The words pushed her over, shocks rushing through her body as she tensed around his fingers, her clit pulsing under his touch. She moaned, not sure if it was words she spoke or just guttural sounds. It didn't matter, none of it mattered but the way Zeke made her feel. The way he made her fall apart and yet come together at the same time.

She gave up all pretense of caressing him, her hands going to his arms, hanging on to those biceps. He pushed her further, making the sweet sensations rock through her again.

"Yeah. Yeah, Jess, that's it," he said, coaxing her into even more intensity. More than she thought she had in her cold, broken heart.

She convulsed on his hand again while those brown eyes met hers.

Dazzling.

Emotions overcame her, pushing out sensation, and she felt what had to be a teardrop slide down her face as her body slowly came down from such a staggering height.

"No, baby, it's okay," he said, then leaned forward and licked the tear from her cheek. "You needed that, that's all." She nodded with him, but she knew it was more than just an intense release.

He leaned forward, taking her to her back, pulling her legs wide while he settled between them. Taking his cock in hand, he guided himself to her and slid in, causing an aftershock that rocked through her, igniting her nerve ends all over again.

"Christ, Jess, you feel so good around me," he said. She clenched her muscles, and he grinned down at her. Cradling her face in his hands, he kissed her as he rocked into her. Drawing her feet up the bed, she wrapped her legs around his hips, wanting him deeper.

But even then he wouldn't give it to her fast, instead taking his time as he moved inside her. No pounding and driving, but instead melding and gliding. Building the tension in her all over again. Never taking his eyes from her.

Her hands went to his firm and sculpted ass. Trying to urge him on, she dug her nails in, but he gave a tiny shake of his head and kept up with his slow, excruciating rhythm. "Zeke," she said, and he smiled down at her.

"My turn. And I want it slow."

His turn in theory, but it quickly became another turn for her as his methodic strokes brought her to the edge once more.

"Together," he said, knowing her body so well. She nodded, and he moved faster. It only took a few more strokes before she shattered in his arms as he pumped himself one last time into her.

His breathing was labored, as was hers, and he watched her as they both came back to earth.

"Beautiful," he whispered, then kissed her once more before rolling from her body.

Beautiful, she thought, wishing the night would never end. But knowing it would.

Twenty-Eight

—w—

"WHY DID YOU REALLY LEAVE THE NAVY?" JESS SAID softly to him as she lay on his chest, their arms around each other, their legs entwined. Her head tipped up to meet his eyes. "You are awake, aren't you? Your breathing changed a few minutes ago."

Yes, he'd awakened moments ago, happy and sated, delighted to find Jess still in his arms hours after they'd made love.

Yeah, made love. That was exactly what that had been.

He nodded, threading his fingers through her hair as she settled back onto his chest.

"So?" she said. "Unless you don't want to tell me."

He was ready with his pat answer, the one he'd given his squadron and his CO, about not wanting to go on to the next step of screening for squadron commander. Or the variation of "time to settle down" he'd given to his parents, Lizzie, and Petey. Both were true, and no one had really questioned him. Hell, his parents and Lizzie had been so happy he was getting out that they'd hurriedly agreed with any reasons he gave them.

But Jess, who had known him for a shorter amount of time than anyone, knew there was more.

"There's more than I told people," he said, then cleared his throat when he realized his words came out scratchy and dense.

"I figured," she said. "It's okay if you don't want to talk about it."

"No. It's not that. It's just, it wasn't any one thing. Well, yeah,

I mean..." He sighed, letting the ragged breath escape, loving Jess's soothing hand as it swept across his chest, her fingers playing in his chest hair. He placed a hand over hers, lacing their fingers, and she squeezed, encouraging him. Or just letting him know she was there.

"So, yeah, the reasons I told you about the night we fell asleep on the couch..."

"The night after I'd had two crank calls," she said.

That thought rushed back now with new meaning. "Do you think that could have been Jim calling you?"

Her hand tensed for a just a second, then relaxed in his. "I don't know. I suppose if I do contact him, see him again, I could ask him. I'm not sure if he'd admit it or not."

Zeke didn't know Jim Peterson very well, but he struck Zeke as a pretty honest guy. He thought Jim would cop to making the calls to Jess if he'd done it. But Zeke kept that thought to himself.

"Enough of that. I don't want to think about Jim Peterson, or James Chapman, or anybody else in any way related to me anymore tonight. We were talking about you and the Navy."

"My subterfuge didn't work, eh?"

"Not hardly. As I said on that night, 'Okay, flyboy, your turn. Spill.'"

"So, yeah, I had no interest in becoming a squadron commander. And I really did want to settle down and not be out on cruise six months at a time. I know a lot of military do it, a lot don't have the choice. But I did have the choice. I have a lot more options coming out as a pilot, one with an engineering degree to boot."

"Right..." She waited for him, and he liked that she did. She was there with him for the ride, and knowing that, something shifted in him, settled.

He knew he'd made the right decision leaving the Navy, even with only six years to go before he got his twenty years in. But lying in Jess's bed, with her glorious body draped over his, he found a peace that he hadn't dared hope was out there.

He knew he would be happy, content, with his life choices. He'd learned to do that in the military, to make the best of any situation. Choose happiness. And really, as long as he was flying, in any kind of aircraft, his life was pretty damn great.

But the feeling he had now, with what he and Jess had come to mean to each other? That, along with being back in the Copper Country around family and friends? And flying every day?

Damn near perfection.

"Those two things certainly had me thinking about getting out," he said.

"But what made you *decide* to get out?" she asked.

It was cool in the loft, and he pulled the comforter up higher on them both, then went under the sheets and rested his hand on her naked hip. "We had a mission. I can't tell you where, or any of the specifics."

"That's okay. I don't need to know details, just how it affected you."

"It was an airstrike. Like hundreds before it. You have a target. You bomb the target. Smart bombs, you know, very few mistakes."

"Right. I've seen the footage. Crazy accurate."

"Yep. There's a level of trust that you've been given a credible, reliable target. And certainly a don't-question-orders mentality."

Her body tensed. Surely she'd seen headlines over the years about strikes gone wrong due to bad intel. Civilian deaths. Schools bombed.

"Yeah, it was that bad," he said, and she tensed more. But instead of pulling away from him, she burrowed deeper into his side, held on tighter.

If there'd been any question before that day—and there wasn't, not really—Zeke now knew that he was in love with Jessica Chapman.

The woman who didn't want a long-term relationship of any kind.

And he couldn't blame bad intel for this mission going so

badly. She'd been honest with him from the start.

"I'm so sorry, Zeke," she said, then gently kissed his collarbone. She moved like she was going to sit up, but he stilled her with the hand on her hip. He didn't want to see those blue eyes. Certainly not filled with pity. And not until he was done.

"The thing is, it wasn't me. I didn't drop the bomb that hit the civilian target. It was a buddy of mine. As soon as we trapped and climbed out of our jets, our skipper met us and we reported to CAG—the airwing commander—still wearing our G-suits and torso harnesses. CAG told us to stand at ease, but he certainly didn't offer us a seat. We were debriefed on the carrier. Even then they knew it was FUBAR and we'd gotten bad intel. The admiral of the battle group was going nuts, trying to cover his ass with the admiral in Bahrain. Trying to put a good spin on it. Ranting about all the bad press that was to come. They weren't even sure how many civilians were dead and they were already trying to circle the wagons.

"It could have happened to any of us. It had happened, to smaller degrees, to each of us before. Nothing this big, though. Or this deadly."

"Your poor friend. He must have been devastated."

Now they were getting to it. How much to say? Could he really explain it to Jess? "Well, it was weird, his reaction. And I think that's the thing that made me realize it was time to get out."

Her head popped up then, and though it was the middle of the night, there was enough moonlight coming through the huge front window for Zeke to see the shining blue of her eyes. See the concern. Concern for a guy she'd never met.

Concern for Zeke as that guy's friend.

"Oh, no, did he…do something? Hurt himself?"

Zeke shook his head. "No. That's just it. It didn't affect him at all. Not…not at *all*."

Confusion spread across her beautiful face. Her brow furrowed, creating a cute little crease between her eyebrows. "I don't get it," she said.

"We learn quickly—are taught, in fact—how to compartmentalize what we do. We rely on our commanders, on their intel and decisions, and carry out our missions to the best of our ability. There's a reason that saying 'above my pay grade' became mainstream."

"Well, you'd almost have to do that, right? Otherwise, there'd be chaos."

"Right. No place for chaos in the military. And the system works. But I think in Keppler's case—that's the guy who was also on the mission—it worked a little too well."

"What do you mean?"

"After our debrief, I went by his quarters to make sure he was okay, see if he wanted to talk. Sometimes we did that. Lots of times, you just dealt with shit on your own."

"The solitariness of a single-seat pilot. You mentioned that before."

"Yeah. It serves us well. But sometimes you need to talk it out, and I wanted to be there if he needed it."

"But he didn't?"

"I wasn't sure at first. He was FaceTiming his wife and kids when I got to his quarters. Which in itself is rare. The bandwidth on the carriers is iffy at best. But I thought that was good, that seeing them would ground him, make him shake off what had happened.

"I tried to leave, but he waved me in to say hi to them all. I knew them, of course. His wife Shelly had had me over for dinner tons of times since we'd been at Oceana together. Had tried to set me up with her friends, all of it."

Did she tense at hearing that he'd been set up with other women? Zeke was just petty enough to hope that maybe it had. But if she reacted at all, she quickly got over it and spread her hand across his chest again. "Go on," she said. No trace of jealousy in her voice. Damn.

"So, I say hi to them all, and he tells me to stick around while he finishes up talking to them. I'm thinking he wants to talk about the mission afterward, so I do. He's great with the family. Laughing, joking, asking the kids all about school and activities. No sign that things had gone horribly wrong earlier that day.

"I was thinking he was the best bullshitter I'd ever seen. Was admiring his ability to hold it together in front of his family so as not to worry them. His wife never questioned that everything wasn't completely A-okay."

"But everything wasn't A-okay," she said.

"No. Innocent people had died that day. Kids. Women. And we were responsible."

"But you said you weren't flying the plane that struck the wrong target."

He sighed, scraping a hand down his face then letting it flop on the outside of the comforter. "I wasn't, but we were a squadron. And beyond that, we're the United States Navy. A fuckup is a fuckup. For all of us."

"So, when he got off his call? Did he lose it?"

"Nope. Just turned to me and started talking about squadron stuff. Who was thinking of transferring, who was going to screen for squadron command. Bitching about our CO. The usual stuff."

"He didn't want to talk about it at all? Not even with you, who'd been there?"

"It wasn't even that. Not that he just didn't want to talk about it, but it wasn't even on his mind anymore. It was like he'd walked out of that debrief and it was gone. As if it never happened."

"So he…what…can compartmentalize like a champ? Isn't that helpful in your line of work?"

"But it went beyond that. I'd flown with him for years. He hadn't always been like that. He'd gotten so good at putting it behind him that he'd lost, I don't know, his sense of empathy."

"Ah," she said. "And that scared you."

It wasn't a question. And he'd never put it in those terms, even in his most secret thoughts. He'd been disgusted by Keppler's lack of emotion—of any kind—that day and the days after. Yeah, Jess had nailed it.

"Yes. I was afraid that would happen to me. Maybe already was happening to me. That I'd have complete lack of empathy, or understanding, when it came to the big picture of what we were doing."

"That wouldn't happen to you," she said, squeezing his waist, plastering herself to him.

"You can't know that," he said.

She kissed his chest, then rested her chin, looking up at him. "I *do* know that. That you went to see if he was okay proves it."

"Maybe."

"No maybes. You care. Maybe too much."

He let out a breath, unaware he'd been holding one in. It felt good to talk about this with Jess. Freeing. And he was able to process thoughts that before had only flitted around in his subconscious, not crystallizing. Probably out of fear, like she said.

"It's not that I don't believe in what we're doing. I was proud—so proud—to serve. The Navy can fuck up, yes, and the decisions made are only as good as the information they're given on which to base them, but…"

"You needed to get out before you became Keppler," she said, summing up the last year of Zeke's life in one little sentence.

"Holy wah, that's exactly it."

She chuckled and kissed his clavicle, slowly working her way up, nuzzling his neck, sprinkling kisses along his jaw, until her face was even with his. "You wouldn't have become Keppler, I'm sure of it. But if there was even a small chance, then I'm glad you got out when you did."

"Yeah, so am I. And the timing worked too, with the way things fell into place with Bobby putting his business up for sale and meeting—" He cut himself off. It looked like he'd dodged a bullet after the whole "let me be your safe place to land" line when they'd parted. He wasn't going to blow it now with talk about their meeting being kismet or something.

Even though he thought it was.

She stared at him, her eyes going from light to dark as the

moonlight shone on them. Bringing her mouth to his, she gave him the lightest of kisses. Something flashed in her eyes. Pain? Regret? Indecision? It was gone before he could ask her about it, replaced with a sly smile.

"I'm glad you met me too," she said. "Now prove exactly how happy you are."

She rolled to her back, taking him with her.

He was happy to follow.

Twenty-Nine

—⁓—

JESS DIDN'T HAVE A STRAIGHT-ON VIEW OF THE SUNRISE from her living room, facing north over Lake Superior, but she sat staring out anyway as light dawned.

After their second round last night—and Zeke's info dump about why he'd been ready to leave the Navy—Jess hadn't been able to go back to sleep. An hour ago, she'd finally decided to leave the loft, curl up on the large chair that faced outdoors, and wait for the morning. Maybe the sun would shed some light on her darkening thoughts.

Thoughts that had been churning and swirling during her hike, topped off with her moment with the wolf. All to have them come crashing down and doing a one-eighty hours later as she lay next to Zeke and thought about how much she cared for him.

And damn if she didn't blame her father for part of it.

Not all of it. It was her own poor choice in husbands and subsequent nasty divorce that made her realize she just didn't have it in her to try anything long term again. Still, being courtside at the demise of her parents' marriage didn't help matters.

And seeing her father yesterday only reminded her of the resolve she once felt about not dragging someone else into anything that she was bound to destroy later.

Especially not someone like Zeke Hampton. Someone she loved.

She'd been ready to commit to more yesterday on the dock,

wrapped in his strong arms. And then seeing her father reminded her of how shitty love could turn. (As if her being in the Copper Country wilderness instead of a Chicago office wasn't an everyday reminder—happy as she was in her choice.)

She knew she had to slow it down with Zeke, had come to that conclusion as he flew them home, his hands steady on the yoke of his seaplane. And if she'd wavered when they'd made love, it became even more painfully obvious when he told her about what he wanted for his future. That he was willing to leave the military—and service to his country, which he believed in and took great pride in—so he wouldn't become an unfeeling, compartmentalized machine.

So he could have a life beyond the shit he'd seen and done. He'd left six years shy of major retirement benefits because he needed to save himself.

So did she, in a way. And she had saved herself. The home where she now sat, sipping coffee and watching the black of Lake Superior turn to blue as the sun came up, was a testament to her salvation.

It was cowardly, she knew, but she wouldn't risk it. Couldn't risk it. The peace and tranquility she now felt had been too hard fought.

She didn't want to become a Keppler either.

It was different, of course, but there were similarities to the rationale.

"Hey," Zeke said softly from the stairs. She hadn't heard him move across the loft, and his tread must have been light coming down the steps. He made his way into the living room. "More of that?" he asked, nodding at her cup.

"Yeah, I made a whole pot, and this is still my first cup," she said.

"Need it topped off?"

She shook her head. She hadn't drunk much as she sat contemplating what needed to be said that morning. The liquid in her mug had cooled, even as she held it tight in her hands so it could warm her. She set it on the table next to the chair, motioning to the ottoman.

She half hoped he didn't take the seat. Maybe he'd get his coffee in a to-go cup and come and tell her he had to leave right away, for business, or family, or babysitting duties. Anything to put off what she knew had to be said.

He didn't say he had to leave, and had a healthy mugful when he came into the living room.

He'd pulled on his jeans and zipped them, but the button on the fly was undone, showing a sprinkling of hair that she knew very well. A chambray work shirt of his had been hung over a chair in the loft, a remnant of an earlier stay, and he wore it now, loose and unbuttoned. His hair, now looking less military officer and more outdoorsman, was tousled from both his sleep and her hands.

"Gorgeous morning," he said, sitting down on the ottoman at her feet. He took a deep drink of coffee, staring out at the lake.

"It is," she agreed. She pulled her legs up tighter under her, not wanting to touch him in any way, not when she was about to hurt him. She wouldn't be as cruel as to do it while having her hands on him—much as she'd like to.

How did she start? How to dump the man you loved for his own good? For her own good? It sounded so stupid even in her head.

"I lost you last night, didn't I?" Zeke said, as always, cutting to the chase. And, as always, knowing her so well. He'd done it that first night, knowing when she'd changed her mind about sleeping with him. And the second time he'd been there, when he knew something had upset her.

"What?" she said.

He still faced the lake, his legs on that side of the ottoman, and she stared at his profile. The straight nose, the strong jaw line. The dimple in his chin was harder to see at this angle, but maybe that was for the best. Less dazzling that way.

Just then, the sun burst through a cloud and shined a light

on Zeke that was straight out of Hollywood. The hero shot, she thought they called it.

Damn sun.

"You heard me. I lost you last night, didn't I?"

"Zeke, I—"

"Was it seeing your father? Or me telling you about leaving the Navy? Or—"

"All of it," she said quickly, not wanting him to go on. Not wanting to hear the deadness in his voice. She'd never heard this Keppler speak, but she imagined his voice sounded a lot like Zeke's had just then.

He nodded. "Can we talk about it, at least?" Less dead, with maybe a tiny bit of hope. She wanted to grab on to that, to fan it back to flames, but knew that would be futile.

"We can. But we've had the discussion before. Nothing's changed. We knew we had an expiration date."

"*You* knew we had an expiration date."

"Yes, that's true. But I was really upfront about that with you."

He turned to her, moving his legs so they fit in the small space between her chair and the edge of the ottoman. He spread his long legs, making them fit better along the open sides, hanging his arms across his knees, hands dangling in front. He didn't lean forward, didn't invade her space, but he was so close, reminding her of how close she'd let him get.

"Jess, I'm not going to call you out on doing exactly what you said you were going to do all along. What kind of dick do you think I am?"

"No kind of dick." He chuckled, and so did she, though she knew there was no humor in what they were doing. "You're not a dick at all, Zeke."

"Thanks for that, I guess." He looked out at the lake, took a deep breath, then turned back to her. "You've been really honest and upfront this whole time." She nodded, and he continued, "So, please be honest with me one last time, okay?"

She studied him, wondering what he was going to ask, but only nodded again.

"Yesterday, on the dock. Before Jim showed up. You were going to say something different than what you're saying this morning, right?"

Yep. He knew her very well. "Yes," she said.

"And you seemed pretty sure about it."

She shook her head. "No. I wasn't sure about it. I was scared to death about it. But maybe it was the hike, the physical toll, seeing the wolf alone…I don't know. But no, I wasn't sure about anything."

"But you were willing to take a chance. Fight through the fear."

She didn't reply. She didn't have to. He knew the truth. Fear had won out in the end.

"Fear and past experience," she said, clarifying as much for herself as him.

"The past doesn't have to dictate the future," he said. It must have sounded futile even to his own ears, because he snorted and rubbed his hands up and down his thighs. "Yeah, okay."

She didn't need to explain it to him. He got it. And yet she wanted to try. "It's just… I haven't been in—or around—good marriages. I know they're out there, your friends and family—"

He held up a hand, then let it drop to his leg when she stopped speaking. "Jesus, Jess, I didn't ask you to marry me."

She waited, raising a brow at him, but he didn't finish, so she did it for him. "There was a 'yet' at the end of that sentence, wasn't there? You just didn't say it."

He sighed and looked out at the lake. She touched his knee, then brought her hand back to her lap, not wanting to keep her hands on him. Well, that wasn't true; she wanted nothing more than to keep her hands on him. Indefinitely. But she wasn't willing to risk her heart. Or her sanity. Not with it having taken three long years to gain both back after James.

"You want more because you're ready for more. That was

obvious with what you told me last night. About getting out of the Navy."

"Should have kept my trap shut," he said.

She shook her head. "No, it wasn't that. It wasn't *just* that. And you didn't tell me anything last night that I didn't already know. You're a great guy, Zeke, who feels things deeply, and who doesn't want to lose that part of himself."

"Jesus, did I just get the 'You're a great guy' talk? Next you'll say 'It's not you, it's me' or some bullshit thing like that."

She smiled at him, though she felt like sobbing. "Well, it wouldn't be untrue."

"Fuck, Jess. This feels so wrong, to let what we've got, how good we are together, get away."

Now she looked at the lake and sighed. "That's not untrue, either," she said softly.

"You're right, though," he said, and she looked back to him. "I do want more. But because of you, I'm willing to take less."

"But you shouldn't have to."

"Let me worry about that. What I said in that house in Dollar Bay still holds. I'll take you any way I can get you."

She wanted to say yes. It'd been so easy to do so that day in Dollar Bay. But that was before she'd fallen in love with him, though she'd probably been well on her way. It'd only taken a few weeks from that day at the house to him being at her place whenever they could manage it, to her finding herself thinking about him all the time. It would only escalate further if they kept on, and she'd find herself deep into a relationship that she had no business being in.

She just didn't have it in her. James, and the bitter years afterward, had sucked it out of her.

"It's a bit like trying to put the genie back in the bottle, right?" she said.

"So, that's it?" he said. There wasn't disbelief in his voice, because he'd known all along this day was coming. But still his words stung.

"Yeah, I think it's best we end things now."

"Before you overcome your fear again?" He held up his hands. "Sorry. I have no right to be shitty about this, I know. Like you said, you were straight from the beginning. I just…" There was nothing left to say, and they both knew it.

He rose from the ottoman, took his mug to the kitchen, and dumped his coffee down the sink. Then he went to the loft, and she heard him rustle around up there, presumably dressing and gathering the belongings that had been left. Finally, he made his way back downstairs, fully dressed, his duffel bag slung over a shoulder.

Coming to her, he bent down and placed a soft kiss on the top of her head. "I understand how you feel, Jess, I really do. But I hate it."

"I know," she said, clearing her throat as she spoke. "So do I."

He nodded once as he straightened, then stared down at her. She wanted to jump in his arms, tell him she'd try. That maybe together they could make it work. But images of fights with James and of covering her ears as she heard her parents argue rushed in front of her, keeping her in the chair, arms at her side.

"See ya 'round, Jess," he said.

"Bye, Zeke," she said. And then he was gone. She heard his truck start up and back out of her long driveway.

She sat in the chair most of the day, just watching the lake, half hoping she'd hear his truck return. Half dreading that he would.

But he didn't. Nor did he call. Or text. After several days, she stopped thinking he might. He was respecting her wishes.

Damn him.

Thirty

—〰—

JESS SAT IN A BOOTH AT THE SEAFARER, REILLY AND PAULA across from her. Reilly studied the spreadsheet she'd given him, and Paula was tackling a burger and fries that looked heavenly. Jess hadn't intended on staying for dinner, but thought maybe she would after all when she and Reilly were done talking business.

The house in Dollar Bay would be closing soon, and she and Reilly wanted to be ready to start working on it as soon as they had the keys and the paperwork was signed.

It had been almost a month since Zeke had left her home, and, small area though the Copper Country was, she hadn't seen him in all that time. The ferries had started running to Isle Royale and traffic there had picked up, though still wouldn't be at its heaviest until schools were out and the weather was nicer. May was iffy in the Copper Country, and even more so in the Harbor and on Isle Royale. But it had been pleasant, with only a few rains needed to clean the salt from the roads. She was working shifts in Houghton mostly, preferring those to the ones on the island since her long hike.

She wasn't necessarily avoiding Zeke—or her father, for that matter—but found herself signing up for few shifts through the park services and spending more time putting together a budget and plan for the Dollar Bay house.

She'd met with Deni Casparich, the woman at Summers and Beck, the engineering firm she'd used for her house, and gotten a thumbs-up on what she had planned for the little house. Deni had liked Jess's thoughts about knocking down a few walls to open it up a bit, and once they had closed, she'd get in there and make sure it was feasible from an architectural standpoint.

Still, busy as she was, when she was out and about, she found herself searching Eagle Harbor and Copper Harbor for a big black truck (there were many) with a U.S. Navy front license plate (there were none). And whenever she heard a plane overhead, she nearly wrenched her neck searching the sky.

That was as close as she'd gotten to Zeke Hampton in a month—looking up in the sky as his seaplane soared overhead.

But, looking at the door that just opened in the Seafarer, she was about to rectify seeing one of the men she'd been dodging. Her father walked into the restaurant and headed toward the bar where Reilly's older sister Tessa, who owned the place, was waiting on customers. Halfway to the bar, Jim looked around the restaurant side of the place and saw Jess with Reilly and Paula. His steps faltered, but then he kept on, nodding in Jess's direction. She nodded back but didn't call him over to their table.

She was discussing business with her partner, after all. That was no place for an attempted family reunion. Her father sat at the bar and said something to Tessa that made her laugh. She went to the coolers behind her and pulled out a bottle of beer for Jim.

"Yeah, this all looks good, Jess. Just like we talked about. Thanks for putting it together so cleanly," Reilly said, handing the paperwork back to her, which she put in the folder she'd brought with her. A quickly expanding folder full of thoughts about the house and research on home sales and prices in the area.

"Of course," she said. "I guess we're just in a waiting game until we close. Then we'll be in a position where we can move at whatever speed we want."

"But Reilly's still going to work as many shifts as he can for the park service, right?" Paula said between bites of her burger. She looked at her boyfriend. "You said you didn't know what kind of money you'd see from this house thing, right? Or when we would see it? We still have bills to pay."

From what Jess had seen, Paula made no contributions to the shared bills the couple had, but was always quick to point out extra shifts Reilly should be taking or other ways he could earn money.

Jess knew that wasn't fair to think that way. People had probably thought the same of her when she'd been married to James and stopped working at the firm, though she'd still held on to clients and worked from home.

The fact was she just didn't care for Paula, and so the constant nagging Paula gave Reilly bugged Jess. Maybe that also reminded her of her relationship with James.

Still, Reilly didn't seem to mind. Maybe Paula was what kept them stable. It really wasn't any of Jess's business, but she reminded herself to make sure that Reilly, and only Reilly, was her business partner. She'd need to look into the legalities of that soon, probably before she closed on the house.

They talked over the few remaining details and timetables, and Tessa came over to remove Paula's empty basket. "All set, hon?" she said to Reilly, who nodded and thanked his sister when she cleared his plate. "Paula?" Paula nodded, and Tessa took her basket. Jess could have been imagining it, but she noticed considerably less warmth when Tessa spoke to Paula than when she did to Reilly. Which was only natural, Jess supposed. But maybe Jess wasn't the only one to think that Reilly could do better in the girlfriend department.

"Jess, how about you? Would you like something to eat after all?" Tessa asked, the warmth now back in her voice.

"You know, that burger looked so good, I'm going to get one too. But make it to go, if that's okay. We're pretty much wrapping up here."

Tessa asked how she wanted her burger, then nodded, cleared the rest of their things away, and left their table.

"We need to go," Paula said. "We have that thing in Hancock."

Reilly looked at his girlfriend blankly, and Jess knew that there was no thing in Hancock. Paula apparently wasn't any fonder of Reilly's partner and sister than they were of her.

"It's fine," Jess said, throwing Reilly a rope. "We're all set, anyway. I'll call you if I know anything more before the closing. Otherwise, we're good to go after the thirtieth."

Reilly rose from his side of the booth, reaching for his wallet while Paula slid out. She put her hand on his. "Don't do that. Your sister won't charge us."

"That's not the point," Reilly said, pulling his hand away from Paula's.

"She'll just be insulted. Better to keep your money and maybe get something nice for her later."

Jess knew there'd be no "later" if Paula had anything to say about it. And she absolutely did. "Well, I have to tip her," Reilly said.

Paula looked at him like he'd grown a second head. "Are you kidding? She's your sister. She used to make you *all* your meals. You didn't tip her then, did you? Come on. Bye, Jess." She grabbed Reilly's wallet and started out of the restaurant.

"Bye, Paula. I'll talk to you soon, Reilly," Jess said.

Reilly nodded to her, and when Paula had started out of the restaurant, he quickly pulled a twenty from his front pocket and left it on the table, giving Jess a wink.

"That kid," Tess said when she brought Jess the glass of wine she'd ordered to have while she waited and saw the twenty Reilly had left. "I told him to save his money."

"He wanted to leave it for you," Jess said. She didn't add that he'd risked Paula's wrath to do it.

"Bet that pissed off Paula," Tessa said, causing Jess to laugh and nod. "Burger will just be a minute." She pocketed the twenty and made her way back to the bar.

She was in her mid-forties and had mostly raised Reilly, he'd once told Jess, after their parents had split up and their father had left the area. Apparently, their mother hadn't been much on child rearing, and Tessa had taken it upon herself to raise Reilly, who was fourteen years younger than she was.

Jess sipped her wine and once again looked through her folder on the house, growing excited for her new venture to begin. Anything she could dive into and get her mind off Zeke Hampton.

"One burger to go," came a voice not belonging to Tessa, as a large brown bag was placed in front of her.

Her father stood at the end of her table. He held another burger in his other hand, stacked in the red plastic basket, just like Paula's burger had been. "Or, if you wanted to stay and eat it here, I'd love to join you."

He wanted to have dinner with her. Here. Now. Just a burger with Dad on a Friday night.

Hardly that simple, but she found herself nodding to the empty seat across from her in the booth and unpacking her burger from the bag, spreading it and her fries in front of her.

"So, how do we do this?" she said. "Where do we start?"

He shrugged and took a bite of his burger, taking his time chewing, then wiping his mouth on a napkin. "We do this any way that you're comfortable with. Do I want to hear about what you've been doing the past seven years? Yes. I know the main points, of course. You and James splitting. You leaving finance and Chicago. Settling up here and becoming a ranger. But I'm guessing there was a lot driving those decisions, and that some of those times were probably pretty scary for you. And I know you were crazy about Cassie, and it's probably eating you up not to be in her life. If you want to talk about that, I'd be happy to listen.

"But I also realize that, given the father I was to you, I may have forfeited the right to have those conversations with you, to share your fears and the stories of how you built a new life."

Wow. She sat back in the booth. She couldn't ever remember her father having been so direct and yet understanding with her. Well, maybe years ago, before he'd become consumed with his firm and making a name for himself.

But that had been many, *many* years ago.

"I…I'm not sure—"

He held up a hand. "I'm not going anywhere, Jess. Like you, I've made a home here for myself. My life has changed, and I'm writing an act two for myself that I never would have imagined. And I'm happy. Most of the time."

There was so much about what he said that she wanted to ask about. But she said, "Why only most of the time?" It was probably a question that she needed to ask herself, but she thought she knew her answer. She was curious if her father's answer would be similar.

"Because some of the time, I think about you, and the regret is so overwhelming that I forget for a minute how happy I am the rest of the time."

Oh. Not what she expected, and not anywhere near her answer. But then, she didn't expect that her father would say something along the lines of "I think I made a huge mistake pushing Zeke Hampton out of my life."

But maybe it was all the same. Regret.

"I don't want to be the reason for your unhappiness," she said, meaning it. It seemed quite natural to let go of the resentment she had had for her father for so many years. It wasn't so easy to judge him for his mistakes when she'd made so many of her own. To chastise him for being a father so consumed with his business that he ignored his daughter. Jess herself had cut herself off from Cassie for what she deemed the girl's own good. Would Jim Peterson have thought that creating and building his business was for his family's well-being?

"You aren't," he said. "My behavior is. Nothing you can do about that."

"What if I said I understand it?"

He shook his head. "I'd say I shouldn't be let off the hook that easily."

"Missing out on the past seven years of each other's lives was probably price enough, don't you think?"

He leaned forward. "So, what are you saying, Jessica? That we can somehow start again?"

"Everything okay here?" Tessa said. Jess hadn't even been aware she'd come to the table. "Can I get you anything? Jim?"

He looked from Jess down to her untouched burger and her nearly empty wine glass. "More wine?" he asked her.

"Yes, please," she said.

"I'm good, Tessa, thanks," her father said. Tessa looked back and forth between them, nodded, and left the table.

Jess looked at her father, who was still waiting for her reply to his question about what she wanted out of their relationship. Instinctively, she knew that he'd accept it if she said she wanted nothing to do with him. And part of her was almost ready to say that. Why rock the boat and all that? But in the past month, since Zeke left, the home that had become her sanctuary had seemed less so, and she knew that she was probably coming out of her islander state of mind.

"I want us to try to forge some sort of relationship," she said. "I don't know what that would look like. But I'm willing to try."

He smiled and sat back in his seat. Her father was a very handsome man, still vibrant at fifty-five. Tessa delivered the wine, and Jess noticed the way the Seafarer's owner looked at her father. Tess definitely noticed that Jim Peterson was a handsome and vibrant man.

"Thanks," Jess said to a quickly retreating Tessa, who just waved over her shoulder.

"Okay," Jim said. "And if you want, we can start slowly. I'm meeting some friends here tomorrow night for dinner. Kelsey and Huck Beck? I'm not sure if you met them last year or not. They worked for me on the boat last summer and are in town on vacation. I'd love for you to join us, meet them. It'd be a nice, low-key way to spend some time together."

"I didn't meet them, no. I'd like that," she said.

"That's great, Jessica. Just great."

"And we can also start by you calling me Jess. That's what I go by now."

He smiled again. "It suits you. Jess."

It did suit her. The name. Her life in the Copper Country. Her home. Her job as a ranger. The fledgling house renovation business.

Zeke. Zeke suited you too. And you pushed him away.

She shook the thought away before it led to others like she'd had over the past month. Like those of Zeke out there right now in the Copper Country, starting the search for his baby mama and life partner.

"Honey? Are you okay?"

A nasty divorce from her mother and years of estrangement apparently hadn't erased her father's ability to know when something was wrong with his daughter.

She nodded and took a bite of her burger. When she'd swallowed and he was still staring at her with concern, she nodded again. "I'm okay, Dad. Really."

The words weren't exactly true, but she hoped that, just like it felt oddly natural to call Jim Peterson Dad again, she'd one day be okay with losing Zeke Hampton.

Thirty-One

—ᴍ—

"THANKS AGAIN FOR GIVING ME A RIDE, ZEKE," Phoebe Robbins said to him from the passenger seat of his truck as they pulled into the parking lot of the Seafarer. It was a Saturday night, and the lot was full, even though it was still early in the season.

A promising season for Hampton Air, if the past month's healthy bookings and future reservations held up. Zeke had been busy with mostly fishing charters, dropping off fishermen—and women—on Isle Royale, or other remote places, and picking them up a few days later, their coolers weighed down with their catch.

"No problem. Happy to have the company," he said, cutting the engine. As was his habit lately, he scanned the parking lot for Jess's Range Rover but didn't see it. Just as well, probably.

Who was he kidding? It still stung like hell when he thought of Jess and her throwing away what they had. What they could have had.

"It really should be Charlie thanking you. You bringing me up here allowed him to finish up something he was working on."

"On a Saturday?" The tourist industry didn't get to take weekends off, but Phoebe's boyfriend, Charlie Simpson, was an engineer at Summers and Beck, so presumably had his weekends free.

"I know, right? That's what I said. But he said he wouldn't make it a regular thing. And really, this is the first weekend he's had to work since we got together, so I can't complain." She got out of the truck, and Zeke met her around front, waiting as she zipped up the front of her jacket and slung her purse strap around her shoulder.

Phoebe was Zeke's brother-in-law Finn's younger sister. He'd met her at Lizzie and Finn's wedding two years ago, but he'd hardly seen her since. He'd been away, and Phoebe had lived downstate (Flint? Saginaw? Zeke couldn't remember) until around Christmastime, when she'd moved home.

Zeke didn't know her well, but he had volunteered to drive her to the Harbor to meet Lizzie and Finn for dinner. His sister and her husband were making a day of it, having driven up earlier in the day. Petey and Alison were having their own outing too, but also meeting them there for dinner.

"You know," Phoebe said as they walked through the parking lot and to the restaurant, "if I wasn't sure that Lizzie knew I was head over heels for Charlie, I wouldn't put it past her to try and arrange a reason for you to have to bring me up. Some elaborate plan to get us together."

He laughed. Lizzie might have only been Phoebe's sister-in-law for two years, but the young woman had Zeke's twin down cold.

"You are absolutely right. This all kind of feels like one of her plans, doesn't it?"

"Yes. But no worries. I'm desperately in love with Charlie Simpson, poor guy."

He smiled at Phoebe, her glee in declaring her love innocent and infectious. And so fucking painful, too. "Lucky guy, I'd say."

"Aw, you're sweet."

He slung one arm around her shoulder, pulling her close. It was kind of like having another sister, though he'd always thought Lizard was more than enough sibling for him. He entered the restaurant and nearly froze on the spot when he saw who was sitting at the table with Lizzie, Petey, and their spouses.

JESS'S FATHER HAD CALLED HER with a time to meet at the Seafarer after he'd spoken with Huck Beck. On the spur of the moment, she'd invited him to come and see her place and have a glass of wine before they went. He accepted, and they'd had a nice conversation while he'd made the appropriate sounds of admiration about her home. She was especially pleased at the attention he paid to the photos that she'd taken on Isle Royale on the walls.

It was probably too cold to do so, but they'd kept their jackets on and had a drink on her deck, watching the lake crash against the rocks below them.

"You know, last summer I used to bring the *Mina* up and down this shoreline. I'd learned you'd built somewhere in here and I…I don't know…wanted to feel closer to you somehow. And a few months back, I finally got up the nerve to call you, but I hung up when you answered."

Ah, so those were the calls that had freaked her out. She supposed she could have found her father's actions creepy, or an invasion of her privacy, but she didn't. In a way, it was comforting to know her father was out there, looking after her in his own way.

They'd talked for a while out on her deck, then decided that she'd ride with Jim to the Seafarer. He'd bring her home after their dinner with Huck and Kelsey Beck.

Their party had grown from a table of four to three times that when first Huck's brothers Twain and Sawyer (whose names cracked Jess up) and Twain's wife Liv and Sawyer's fiancée Deni Casparich had walked in. They weren't going to intrude, but when it became obvious that Jess knew Deni from Summers and Beck's work on her house, it seemed natural to pull a table up to theirs and make their foursome eight.

Which was great until Petey and Alison walked in, followed a few minutes later by Lizzie Robbins and her husband Finn. (Finn, who wasn't even related to those Samuel Clemens-named brothers!) They all knew each other, most from way back, and even her father knew them from a sunset cruise of a year ago. Jess hadn't met Lizzie's husband, and when introductions were made and Jess said her name, she knew from the look that passed from Finn to his wife that Lizzie had mentioned Jess before.

But it was still all good. She talked with Deni a little about the Dollar Bay house. And then with Huck's brother Twain about the house flipping he'd done before going back to work at the engineering firm full time a year ago. He said he'd gotten out of it because there wasn't a lot of money in it, which concerned Jess. She wasn't doing it to get rich, but she didn't want to lose any of her savings, either. But then he explained that he was doing really large homes, some of the old mining mansions, and when they were completed there just weren't the number of buyers around that could afford something that grand, especially if it wasn't on the water.

She felt a little better after talking to him.

And she felt even better after talking about her estrangement from Cassie with Alison, who was a therapist and a very good listener. Jess wasn't even sure how it'd come up, but it somehow grew from the revelation to the table that Jim was her father. That went into a brief history of her life that she shared with the table, even though Lizzie, Petey, and Alison had heard it the night she'd sat with them at the Commodore.

"It's a more common phenomenon than you'd think," Alison told her. "With the divorce rate of second marriages at sixty-seven percent, there are a lot of step-relationships that are ending, with no clear way of maintaining those bonds. Particularly if there are no children—no half-sibs of the child—from the second marriage."

"That was my case. We didn't have our own, but Cassie was in my life from five to twelve years old."

Jess explained how she'd ended contact with Cassie and was relieved to hear that Alison agreed with her decision. She was also grateful the Beck contingent were talking amongst themselves, so few people heard her and Alison's side conversation. "Trying to maintain a relationship in secret—and it's obvious neither of her parents wanted her to continue contact with you—is hard on a child," Alison said. "Particularly a preteen or teen, because of all the other social changes they're going through at those ages. Give her time, and then if you want, reach out to her when she's in college. Just let her know you were giving her space, and if she'd like to be in contact, you would like it. Don't push it, though. She might not be over a sense of abandonment from you."

That hurt like hell. Jess's father must have known it, because he put a hand on her shoulder and squeezed.

But hearing the words from a trained therapist was helpful. It was what Zeke had said too, when she'd told him about losing Cassie from her life.

And as if she'd conjured him up, he then walked through the door of the Seafarer with his arm around a young woman. A woman younger than Jess. One that was probably rich with eggs and ready to ovulate at any moment. One who was probably itching to get a ring on her finger and a baby in her belly.

Zeke halted at the sight of her, and his friends and sister looked her way, while the Becks looked confused.

Lizzie saved the day. "I know, I know. A lot more people than we originally thought. But you know me. I can't resist a good get-together. Here, we saved you seats down on our end."

Zeke made his way around the table, nodding to most, hugging Twain Beck and kissing Liv on the cheek. A nod to Jess, a handshake to her father, and then he was sitting at the far end from her of the four pushed-together tables. Unfortunately, he was across from her, so, though she had to glace down the table, she still had a pretty good line of sight to him—Zeke and Phoebe Robbins, as Jess learned when the young woman said hello to everyone.

"Who was that?" Kelsey Beck softly asked Huck once Phoebe was out of earshot. "How is she connected to this crew?"

"Phoebe is Finn's sister," Huck replied. "She's my age. We were in the same year, but she went to Houghton. I kind of knew her in high school, but not really well. I think she moved away after she graduated."

"She seems very nice," said Sawyer. "We met her at Petey's Christmas party."

"You mean at Petey and Alison's wedding," Deni said, laughing.

Sawyer leaned over to Deni, who was sitting next to Jess, and whispered, "No, I mean at the thing we went to after you agreed to be my wife." Deni smiled and kissed her fiancé.

Jess would have smiled at the lovebirds next to her (just because she'd sworn off marriage for herself didn't mean others couldn't be happy), but she was wrapping her mind around the fact that the woman who Zeke had had his arm around—the woman who even now was saying something low for his hearing only, causing him to bend his head close to hers—was Lizzie's sister-in-law.

How all in the family could you get?

The night went on, and all the different connections were solved for Jess by the context clues she picked up, mostly by being quiet. And drinking *a lot* of wine.

The Becks were brothers; that was obvious. Lizzie, Finn, Alison, and Petey had gone to high school together and remained good friends. Petey, Twain, and Zeke had been freshmen at Tech together. Though from what she pieced together, Twain hadn't finished school. That might have something to do with his and Liv's son Matty, whom they talked about. There was a large age gap between him and their nearly five-month-old little girl, Faith, whom Kelsey begged to see photos of on Liv's phone.

And in another weird connection, Deni privately shared with Jess that Alison was her therapist, and she had treated Sawyer as well after his first wife had passed. She told Jess this after Alison had spoken to Jess about Cassie, as if vouching for Alison's advice. Which Jess appreciated.

Huck and Kelsey had worked for her father last summer. Twain had made something for Petey's driving range business, which both Sawyer and Deni had designed at Summers and Beck.

Jess knew the Copper Country was a small area, but the table was like one tiny game of six degrees of separation. It seemed like Petey Ryan was this group's Kevin Bacon.

And through it all, Jess tried not to watch Zeke and Phoebe interact with the others, thankfully mostly at the other end of the table. Phoebe was animated while telling her brother and Lizzie a story, her smile bright and infectious. When she was done, the four of them laughed, and the sound cut through Jess, making her put her wine glass down hard.

"You okay, Jess?" her father asked her. He'd seen her hugging Zeke on the dock at Windigo, but when he'd asked about Zeke earlier that evening at her place, she'd told him it had been a short-term thing that had run its course. Her choice.

All true.

And yet that didn't stop her father from placing a hand on the center of her back. "Do you want to go?" he asked.

They'd taken their time ordering, having a couple rounds of drinks first, and their food was only now arriving. Tessa had taken a hand in getting all the tables moved together to accommodate the large, unplanned group, but had then handed the table off to one of her waitresses while she tended bar.

"No," Jess said. "Our dinners just arrived."

"That doesn't matter. If you'd rather leave, that's fine. We can have Tessa box this up and take it to your place. Or to the marina and eat on the boat."

Though the thought of getting a good look at her father's boat appealed to her—as did the thought of getting away from Zeke and Phoebe—she didn't want Jim to miss out on catching up with his former crew.

"I'm fine. Really. But I think I might just step out for a second. Get some fresh air." She'd ordered a seafood salad, so there was no objection from others of her dinner getting cold when she excused herself, grabbed her fleece pullover from the back of her chair, and made her way out the door.

She didn't look at Zeke as she passed by his end of the table, but she was sure she felt his eyes on her.

Or maybe that was just hope. Hope that he hadn't forgotten her already, even though it seemed as if it was open season on his wife hunt.

Thirty-Two

HE DIDN'T FOLLOW HER. GOD, HE WANTED TO. Wanted to get out of his wooden chair and follow Jess right out of the Seafarer to wherever she'd lead him.

But she didn't want him to. Didn't even want to be in the same room with him.

He did exchange a mouthed "She okay?" to Jim at the other end of the table. Jim gave a nod to Zeke, then narrowed his eyes at him, like it had been Jess who'd had her heart ripped out instead of Zeke.

Whatever. He didn't know what Jess had told her father, and it didn't matter, not really. Not when the outcome was the same. Sitting at different ends of a huge table of people, trying not to make eye contact with each other. She because who wanted to look at the loser they'd dumped. He because…because seeing her sitting there, her hair down and loose around her shoulders, wearing a gray sweater and the rarely worn greenstone necklace, had ripped him apart every time he glanced in that direction.

So no, he didn't follow her, even after Lizzie had kicked him under the table and motioned with her head to the door. And then a thought occurred to him.

"Was this some sort of plan of yours?" he said to his sister. "Did you know she'd be here?"

His twin looked affronted, and he raised a brow. "No, it wasn't a plan. Why would you even ask that?" He raised his other brow in answer. She waved a hand in his direction. "Please. I'm much subtler than that. You wouldn't see a plan of mine coming a mile away."

"Yeah, right," he said, but let it drop. He believed Lizzie. This time.

So he sat while stories went on around him, smiling when others laughed, hoping they wouldn't call him out on the fact that he wasn't listening to a word anyone said.

Until Charlie Simpson walked in. Phoebe sighed next to Finn at the sight of her boyfriend, who walked toward the table, looking a bit dumbstruck. "There are a lot of people here," he said. He waved down the table, making special note of his coworker Deni, and his boss, Sawyer. "Hey, guys. Didn't know you'd be here."

"It all just happened," Deni said. "So weird."

Charlie coughed, then took the seat at the head of their side of the table, with Phoebe on his right. "Yeah, weird."

Phoebe leaned over, placed her hand on his arm, and moved in for a quick kiss. "Did you get everything done you needed?"

"Uh, yeah."

"So you won't have to go in tomorrow?"

He shook his head and nervously looked down the table. A table that was in a lull in conversation, causing Phoebe and Charlie to be overheard at the other end.

"You were in the office, Charlie?" Deni asked. "Why? What's going on?"

"Um, you know, just...stuff."

Zeke had only met Charlie a handful of times when he'd been at Lizzie and Finn's house, and didn't know the guy very well. But even he knew that something was off with Charlie.

"You shouldn't have to go in on a weekend, Charlie," Sawyer said. "Is there a problem with a deadline or something? Because we can look at—"

"No, no. That's not it. I mean, everything's cool at work." At his boss's confused face, Charlie slumped in his chair. "I wasn't at the office." He looked at Phoebe. "I'm sorry I said that's where I was."

Zeke felt Phoebe tense next to him. Oh, shit. This whole dinner could turn south quickly. Maybe he should have followed Jess out, whether she wanted him to or not.

"What's going on, Charlie?" Phoebe asked. Zeke was hopeful when he heard concern in her voice and not suspicion. "Are you okay?" She ran her hand up and down the sleeve of Charlie's sweater. It was a simple, kind gesture, but it made Zeke's heart pang at the intimacy of it.

Like Zeke and Jess, Charlie and Phoebe hadn't known each other all that long, having only met around Thanksgiving. But, also like he and Jess, their connection was strong and undeniable.

The difference was they were in the present tense. He and Jess were not.

Charlie looked over at Finn, who gave a small nod. Charlie then took a deep breath. "I thought it would just be your family here," he said quietly.

"It can wait, if you have something to tell me," Phoebe said. "Unless… Is it something bad, Charlie?" The sweetness of her voice was unbearable to Zeke, and also to Charlie, who quickly shook his head.

Even as he got out of his seat and dropped to one knee in front of Phoebe.

"I was late because I was picking this up, and they'd sized it wrong." His words could not be heard at the other end of the table over Phoebe's—and every other woman at the table's—gasp.

"Phoebe Robbins, you have already made me the happiest man alive, but would you raise the stakes and agree to become my wife?"

There were cheers that drowned out Phoebe's "Yes," which was also muffled by her sob. Then she dropped to her knees and hugged her fiancé.

That was when Zeke got up and walked out of the Seafarer.

"DID MY FATHER SEND YOU AFTER ME?" Jess asked Zeke when he neared her on the dock in front of the restaurant. She honestly wasn't sure whether she was glad or pissed that he had followed her.

Took him long enough.

Okay, so not exactly pissed.

He shook his head. "No, he said you were fine by yourself. And really, I wasn't following you. I just had to get out of there."

"Things not going well with Phoebe?" she said, then wished she could pull the words back. One, because it was none of her business. She'd forfeited the right to ask. And two, because she hated the sound of pettiness in her voice. She wasn't a petty person. Or she hadn't *thought* she was.

Zeke looked at her, tilting his head, as if trying to figure her out. Yeah, he wasn't used to her being petty either. Then a slow smile crossed his face. Damn, those dimples. "Actually, things are going great *for* Phoebe. She just became engaged."

"What?" Beyond petty, she sputtered, "Are you kidding me?"

"To her boyfriend, Charlie Simpson, who finally showed up."

She was processing what he was saying, but the profound sense of relief that rushed through her precluded her muddled mind from grasping it.

"You thought she was *with* me?" There was pleasure in his voice that Jess found unflattering.

"What was I supposed to think when you walked in with your arm around her, meeting two other couples?"

He looked to the sky, obviously trying to remember his entrance with Phoebe. Phoebe, who was not his date. Who was now somebody else's fiancée. He nodded, apparently acknowledging how she could have misunderstood. Then he smiled. Broadly.

The ass.

"Nope. Not with me. I just gave Phoebe a ride up here because her boyfriend had to work. But he didn't really. He was picking up the ring to pop the question tonight in front of her brother and sister-in-law. I was the fifth wheel tonight."

"It was a pretty couple-y table." But not completely. Not the couple that mattered to Jess.

"That it was," Zeke said. "Another reason to get out of there."

"Amen," she said softly.

"Did you come with your dad?"

She nodded and recapped her evening with Jim for Zeke. He leaned against one of the rails on the dock, his hands in his jeans pockets, seemingly content to just stand in the brisk evening air and listen to her talk about her relationship with her father.

"That's nice, that you're…in contact. And I see you're wearing the greenstone necklace. Was that a gift from him?"

He couldn't see it now because her fleece was zipped too high. He must have noticed it earlier, though he'd been at the other end of a table of twelve. "Yes. He gave it to me for my fifteenth birthday. We'd been here a few times when I was younger. Before… Anyway, I thought he'd be happy I wore it." He nodded, and she thought on it. "*I'm* happy I wore it."

"Probably won't get hauled away by the greenstone police tonight in the Seafarer. Seems like Tessa would offer you sanctuary or something."

She laughed. God, it felt good to laugh. It felt like the last month had been nothing but misty eyes and deep sighs. "Except I *am* the greenstone police. Sort of."

He placed a finger to his pursed lips in the "shhh" sign. "I won't tell if you won't. I spent a week at Survival, Evasion, Resistance, and Escape school. The National Park Service can put me on a waterboard and rip out my fingernails, but I'll never tell."

Standing there, relaxed and smiling, he looked so damn good. She wanted to take the three steps to him and wrap her arms around his waist, bury her head into his chest.

She knew if she did that he'd wrap those strong arms around her, probably kiss the top of her head. And she'd have him back.

It would be so easy. And it would feel so fucking good.

But she wouldn't do it. Because she loved him.

And even if it wasn't Phoebe, or tonight, at some point, Zeke would need to start looking for a woman to spend the rest of his life with. And she'd known all along that that couldn't be her. She'd had a moment of denial—which she'd assumed was clarity—on the island with the wolf, but that moment was gone, replaced by the glaring fact that she was just like her parents. Incapable of sustaining a long-term relationship.

Like he'd known the last time they'd made love, he knew now, and stepped away from the railing. "I'm not going to beg," he said.

"No, of course not," she said. "You should never have to beg to be loved."

"Oh, I know I'm loved," he said, and she nearly gasped. Of course he knew. It wasn't something she could hide. No more than he could hide that he loved her. "That's not what I'd be begging for. It'd be for a future."

"Nobody should have to beg for that, either."

He watched her, and she tried to convey how bad she felt without speaking. She wasn't sure something entirely different wouldn't come out if she opened her mouth.

Something like "I suck at all this, and it will end up with us despising each other and our kids being shuttled back and forth between homes, but hey, it feels good being together, so let's roll the dice." Yeah, no. She'd keep her mouth shut.

He sighed, shook his head, and headed further out onto the dock area. Away from her. "It was good to see you, Jess."

"You too, Zeke. Take care," she said, and then walked back to the restaurant, leaving the man she loved alone.

Though she was sure that he wouldn't be alone in life for much longer.

"EVERYTHING ALL RIGHT OUT HERE?" Zeke heard from behind him, and turned to find Jim Peterson.

"Yeah," Zeke answered. "Jess went back inside about ten minutes ago." Then he grew concerned, looking toward the stone walkway between the Seafarer and the docks. "Didn't she?"

Jim nodded. He walked out to where Zeke stood looking out at the harbor. "Calm tonight," Jim said. Zeke only nodded and jammed his hands into his pockets. It was a cool evening, and standing out there feeling sorry for himself had only made him colder.

"I owe you an apology," Zeke said. "For the way I spoke to you, put hands on you, on Isle Royale."

Jim waved the words away. "You thought you were protecting my daughter. I should be thanking you. I *am* thanking you."

"Still…"

"Forget it. I have." After a minute or two, Jim turned to Zeke. "It feels pretty hypocritical for me to say this, given the relationship I have with Jess myself, but what exactly are your intentions toward my daughter?"

"What did she say about us?"

He shook his head. "Not much. Obviously, I saw you two at the Windigo dock. And you had said before that you were meeting 'your girl,' but she gave me the impression that…"

"It was over?" Zeke finished.

"Yes."

"So why then are you asking me my intentions toward her?"

"Because her ex-husband made her life hell when she ended it with him. I wasn't around to be there for her then. I am now."

The words almost felt like a physical blow. In fact, they caused Zeke to take a step back, as if he'd needed to duck another oncoming punch. "I would never hurt Jess. She was the one who ended things, yes. But my God, I would…" He shook his head, trying to even wrap his mind around what Jim was suggesting.

But what he was suggesting wasn't out of the realm of possibility, because it had happened to Jess.

Zeke knew, and understood, Jess's reasons for not wanting to get involved more deeply than they were. But Jim's words drove that point home even more.

He turned fully to Jim. "Jim. I am in love with your daughter. But more than that, I respect her. And if she doesn't want to pursue something further with me, then I have to respect that."

Jess's father studied him. Zeke could see Jess in her father's face. The straight nose, the blue eyes, though hers were of a deeper, stormier blue than her father's. The fair skin and red hair must have come from her mother.

"You're in love with her." It wasn't a question, but Zeke answered him anyway.

"Yes. Deeply."

"And what are you going to do about that?"

Zeke put his hands up in the air and groaned. "I just told you she doesn't *want* me to do anything about it. You just *warned* me not to do anything about it."

Jim smiled. "I know. But maybe I was wrong."

Zeke chuckled, then sighed. "You Petersons are quite the challenge, you know that?"

Jim started walking back down the dock, away from Zeke. "You were a Navy pilot, right?"

"Yeah. A Navy *fighter* pilot," Zeke said. "So?"

He saw Jim shrug. "Nothing. I just figured maybe you were up to a challenge. Maybe I'm wrong." Jim stepped off the dock and headed up the stone walkway back to the restaurant.

His words rang in Zeke's ears.

Thirty-Three

—◊◊—

IT'D BEEN A COUPLE OF WEEKS SINCE THE NIGHT AT THE
Seafarer when Zeke had last seen Jess. He'd stopped looking for
her Range Rover in parking lots in the Harbor and didn't spend
a lot of time around Rock Harbor when he was flying in and out
of Isle Royale. No reason to keep ripping the scab off the wound
by seeing her.

Nothing had changed. Nothing would change.

He took a sip from his beer as the waitress at the Commodore
brought out the pizzas that the group had ordered. He couldn't
believe he'd agreed to come out tonight when Lizzie said that a
woman they'd known for years would be with the group too.

He hadn't been ambushed, exactly, and Lizzie had promised
that it wasn't a setup, that she and Finn had to talk with Margo
Karstuu about the foundation in Annie's name. They'd decided to
do it over dinner, since the board members were pretty much all
friends of theirs.

It wasn't an official board meeting, but Petey and Alison,
Lizzie and Finn, and Margo, and Zeke, though he wasn't on the
board, were there enjoying a night out while nailing down some
specifics on the Annie Aid fundraiser that would take place later
in the summer.

Summer. It was almost there, the first week of June turning
the Copper Country into an explosion of greens.

He sat, having a very grown-up couples dinner with Margo,

who was their age but had gone to Houghton with Petey. She was now a vice president at the local bank.

And apparently his date.

Lizzie had said that Margo was single, but wasn't treating this like a fix-up, which seemed apparent from the lack of attention she was paying Zeke. She wasn't ignoring him, but she wasn't making a move or anything.

For which Zeke was deeply grateful.

Maybe he had that "I've just had my heart handed to me and can't deal" look about him. Maybe it was nothing more than Margo just wanting to have dinner with old friends while talking business. Either way, it was a low-pressure night, and Zeke was happy to be with friends and family.

And the pizza. He was very happy to be diving into the pizza.

"Hey, isn't that Charlotte?" Lizzie said when they'd demolished the three large pizzas. "I haven't seen her in forever. I'm going to go say hi," she said, rising from the table. "Me too," Alison said.

"Must be a Bulldog," Margo said, and Zeke nodded, confirming that Charlotte had indeed graduated from Hancock like he, Lizard, and Al had. "Good time for me to use the restroom, then," she said, and left the table as well.

"Quick, we've got a few minutes to be guys," Petey said, looking over his shoulder at the women as they left the side of the restaurant where they sat. "Start scratching, farting, and swearing."

"Like you've refrained from any of that for the past hour," Zeke said, and Petey flipped him the bird. Finn laughed and took a sip of his beer.

Zeke's brother-in-law was a quiet guy. Zeke liked him, though they didn't have much in common. But Finn loved Lizzie and made her happy, so that was all Zeke could really hope for. He didn't have to be drinking buddies with him. Zeke had Petey for that.

Besides, with Sam, Annie, and Stevie at home, Finn and Lizzie didn't have much time for anything other than their little family unit.

Which was fine with Zeke most of the time, though it had made the sting of losing Jess that much sharper.

"How ya doing, Zeke?" Petey asked. "Anything there with Margo?"

Zeke shrugged. "Naw, man. I'm just happy to be out with everyone. And she's great and everything, but…"

"Not ready yet, I get it. No shame in that. Even if it does make you a pussy," Petey said.

It was Zeke's turn to flip the bird.

"Lizzie's worried about you, you know," Finn said softly. So softly that Petey had to lean across the table to hear him. Zeke was sitting next to him, so the words were clear. Very clear.

"I know," Zeke said. "She's called. But thankfully, I've been pretty busy with charters, so that's been good."

"I saw Jess's face when she came back into the Seafarer that night, you know," Petey said. "She's crazy about you. You should totally put on the full-court press. She won't be able to resist you. Maybe pull out your dress whites or something. Oh, pull a Gere. Yeah, totally pull a Gere. With the hat and everything."

"I'm not pulling a Gere."

"Dude, totally Gere her."

"Jesus, Petey, shut the fuck up."

Petey held his hands up in surrender but still had a shit-eating grin on his giant mug. "Just trying to help, bro."

"It's not helping." Zeke leaned forward, moving his bottle out of the way and putting his forearms on the table. "She might be crazy about me, but she doesn't want what I do. So, I talk her into being with me, and in a few years, one of us wakes up pissed as hell that we're with the person we want to be but not in the life we want to be? I won't do it to her. I won't do it to me."

Petey waved a hand. "Fuck a few years from now. You think we know what's going to happen a few years from now? You love her? Get her."

Zeke rolled his eyes at his best friend and turned to Finn. "Help me out here."

Finn was quiet, pushing his napkin around his empty plate. Zeke was about to turn away from him when he finally spoke. "I think it's admirable that you're respecting Jess's wishes. And that you both are so sure of what you want out of life."

Zeke turned to Petey. "See? Fuck you."

"But," Finn added, "I thought I knew what I wanted out of my life three years ago. I wanted to protect my kids, make sure they would never be hurt again. That's it. That's all I wanted. Love? Marriage? So not what I wanted to bring into my life."

Petey sat back in his chair, crossed his arms across his mammoth chest, and raised a brow at Zeke as Finn continued.

"And then I was given a second chance. Your sister came into my life, and I thought, 'Yeah, okay, this will be a fun little escape from reality for a summer,' never intending for it to come anywhere near my family. Or to last."

"And look at ya now," Petey said.

Finn gave a half-smile and turned to Zeke. "Your sister is the best thing that ever happened to my family, and I include myself, Phoebe, and my grandmother in that statement."

"Yeah, but—" Zeke was about to point out that Lizzie and Finn had a shared history—they'd dated in high school. But Petey cut him off.

"So, Finn, the moral of your story is…?"

Finn shrugged. "I guess that you can know what you want, think you want certain things, but if you wrap yourself up in that, and only that, you could miss something that turns out to be even better than what you thought you wanted."

"Exactly," Petey said. "And how long did it take before you got that second chance with Lizzie?"

"About eighteen years," Finn said, a melancholy tinge to his voice.

"Right. And it was a little longer than that for me and Al." Petey looked at Zeke, leaning closer because the women were all now approaching their table. "You want to take that chance? Hope you get a second chance with Jess down the road? Pray that it doesn't take eighteen years?"

"What'd we miss?" Al said as she took her seat next to her husband. Then she looked around at the men when they didn't answer. "Babe?" she said to Petey, who only stared at Zeke.

Lizzie and Margo took their seats but sensed something was going on, so they looked around the table too, not saying anything.

"Fuck!" Zeke said, slapping his hands down. He pushed away from the table, grabbing his pullover from the chair. He pulled out his wallet, but Petey had a hand up.

"I got it. Next one's on you. Just go."

Zeke nodded and moved around the table. Looking back at Lizzie, he said, "I'm sorry. Petey can explain it. Later." His sister nodded. To Margo, he said, "I'm sorry. It was good to see you again, Margo. But there's something I really need to do." She nodded too, and he quickly walked out of the restaurant.

LIZZIE LEANED FORWARD AND looked at Petey across the table from her. "Was that what I think it was?"

"If what you think it was is him getting his head out of his ass and going after the woman he loves, then yeah."

She high-fived her friend, but he nodded toward her husband. "It was Finn, mostly, who made him see the light. I just poked the bear a little bit."

Lizzie put a hand on her husband's thigh. "Thank you. I know you hate this kind of stuff."

He covered his wife's hand with his and squeezed. "Anything for family, right?" Lizzie leaned in and kissed her man, even with Petey groaning at their PDA. When she finally broke away from Finn, Lizzie turned to Margo.

"Sorry. But you don't want Zeke, anyway."

"Well, I certainly don't want someone who's in love with someone else, that's for sure," Margo said.

"And he definitely is," Petey said.

Margo pointed at Lizzie. "But you owe me one *eligible* man."

"I'm on it," Lizzie said.

She sat back in her chair, Finn's arm immediately coming around her. Crossing her arms, she sighed contentedly. "I told him. He'd never see one of my plans coming."

They all laughed, raised their beer bottles in toast of the master planner, and then ordered another round.

Thirty-Four

—⁓—

JESS WASN'T SURE WHAT THE PROTOCOL WAS FOR approaching a boat the size of the *Mina*. You'd have to be on deck to actually knock on the door, and that seemed like an intrusion. She'd been so happy to see the boat docked at Rock Harbor when she was done with her shift. She needed someone to share the shitty way she was feeling.

"Um…Dad? Permission to come aboard?" Should she just walk to the cabin loudly?

She ended up not having to make the decision. Her dad poked his head out of the bridge, looking down at her. "Jess? What a nice surprise. Permission to board," he said, smiling as he waved her onto his boat. "Always permission to board. You don't have to ask."

"Okay," she said, making her way across the deck of the boat as her father climbed down the stairs to the bridge.

"It's good to see you."

"I hope it's okay. You're not in the middle of a charter or anything?"

Her father shook his head. "They're camping on the island. Pickup is for tomorrow morning. I decided to spend the night instead of getting up early. I didn't even bring any help, just wanted a night out here for a change."

"And here I am, ruining that solitude."

"Not at all. I'm happy you found me. Wine?"

"That would be great, thanks," she said.

Jim nodded and led her to the cabin. It was a comfortable area with a main room, small galley kitchen, and what looked like two berths. Jess sat at the small table used for meals and waited for her father to pour her a glass of wine. When he brought it to her, he studied her. "Everything okay, Jess?"

"It's been a bad day, that's all."

He nodded, took his glass, and sat across the table from her. "Want to talk about it?"

She shook her head. "Maybe later. Right now, I just want a healthy sip of this and to think about something else."

"To better days," he said, raising his glass. She clinked hers against his, then took that sip, which turned out to be way more than healthy.

"To better days," she said when she was done. Setting the wine on the table, she circled the bottom of her glass with a finger. "I called Mom a few days ago."

"Oh? How is she?" Jim asked. There was no bitterness or scorn in his voice for his ex-wife, for which Jess was grateful.

"She's good. I guess. She's in France right now."

A slow, wistful smile crept across her father's face. "She always wanted to go to Paris. I was too busy making sure we could afford places like Paris—and in style, no less—to actually have the time to take her. I'm glad she's there now."

Jess didn't comment on how many times her mother had been to Europe over the years—or with how many different husbands.

"She seems to be enjoying it. I let her know that you and I are…back in touch."

He looked beyond Jess, slowly nodding. "Yes, that seems right." Then he looked at her. "The last thing I want to do is put you in the middle of any kind of *situation*, Jess. I hold no ill will toward your mother. It ended very badly, but I really do wish her the best."

"How long did it take you to get to that place with her?" Jess asked. She didn't add that her mother hadn't seemed quite so resolved. But that was one thing that seemed very obvious during the time she'd spent with her father over the past month—he was a man at peace with himself.

Oh, he had regrets. He'd let Jess know that the time they'd been estranged had been the most painful time of his life. And he also had told her about the demise of his second marriage and how that had made him re-evaluate his life.

"Too long, it seems. A lot of time wasted." He took another sip of wine. "Are you wondering if you'll ever get to that place with James?"

She nearly snorted. "God, no. Although I guess I should, right? You seem very Zen about life since you let go of all the baggage."

"I had a lot more years to get to this point. And neither of my exes are people like James." He quickly held up a hand. "I know. I told myself to stay out of your marriage. I don't want a repeat of seven years ago."

This time she did snort. "Please. I should have listened to you then. I think, on some level, I knew you were right but wasn't willing to admit it."

"You were in love and committed. And you never were a quitter."

A small, sad smile formed on her face. She was, though. A quitter. She'd quit with Zeke.

"Yeah, I guess," she said without much conviction.

"So, this bad day? Does it have something to do with Zeke Hampton? Did you see him out here?"

If only she'd seen Zeke today. To take comfort in his strong, warm arms. To feel his hand on the back of her head as she burrowed into him. She shook her head. "No. I haven't seen him since that night at the Seafarer. But I... No, it wasn't about Zeke."

"Office politics?" he said in a teasing voice. "The corporate climate at the visitor center doing you in?"

She laughed, the sound hollow. "Yeah, rangers walking all over each other's backs to get the Keweenaw Cruise shift. It's a dog-eat-dog world."

He smiled with her, both of them probably thinking of the way they'd made their living previously, where selling out a coworker to get ahead was part of the norm.

"A moose emergency?"

Jess laughed a little. She missed Zeke. She knew her father would be sympathetic when she told him what had happened today, but he wouldn't get it like Zeke would. Wouldn't know what it meant to her. She was still grappling with that herself.

"No, not that. We found out today…one of the other rangers found out…one of the two remaining wolves died," she said, and promptly burst into tears.

Thirty-Five

—ɯ—

"JESS? ARE YOU OKAY?" ZEKE ASKED AS HE CAME INTO the cabin of the *Mina*. He'd called down from the deck, and Jim had told him to come aboard. He was hoping Jim would know where to find Jess, and then Zeke got lucky to see her being consoled by her father.

Her head whipped around at his voice. Apparently, she hadn't heard him call to Jim. Yeah, how could she, over the sound of her crying?

God, it gutted him to see her hurting like that.

"I heard," he said. She nodded, then disentangled herself from her father and walked the space of the small cabin toward him. He opened his arms and—God, it was so sweet—she walked right into them, circling her arms around his waist and laying her head on his chest. "I'm so sorry," he whispered in her hair. She just continued to sniffle while he held her.

Jim nodded to him, then walked past them and into one of the other rooms on the boat, closing the door behind him.

Zeke held Jess, hoping it helped her, but selfishly wishing she'd cling to him forever.

It wasn't forever, and she finally pulled away. "I'm so sorry," she said, walking to the galley, where she took a Kleenex—okay, four—wiped her eyes, and blew her nose. "I don't know why the news hit me like it did. I wasn't part of the study or anything. I hadn't spent years and years following him like others have."

"So it was the male, then?" Zeke asked, and she nodded. He didn't know why that made him feel better, but it did. Maybe because Jess had seemed bonded to the female more, having been so close recently?

"Is it weird that I'm glad it was him? And not her?"

He shook his head. "No. I was thinking the same thing."

She crossed to the small seating area and sat down. It wasn't really a couch. More like a loveseat built into the side of the boat. There was room next to her for Zeke, so he joined her, putting an arm around her shoulder. She huddled into his side, still dabbing a little at her eyes.

"You know what else is weird?" she asked.

"What?"

"I was just thinking how much I wished you were here, how I knew you'd get what this meant to me. And then…here you are."

He pulled back, forcing her to look up at him. "I do know what that wolf dying means to you. And as soon as I heard, I had to find you."

"Could you… Would you…"

"What? Anything. You know that."

She repeated the words she said to him the day they met, alone in the hangar after their flight to view the wolves. "Would you come home with me?"

"Let's say goodbye to your dad and get out of here," he said, rising from the seat.

"THIS DOESN'T MESS UP A FLIGHT for you, does it?" she asked an hour later as they flew from Isle Royale back to Copper Harbor. The days were longer now, and the sun was still out even though it was nine at night.

"No. I don't have anything scheduled for two days."

"So you were finishing up a charter?"

He shook his head. "No."

"Why were you on the island? You couldn't have heard and then made it there in that amount of time."

He hadn't planned on having this conversation three hundred feet above the waters of Lake Superior, but maybe it was just as well. This way, she couldn't exactly walk away from him when she found out what he had to say.

"I came to see you. When I went to the visitor center to see if you were still on shift, I found out about the wolf. Then I double-timed it to find you."

She turned to him. "Why did you want to see me?" Was that hope in her voice, or was that just wishful thinking on his part?

"I told you on the dock at the Seafarer that I wouldn't beg," he said.

"Yesssss?" Yeah, maybe it *was* hope.

"I lied."

She stared at him, and he pulled out the best grin he could. Finally, she returned it with a soft smile. "Zeke," she said softly. It wasn't quite in a "You poor, poor fool" tone, but it wasn't "At long last" euphoria, either.

"I am going to beg, Jess, and I'll tell you why." It would be easier if he could do this more face-to-face than he was willing to do with him flying a plane. He was a damn good pilot, but even he couldn't handle the Cessna while wrapping Jess up in his arms and gazing deep into her eyes while he made his case.

"Take a look below us," he said, winging it now, figuratively and literally. He'd had the whole flight to the island to think about what he wanted to say, but when he'd walked in to find her in tears and then held her as she'd cried, all sane thought had gone out of his head. Even being up there in the sky—where his mind was clearest—wasn't much help. "Look at how huge Lake Superior is, how vast. And it's just one of five Great Lakes. Not even an ocean."

"Okay?"

Yeah, she was onto him and the fact that he was rambling.

Focus, Zeke. Lock on to your target. This is the biggest mission of your life.

"Okay. And we found each other. Yes, it's a small area here

in the Copper Country. But I've been all over the world the past fourteen years, and you've been in Chicago, and, were basically a hermit here."

"I wouldn't exactly say a—"

"Work with me here," he said with a smile. She smiled back. That had to be good, right? "My point is, when you find someone who you connect with like we do, you don't throw it away. Even if it isn't exactly what you want. Even if it isn't in your plans." He looked away from the horizon and into her eyes. "You don't throw away the love we have."

There, he'd said it. Love. And what was more, it felt right. What was *even more*, she knew that it was right.

"If it's kids you're worried about, don't. I love being an uncle, and that can be enough for me."

"Zeke. I—"

There was no way he was going to let her in with something as stupid as a sound argument. "And we don't even have to live together if it's your freedom you're afraid of losing. Keep the color towels you want. I don't give a shit."

She laughed. "But Zeke—"

"Hell, we just date for the rest of our lives if that's what you're comfortable with. We make up our own rules about what commitment means."

"Zeke, I—"

"I only know there's no one else for me, Jess. I love you, and I want to be with you forever, in whatever form that takes."

He looked up from the controls to see her crying again. Oh, shit, he hadn't wanted to make her cry, to cause her more pain. But the stormy blue of her eyes turned sunny, and she was nodding even as the tears fell down her pale cheeks and over her pink lips. Lips that parted in a huge smile. For the first time since he'd met her, he felt the peace he'd been searching for after he left the Navy.

"Jess?" he said, and she nodded faster. He laughed, the relief was so strong. "Let me guess. I had you at hello?"

She let out a half laugh/half sob. "Not exactly at hello, but you had me the moment you walked into my dad's boat, knowing what you'd find, what state I'd be in."

"Baby, I knew you'd be hurting. I couldn't let you do that alone."

"I know. That's why I love you."

"I know you love me. Are you saying you still want to *date* me?" The absurdity of his question had them both laughing.

"Yes, that's what I'm saying," she said. "You're right. We can figure it out. I'll try to let go of my fear."

"It's okay to be afraid. I'll be right by your side."

She leaned closer to him, but her seatbelt held her in place. Damn safety.

"Hey, flyboy, are you pilot enough to take this plane down anywhere?" she asked, her voice low and full of promise.

"Yep," he said. "Lieutenant Commander Zeke Hampton, at your service."

"Then land the plane, Zeke," she said, already looking behind her to the passenger seats. The ones with a little more legroom than where they currently sat.

"Here? Now?" He was already moving his hands on the yoke, checking gauges. Thinking about the sturdiness of the seaplane floats, for they were about to get a workout.

Thirty-Six

—⚏—

THE MINUTE HE CUT THE ENGINE AND GAVE HER A nod, she was out of the seatbelt, off the seat, and headed for the passenger row behind them. It was going to be tricky, the logistics in the small plane. But hey, people did it in those tiny airplane bathrooms, right? They had more room than that.

So, not the Mile-High Club. More like the Wavy Superior Club.

She'd take it. Take it all, with Zeke.

She hovered over the seat, stepping out of the way while he moved to the back with her. Letting him sit in the chair, shimmying out of her green uniform pants while he unzipped.

"The hat," he said. "Where's that hat?"

Her uniform hat? She wasn't sure where she'd left it, but it wasn't in her pack. Or on the floor of the plane with her stuff. It was either still at the visitor center or on her dad's boat. "I don't know. Why?" she asked.

He smirked. "I've had fantasies of you riding me with nothing but that hat on."

She barked out a laugh, the sound scratchy after her tears. "God, seriously? *That* hat?"

"Hey, don't judge my kink."

She laughed again, tugging her work shirt from her body, her eyes greedily devouring him as he pulled his cock, already hard, from his jeans. She stripped off her panties but didn't even bother with her bra, then stepped to his seat and arranged herself over him, careful of the seat arms.

An arm snaked around her waist, pulling her closer. His other hand pulled the cups of her bra down over her breasts, and his mouth was on her with the precision and heat of one of his smart bombs.

She arched back, knowing Zeke's strong arm would keep her safe, not allowing her to tumble to the floor of the seaplane.

The waves rocked around them, creating a motion their bodies quickly picked up as she held Zeke's head to her, growing wet as he tugged and sucked at her. He moved from one breast to the other, the cool air causing the wet nipple to pucker when he left it. The position they were in reminded her of the last time they made love, when on some level, she knew they'd never be together again.

It had been sweet and yet soul-crushing.

Now, it was sweet, yes, but intense and soul-affirming because she knew it wasn't the last time.

It was the first time. The first time in their newly committed, in-it-for-the-long-haul relationship.

She rocked her hips into his, nudging his cock, but not willing to take her hands from his hair. He pulled back from her tits, licking one last time. "Baby, we can't," he said. She looked at him like he'd grown two heads. "No condoms. I don't have much call for them on the plane," he joked. "A situation I will rectify as soon as we dock."

She stared down into his face, and he must have misinterpreted the thoughts running through her head as regret. "But we can do other stuff. I can get you off, you know that for sure." His hand moved from her hip around to her front, but she quickly reached down, grasping it in hers, holding it still.

"It's okay," she said. "I want you inside me. Without the condom."

The love in his eyes nearly did her in. "Jess. Are you sure?"

He was asking her more than just if she felt safe going

bareback this one time. And she knew her answer was more than just the nod she gave him.

"Jess? Say the words. I need to hear them."

She wasn't thinking irresponsibly. Her responsible brain was firing on all cylinders—just like her body. "I'm sure. It's a safe time of the month for me, but…"

"But?"

She held his handsome face in her hands, her thumb gliding into the dimple in his chin. "But even if it's not safe, I know what I'm doing."

"Jess," he whispered, the love she knew he felt for her coming through with the soft sound.

"If I do get pregnant, you're there for me, right? We're in this together?"

He snorted. "Woman, I've been trying to get you to be *in this together* since the moment we met. If getting you knocked up is an easy in, then I'm more than willing to fuck you silly in the middle of Lake Superior to get there."

She giggled, surprised at the girlish sound that emanated from her. Then the thought of what they were actually contemplating hit her full force. "But Zeke, seriously—"

He stilled her with a firm grasp on her hips. "Seriously, Jess, I am in love with you and want you in my life. Forever. Kids. No kids. Forever. Got it?"

"Roger that," she said, causing him to smile.

"Never thought Navy jargon would get me so hard," he said. He positioned himself below her and let her make the final decision.

As she lowered herself onto him, feeling the delicious glide of uncovered Zeke deep inside her, they both moaned. "Bombs away," she said, and he chuckled, wrapping his arms tightly around her.

His mouth again returned to her breast, and she held on to him as she moved on top of him. "Swab the decks," she said, and he nipped at her nipple, then soothed her with his tongue.

"I feel the need, the need for speed," she said, and rose quicker, plunging down harder.

She heard him gasp, but he didn't say a word, seemingly content to let her make a fool of herself throwing out anything she could remember from any movie she'd ever seen.

"Aye, matey," she said as his cock hit a particularly sensitive spot. A motion she quickly re-created.

"Okay, now you're just doing pirates," he said, pulling away from her chest.

She laughed, the sound quickly turning to a gasp as Zeke's hand moved to where they were joined and pressed on her clit.

"Target engaged," he said, "That's always a good one."

She exploded in his arms, rockets going off in her head. Smart bombs detonating right on target. When she came back to earth, the waves still rocking the plane in a motion that prolonged her climax, she said, "Yes, that's always a good one."

He laughed, then moved her hips, making her glide up and down him again. "You're sure?" he asked, and she nodded. He pumped a few more times, his ass coming off the seat, his legs leveraged by his feet on the floor, and came inside her.

Unprotected, but very safe.

Exactly how she felt about her future with Zeke. Scared as hell, but very, very safe.

Thirty-Seven

———

ZEKE CARRIED IN THE LAST BOX AND TOOK IT TO WHERE Jess pointed. "That's all of it," he said.

"Really? I thought there'd be more. What, did you live in some sad, spartan apartment with rental furniture for fourteen years?" Jess asked.

"Not quite spartan. But being gone so much, I didn't spend a lot of money on furnishings. A great couch and an awesome TV were all I really needed."

"And where are those?" she asked.

"Sold 'em. There are always people looking for a good deal on that kind of stuff near a naval base."

He couldn't believe it, but he was moving in with Jessica Chapman. And *she'd* asked *him*!

It was early July, and she'd mentioned it a week ago. Before she could change her mind, he'd cleared his schedule and driven to Virginia Beach. He'd picked up the things he had in storage that he'd wanted to keep, sold the rest, and drove home to Jess.

Home. Their home.

They'd had the discussion about money, since he wasn't entirely comfortable with moving in to a home she'd spent a small fortune building for herself. Now that he had some money coming in from the business and wasn't living off savings, they'd agreed that to even the playing field, the household expenses would be covered by him. Too bad, because he'd kind of liked calling her his sugar mama.

But not a mama yet.

He'd felt a deep sadness when she'd texted him that she'd gotten her period while he'd been on the road. He'd pulled the truck over and called her, wanting to hear her voice, wanting to know if it was relief or regret that she felt.

Turned out, just like him, it was a little of both.

Since that day on the plane, they'd gone back to using condoms. Mostly. But when they both admitted to feeling a little bit of sadness when Jess got her period, the thought that "mostly" might turn to "mostly not" was discussed.

"Here, this is for you," he said, pulling a large box from under the load he'd brought in earlier. A big bow was across the gift box. "Happy move-in day," he said.

"Oh, please. You've been living here since the day on the plane," she said. "And if anything, I should be getting something for you on move-in day."

"You're gift enough," he said, and she rolled her eyes. "Here, open it." She took the box from him, slid off the bow, and took off the lid.

"Towels? *Black* towels?"

"No room for any ambiguity," he said.

She burst out laughing, dropped the box to the floor, and wrapped her arms around his neck, kissing him soundly. "God, I love you."

"I love you too," he said.

She left his arms, picked up the towels, and put the lid back on the box, a smile on her face the whole time. He moved to the large box that held his hanging clothes to continue the unpacking.

"So, if not the awesome TV and comfy couch, what was worth moving up here?" she asked as she neared where he'd started to unbox his uniforms. A small gasp escaped her. "Is that... Are those...dress whites?"

"Yes, ma'am," he said, saluting her.

"Is there... Do you have the hat, too?" Her eyes were lit up, and a flush crept up her neck. Yeah, he knew that look. He'd seen it a lot in the past month since they'd gotten back together.

For good.

"I do indeed." He waited, but she only pursed her lips and then bit the lower one. Apparently, he wasn't the only one of the two to have hat fantasies. "You want me to Gere you, don't you?"

A small nod, and then a huge smile.

"Give me five minutes," he said, then pulled the uniform from the hanging box. As he dashed to the stairs of the loft, he swore he heard her squeal.

"WHAT'S THIS?" HE ASKED LATER. Much, much later. He'd brought her a bottle of water and set it down next to her and then moved over to the desk in the office area of the loft to sit down at the chair. He didn't trust himself to get too close to her. Wearing only his naval officer's hat, she was too delectable, and they were due to meet the gang at the Seafarer in an hour. Katie and Darío would also be there. They'd been back in da Yoop for a few weeks now that Katie was close to her due date. Jess hadn't met them yet, and Zeke couldn't wait for her to meet the rest of his close-knit group of friends.

"What's what? Oh, that. Forms to change my name back to Peterson."

He looked at the forms, back at her, and smiled. "Your dad will like that."

She nodded and sat up in the bed, wrapping the sheet around her, her red hair falling about her shoulders. "He will. But it wasn't only for him. It was time to put Jessica Chapman behind me."

"And fully embrace Jess Peterson?"

"Something like that."

He looked at the papers. The date at the top of the form was a few days ago, when he'd been gone. Then he glanced at the bottom of the last page. Blank. "You haven't signed them," he said.

A moment of unease zipped through him. He knew Jess

was all in on their life together. He had no reason to think she would—in *any* universe—want to hang on to James Chapman and the life they had.

"Yeah, I decided to hold off on that," she said. His head moved back, like she'd punched him. "Because…" she continued in a tone that had his head firmly back in place and him leaning forward, resting his elbows on his knees. "It didn't make sense to change it back to Peterson, *if* I might be changing it again anyway."

He grinned, rose from the chair, and walked to the edge of the bed, looking down at her. "Did you just ask me to marry you?" he said.

She scoffed. "I did *not* ask you to marry me."

He smiled even bigger. "There was a 'yet' at the end of that sentence, wasn't there? You just didn't say it."

"Maybe," she said. She rose to her knees, putting her almost at kissing level. Hell, with just a small knee bend on his part, they'd be lip-locked. "I'm just saying that I'm not taking anything off the table at this point."

"So marriage is on the table?" he asked. He took the sheet where it was tucked around her bust and gave it a gentle tug, pulling it free and letting it drop to the bed.

"I think *everything* is on the table with you, flyboy," she said.

He knelt on the bed and wrapped an arm around her bare waist, crushing her body to his. Once again, he threw her words back at her.

"Prove it."

—◊◊◊—

Acknowledgments

I was lucky to have my very own former Navy pilot as a source to draw from: my brother, Tyler Kearly. A very big thank you to him for sharing some of the jargon and experiences. Any inaccuracies and misrepresentations are mine. Also, a HUGE thank you, Tyler, for your service.

As luck would have it, while flying as a passenger to the Copper Country, Tyler was on a flight with another pilot, Christine Hamilton Rector, whose husband happens to own a seaplane charter business which flies to Isle Royale. Worth The Flight was already percolating in my head when Tyler let me know about Jon Rector and Christine's business, Isle Royale Seaplanes. I was able to get most of my info about what type of seaplane Zeke Hampton would fly from just their very informative website. I hope to make it on one of their flights out to Isle Royale soon.

Also, they were gracious enough to let us take photos of their docked plane, which, with some design help, became the cover shot of Worth The Flight. Many thanks, Jon and Christine.

Beta readers Holli Bertram, Liz Kelly and Patti Kearly were invaluable in their feedback. The editing at Word Wolfe and Editing 720 was, as always, top notch. And a big thank you to my last-look editor, Margo Burrage.

More WORTH books are coming!

In the meantime, try Mara's New Adult Romance Series

IN TOO DEEP
FRESHMAN ROOMMATES TRILOGY, BOOK 1

IN TOO FAST
FRESHMAN ROOMMATES TRILOGY, BOOK 2

IN TOO HARD
FRESHMAN ROOMMATES TRILOGY, BOOK 3

Mara Jacobs is the *New York Times* and *USA Today* bestselling author of The Worth Series

After graduating from Michigan State University with a degree in advertising, Mara spent several years working at daily newspapers in advertising sales and production. This certainly prepared her for the world of deadlines!

She writes mysteries with romance, thrillers with romance, and romances with…well, you get it.

Forever a Yooper (someone who hails from Michigan's glorious Upper Peninsula), Mara now splits her time between the Copper Country, Las Vegas, and East Lansing, where she is better able to root on her beloved Spartans.

You can find out more about Mara's books at
www.marajacobs.com

Mara loves to hear from readers. Contact her at
mara@marajacobs.com

www.ingramcontent.com/pod-product-compliance
Lightning Source LLC
Chambersburg PA
CBHW031716170626
46808CB00005B/1767